"Glas has become almost disturbingly indispensable. The texts and voices out of Russia come through with formidable insistence. More now than ever before, precisely because hopes on their native ground are again precarious."

GEORGE STEINER

"Together these two novels, saturated with an emotional intensity and inescapable horror, chart the traumatic decades of Stalinism which today's 'scared generation' of middle-aged Russians must now put behind them."

World Literature Today

"These novels, in their different ways, explore the inner powerlessness of the victims. Crushed and tormented by the totalitarian system they begin to feel that they must be responsible for their own ill fate... Written in an intense, suffocating style they make a powerful reading."

Moscow Times

GLAS NEW RUSSIAN WRITING

contemporary Russian literature

in English translation

Volume 37

The Manhunt by Vasil Bykov
Translated by *Rachel Polonsky*

The Old Arbat by Boris Yampolsy
Translated by *John Dewey*

glas

GLAS Publishers
tel./fax: +7(095)441-9157
perova@glas.msk.su
www.russianpress.com/glas

Glas is distributed in North America by
NORTHWESTERN UNIVERSITY PRESS
Chicago Distribution Center,
tel: 1-800-621-2736 or (773) 702-7000
fax: 1-800-621-8476 or (773)-702-7212
pubnet@202-5280
www.nupress.northwestern.edu

in the UK and Europe by
INPRESS LIMITED
Tel: 020 8832 7464
Fax: 020 8832 7465
stephanie@inpressbooks.co.uk
www.inpressbooks.co.uk

Edited by Natasha Perova and Joanne Turnbull
Cover design by Emma Ipolitova
Camera-ready copy by Tatiana Shaposhnikova

ISBN 5-7172-0071-4

Contents:

THE SCARED GENERATION

The first person we meet in Boris Yampolsky's *The Old Arbat* is a self-satisfied young lieutenant just out of KGB college, admiring the elegance of his handwriting as he fills out an arrest warrant for an innocent man. The first question the novel asks is, 'What really did happen then?' Now, when men and women from the KGB, who take open pride in its history and traditions, have returned to political power, the question has acquired a new urgency. It is in this context that the editors of GLAS have chosen to reissue *The Scared Generation*, ten years after its first publication.

The Soviet myth was a highly-wrought construction which survived by cultivating mass indifference to the reality of the past and present. In the former Soviet homelands of both Yampolsky and Vasil Bykov, the myth has proved easy to reconstruct in the form of nostalgia, while the mechanisms of political control have been manoeuvered back into place. The elevating story of Soviet greatness, enacted in parades, light entertainment, monuments, and solemn speeches, promises to lift people out of weariness, sorrow, and shame, to erase memory. Now, as then, the amnesiac fantasy is underpinned by repression, subtle and overt. Now, as then, the maintenance of the system requires the invention and destruction of 'enemies', both internal and external.

'They fear memory,' the dissident writer Lydia Chukovskaya wrote in 1967, 'even now the authorities still will not tolerate any mention of 1937.' Yampolsky's *Old Arbat*, written in the 1960s, comemmorates a later phase of Stalinist repression, the 'Doctors' Plot'. 'This has happened before, in 1937', the hero thinks, as he destroys his notebook, letters, and photographs: 'everything was electrified, the whole atmosphere became stifling and laden with fear, and there were universal demands for sacrificial victims'. He is an intellectual, a writer. Living in a room 'like a prison cell', perched above the 'wailing and snarling' din of central Moscow, he attempts to give his life a deeper meaning through literature, experiencing the sense of isolation and abandonment of the individual who cannot submit to the blind ideological machine. 'What was all this: vanity and ambition, overwrought nerves, the natural urge to work?', Yampolsky's hero asks of his daily compulsion to write, 'or was it a sense of responsibility, a hungering after truth and justice, a contempt for all that was base and vile? Most likely it was a combination of all these things...'.

Like the writers and dissidents interviewed at the end of this volume, Yampolsky's writer-hero acknowledges the problem of inner freedom in circumstances of political repression. 'You can destroy my spirit with fear and a feeling of uncomprehended guilt', his inner voice affirms in words of archetypal resistance, 'yet it is not in your power to make of me a lickspittle and amoral cripple'. In his candid and nuanced 'Confessions of the Sixties Generation', Lev Anninsky describes how he learned to maintain inner freedom within the climate of all-pervading fear in which his generation was raised. Valery Agranovsky's painful reminiscences of a Soviet father-son relationship confront the damage done to a child's sense of truth by a system dedicated to the 'reforging of souls'. At the same time, Agranovsky pays tribute to the goodness of certain individuals at the very heart of that system. The darkly amusing tale of Vladimir Moroz, a 'dissident art collector', reveals that, then as now, avarice can masquerade as ideology in the law enforcement activities of the security services:

'During the trial every effort was made to fabricate a case for confiscating his property. His lifestyle was categorized as bourgeois, and this was amply corroborated by evidence collected by the KGB. ... While Moroz refused to admit his guilt, two hundred witnesses, their names taken from his diary, were interrogated. His own interrogations lasted for many hours. It soon became clear to him that what his jailers were after was his art collection.'

As the dissident writer Yuri Glazov wrote in *The Russian Mind since Stalin's Death*, many people who submit to totalitarian myth-making 'do not want to know the truth' not because they 'trust the media's description', but 'because they have become tired and felt discouraged long ago from knowing the truth'.

The Belorussian writer Vasil Bykov was a rare individual who, up to the very end of his life, refused to allow fatigue or discouragement to prevent him from bearing witness, through imaginative literature, to the truth of Soviet history. Bykov hungered after truth and justice in his writing, a stoic sage, retaining the austere courage of witness against official lies about the Soviet past. Though he claimed to regard evil as 'infinite' and 'prone to mimicry', and human beings as impotent in the face of cruelty and intractably resistant to self-scrutiny, he continued to write about World War Two and Stalin's collectivization from the point of view of their least remarkable, least remarked victims. A truly 'Soviet' writer, he wrote in his native Belorussian and translated his prose into Russian himself.

Bykov's peasant-hero, Khvedor Rovba, is no intellectual. Yet his inner life is rich and affecting. From his quiet observations of 'all sorts of people and bosses', both 'at home and in exile', he perceives Marxist-Leninist theory in all its moral nullity: 'he understood that you find goodness where you find justice and truth. And where there was class struggle, that unreconciled state where everyone on top does what he wants with the people beneath him, where was goodness?' Khvedor loves his home and his own freedom with an instinctive intelligence. He knows why the land thrives and how it dies. Hunted down in terror by his own son in the swamps of his native land, his death is at once submissive and defiant.

The decade since the publication in GLAS of *The Manhunt* has seen the hardening of dictatorship in Bykov's native Belarus. Political opposition and independent media have been suppressed, Soviet symbols restored. Bykov drew active official disfavour for his clear resistance to the 'Soviet colonels with a communist mentality' whom he accused of destroying his nation's culture and restoring Soviet ideology. He became a dissident again, subject to vicious hate campaigns in the media, labelled 'politically retarded' by a state-run literary magazine. His funeral in 2003 was a politically-charged event which led directly to the expulsion from Belarus of Russian TV journalist, Pavel Selin, for a report that was allegedly 'unobjective, biased and provocative information aimed at tarnishing the image of the authorities'. More recently, a group of activists was detained by security services in Bykov's birthplace, Grodno, for gathering in a public place to advance the politically provocative suggestion that the town name a street after its illustrious native son.

So why do the 'Soviet colonels' still pay literature this tribute of fear? They fear literature precisely because literature does not fear them. Writing compelled by a free conscience – like Yampolsky's novel about Stalin's terror, kept in the drawer unpublished until long after his death; or the stories of collectivization and war which earned Bykov exile and vilification – reverses the corruption of language on which the Soviet myth depends. It dares to tell us what really did happen then.

Rachel Polonsky
Moscow, July 2005

Vasil
BYKOV

THE MANHUNT

Translated by Rachel Polonsky

Chapter One

A Man on the Village Outskirts

The water meadow by the river, scattered with wide spinneys of willowherb, was steadily turning green with late autumn aftermath. Since the recent rains the neighbouring marshes had overflowed. The stream, which never ran deep in summer, had burst its banks and flooded the meadow. It was marshy and swollen with soft, young moss. The moss sank pliantly underfoot and seeped muddy water, but did not give way; there were no quagmires here. It was autumn now, the water meadow oozed moisture; in summer, at haymaking time, it was dry here; the mowers walked about freely and carts laden with hay drove across it. Wheelmarks and hoofprints still shone faintly with black water in the fresh grass. There was water everywhere. It corroded the leather of his boots like alkali and seeped through his footcloths. He should have sat down and changed his footwear, but paying no heed to the wet or the lack of a path the man headed straight across the swamped meadow.

The autumn day was drawing to a close in a windy hush. There wasn't a living soul about. There were people working in the field, digging potatoes, but nobody had any cause to go to the far off water meadow. The man was aware of this, but he was uneasy all the same, almost alarmed. There was something unnaturally tense in his hurried step; his inveterate, chronic anxiety, revealed momentarily by a tenacious, watchful glance, was usually concealed by a gloomy, aged countenance, greyed with stubble. His mouth was half open, from fatigue or constant tension. His two bottom teeth were visible beneath a drooping moustache, the upper ones were partly covered. The man's breathing was hoarse and rapid: walking across the marsh wasn't easy. He wore a home-spun peasant coat, rusty-

brown with age, with a patched collar; a narrow thong, its end
dangling, was tied round his skinny middle. A tight, black cap,
which had lost its shape long ago, was pulled down low on his
head: this was obviously not its first year of wear. The same
went for his trousers, a motley ancient-looking patchwork
affair. His boots were another matter. Although limp and
sodden, they were cut from firm raw hide, stretched over his
ankles with new string laces and dexterously fastened again
below his wet trouser legs. The man carried no bag or bundle,
his free hands were clenched vigilantly. He had been walking
alone a long time, avoiding other people, growing used to
solitude. People presented the greatest danger to him in the
fields and villages and on the roads, and he chose roundabout
ways — through copses and fields or, better still, through the
forest. During his time of solitude he had grown unaccustomed
to the sound of human voices. He was perpetually silent,
thinking till his head ached, now and then hurriedly eyeing his
surroundings. His hearing had become so acute that he could
easily make out the rustle of birds in the branches or pick up
the sound of wheels on the road a mile off, and the dim voices
of children in the distance told him exactly where a village
herd was grazing. He had no fear of herds. On three occasions
he had obtained food from cowherds — bread or potatoes,
and once he had had the luck to be given a small piece of salt-
pork by some little girls tending cows near the wood. Emerging
from the bushes, he had first enquired about the village nearby
and the little girls' names, then asked for bread. He could see
that they were frightened, but the eldest took a piece of bread
and some salt-pork out of the pocket of her jacket and silently
held it out to him. He took the morsel and walked away and,
although he was as hungry as a wolf, he could not eat it
immediately — the frightened glance of the girl had troubled
him so, reminding him unexpectedly of Olga. He made his way
into the depths of the fir forest and wept — perhaps for the

first time since the day he had buried his little daughter. She had not been destined to see her native land, God had claimed her in a foreign place.

But her father had seen it.

The hay fields with their willowherb and the little river parted company up ahead, above the meadow scrubs a pine grove shone green on the hill, and Khvedor slowed his pace, struck unexpectedly by the view spread out before him. From a long way off he could see the clump of aged pine trees standing tall on the little hill, below it lay the high road on which he had so often driven to the station or the borough town to buy things, to go to market to pay his grain levies or plead with the authorities. All his solicitations had proved in vain, the taxes had to be paid in full: then they had imposed a levy he could not pay. That had been the end of his good fortune... The hill did not appear to have changed in the years of his exile, the fresh green of the pine trees stood out elegantly from the grey autumnal scrub. The pine trees seemed to be greeting him from that sad day when he had bade them farewell on his way to the station. Khvedor longed to turn towards the familiar hill, climb its steep slope, breathe in the resinous scent of the conifers and touch the rough bark of the pines with his hands, but he did not. It was so close and he longed for it, but there were other places he knew awaiting him further on, and on the highroad beyond the hill he might meet people, his own people, the people he knew, the villagers. He feared meeting his own people more than anything now.

So that was how life had turned out. Fate had torn him away from the place of his birth and landed him in places of which he had never even heard. He had tried to run away twice in the past year — like a fool, without the slightest chance of success. But then, just as hope seemed to have abandoned him and he was ready to reconcile himself with captivity, he had been lucky. Could it really be that he would soon see his native home: what had once been his own field, the village roofs of Nedolishche with its poor soil, the marshy common pasture, the impassable elder thickets by the stream? Here he had been born and spent his early years, and here his future had shone before him with sweet, delusive hope.

He had to walk round the hill and creep across the narrow, overgrown hollow to the other side of the highroad; on the other side, along the stream, the now impassable, overflowing marsh began. He knew the country well: he didn't need to ask the way. He had rarely asked directions from anyone except child cowherds in the fields, once he had stopped an elderly woman carrying brushwood. But he never asked men or young lads who he knew might detain him and hand him over to the police. There was no hope for the young. They were all members of the Komsomol now, brought up in hatred and suspicion of anyone strange and unknown. And it was all the worse for anyone they did know, like himself.

He managed to get across the highroad without being seen and, concealed in the elder bushes, he came out by the pine trees on the edge of the forest. This was the edge of the vast state forest where the trees had once been allocated to the village folk for building their dwellings. He had sawed pines here himself for his hut, after the revolution, when he was building on the plot he had received from the village Soviet, — thirty acres of land.

They had allocated five acres a head and he had a family of six by then: himself and his wife Ganna, her two old parents, his son Mikolka, and little Olga, born that year. So one spring morning he, a farm labourer, had become the proprietor of an arable plot from the former master's field near the forest. His heart had cried out in happiness, the whole world had seemed a sunny heaven. He had built a house, a threshing floor and a cattle shed, and bought himself a cow. At times it had been devilishly hard, he had thought he would never hold up. But he was young and strong and he endured, and after a while he made a fair profit.

Somewhere on that side of the forest was an old footpath hidden by the undergrowth, but he made no effort to seek it out, he walked straight on. Tired and hungry, with wet feet, he was unable to contain his feverish impatience as he forged ahead, not minding where he stepped. Sometimes, almost forgetting caution, he tore noisily through the undergrowth and the bushes and ran, trampling the frozen twigs and conifer branches under his boots. He passed a narrow birch grove amid the pines and emerged in an almost clear strip scattered with old pine stumps. It was the very spot where, in winter, he and his brother-in-law Tomash had sawed timber for the house. Mikolka, by then in his teens, had lit a bonfire beside it and helped to hew the branches. But the place held little interest for him now, he was wholly engrossed by the proximity of his desired goal.

He ran the last few hundred metres along a half over-grown forest path — he no longer had the strength to walk calmly, everything in him strained with impatience. The edge of the forest should come into sight here, from there he would see the field and his deserted farmstead. He knew it was unlikely that the farmstead would be empty now, someone would be occupying it, maybe even one of the villagers he knew. But the main thing was to see the shingle roof with its red brick chimney, the straw eaves of the sheds, the front garden under the windows which had once been full of bright autumn dahlias, and the apple trees in the garden above the pond. He had grafted the slender saplings when they were still small — they should be bearing fruit by now...

He came out on the edge of the forest near an old, hollow pear tree which he remembered from childhood, the trampled grass beneath it was colourful with a wealth of fallen fruit. No one had been picking it and it was all rotting on the ground or going white on the tree among the thinning leaves. From here the wide expanse of autumnal ploughed fields was clearly visible. Khvedor walked slowly along the forest edge, his gaze fixed on the expanse of fields, a little way beyond which his deserted farmstead also lay. Soon the houses on the edge of Nedolishche emerged in the distance, along with the roofs of the cattle sheds, the gardens and the vegetable plots which ran down to common pasture. On the furthest of them a woman in a red kerchief was bent over digging in the ground — probably one of Antosev's women picking potatoes. But where was his farmstead? The hut, the threshing floor, the outhouses? On the flat field sloping gently down from the forest with the pale green winter crop there were a few fruit trees rustling in the wind, but not a single building. The bare field stretched away in all directions — from the forest all the way down to the pond.

Shuffling through the dry weeds, Khvedor made his way along the edge of the forest. His strength was failing rapidly and his step was getting heavier, he stopped and sank feebly to the ground.

He had made it. He had walked and run and dragged himself for three months of this improbable journey of torment and endurance, and what did he have to hope for? What did he desire? What had he thought he would find here? Most of all he wanted to see. And now he had seen. Had they been expecting him to come back? Were they bound to look after a deserted farmstead for him? It might have been transported to another place where perhaps it sheltered good people — children and old people. They were bound to be more fortunate than he. And the land?.. The land was still the same and the winter crop was a joyous green. It didn't look a bad crop, but at the other end, near the pond, the damp had darkened it. It had always been wet there when it belonged to him. He had tried to plant potatoes there and twice sowed hemp. Cereal crops would not grow near the pond. The new farmers, obviously not knowing this, had sown rye.

Exhausted and dispirited, he sat and gazed at the field and the village he had not seen in so long. He had dreamed of them every night when they had been far away, out of reach. And here they were, so close. The early twilight was thickening around him, the thick rustling of conifers drifted from the forest, wind-torn rainclouds flew above him. There was no one about in the field or near the village; he could sense the vague presence of people in the village — in the vegetable plots and the courtyards behind the fences. A cart appeared from the outermost hut; it was driven by a young lad, standing upright, lashing a bay horse. The cart disappeared into the hollow in the distance with a dying clatter. Khvedor no longer hoped he would recognize the lad, though he had once known everyone here, old and young alike, but with the years the old men would have departed for the next world and the children grown up; it would be hard to recognize them, especially from a distance. But God forbid they should recognize him — or spot him in the field. Struck by the realization that he could be seen from the village, Khvedor slid down lower in the weeds. His anxiety slowly began to subside, he could already look at the familiar field more calmly — the shoots of the winter crop, the occasional, solitary saplings where the boundaries had once been, the bushes in the low parts near the marsh. At the far end of the village was a hill with a small pine copse on it, something shone dimly white under the trees. It was the ancient village cemetery which held all Khvedor's kin — his grandfathers and great grandfathers, all his ancestors. Like many village families they had died after suffering on that land. All the same, it's an enviable lot, Khvedor thought: to remain with your own people on your native land after you die. And his poor Ganna lay in an icy marsh a thousand miles from here, near frozen Kotlas. Who would have dreamed of such a fate? They had never even heard of such a place, but it had been Ganna's fate. And his too.

Khvedor stayed sitting on the overgrown, bushy forest edge gazing into the evening distance. His wet feet began to freeze and he felt chilly — as evening approached it had started to get perceptibly colder. Life in the village was following its everyday course. People were driving their cattle home from the field, busying themselves with everyday household chores. An old woman carrying a yoke appeared on the footpath leading to the well. She drew water, looked around, and carried the water towards a cowshed with a heavy tread. People had begun lighting their stoves in the huts, and the wind carried torn shreds of smoke across the eaves. Khvedor watched the neighbouring fields and the village avidly, but his gaze was most drawn to the place where his farmstead had once been. It looked as though some vague trace of the buildings remained near the surviving apple trees, not everything had been destroyed. He could see dark, overgrown weeds. Something was piled up on the site of the foundation. He had to get closer, to look, to step on the land which had once promised him so much joy and given him only grief. But it was still light, he had to wait. He waited patiently. Once the village huts were shrouded in evening twilight and not much could be seen in the field, he got up and stumbled down towards the saplings.

As he had imagined, the farmstead had not been ploughed over, the courtyard had been left untouched, the foundations had survived and the cornerstones of the barn were still in place. The barn stones were enormous, particularly the one which lay under the lower corner of the building. He and Tomash had brought it all the way from Goranya, they had only just managed to heave it on to the cart. Its smooth side could still be seen among the nettles. The foundations of the house were crumbling in places and overgrown with weeds; there was no longer any porch — it had obviously been taken somewhere along with the house. A heap of bricks overgrown with wormwood was piled up where the stove had once stood

— that was all that remained of it. That was understandable too: the bricks from the stove were no good for anything, they were badly fired. He had not been able to find any better that autumn — there had been a fuel shortage in the brickworks — but Khvedor had been told they would do for a stove. They did fine, the stove had stood there for eight years, all he had to do was build a flue, for which he had bought a hundred old bricks made from pre-revolutionary casts in the borough town. Wandering through the ruined farmstead, he felt bitter; his soul brimmed with bloody tears. The one thing that brought him joy was the young orchard where the trees were just coming to full strength, carelessly shaking their leaves in the wind. He had planted three winter apple trees in the third year of his life on the farmstead, and two pear trees a year later. He had got the cuttings in Farinov from a teacher at the station. The first graft had not taken and he had planted them again in the autumn. He walked round the little trees and plucked at their firm, solid trunks as though greeting them one by one. It was already dark and he wanted to try the apples — maybe there were some left on the branches? Peering into the dark foliage, he touched the lower branches and gently shook the outer tree. Nothing stirred, nothing fell to the ground. Maybe the crop had already been picked? Then Khvedor saw an apple bough pulled off, hanging down. Another lay on the grass at his feet and he realized that there hadn't been apples here in a long time. Well, how were they supposed to grow here in this orchard in the middle of this bare field, with no one to tend them? Apple trees are like flowers, they will not grow without human care.

Khvedor walked round the farmstead. On the place where he had once dug a well a black pit gaped overgrown with nettles. No trace of the framework or the windlass remained. A few sticks were scattered on the grass where the woodpile used to be, but there was no longer any firewood there. He stood on the heap of broken brick among the weeds, remembering how he used to warm himself on the stove after returning from the forest in winter, or from the field in autumn; how his old men had slept here, and Ganna had sometimes warmed herself. But the poor creature was much too busy bustling about the house, trying to feed her family, which was already quite large in those days, or carrying heavy pails of feed to the cows. Ganna had never had a moment to warm herself at home and she would now be forever cold in the frozen earth on the edge of the marshy cemetery. She had not been ill for long. Before she fell ill she had been doing forced labour in a forestry, since the autumn; there, with a team of other deportees, she had gathered firewood. Of course, she had not been in good health for a long time; since the Feast of Our Lady's Veil she had coughed hard through the winter nights and she complained of a pain in her side. She would not see a doctor — she had a fear of doctors, just as she had of bosses; she tried not to have anything to do with them if she could help it. For a while she had felt a little better after using one of Banadysikha's charms but not for long. One fine Thursday, she had dragged herself back from work and lain down for the last time. Khvedor could not nurse her, they drove him out to work every day; they were preparing a float and there was a great deal to do to get the timber ready. The foreman never gave them a moment to catch their breath and the team worked in the forest from dawn till dusk. Reluctantly he left his wife with Olga, who wept and sang her mother her favourite song, about a little duck, in a thin, childish voice for days on end. This must have been how Ganna had departed this world, to the piteous singing of her daughter. When he dragged himself back to the hut in the evening, Olga told him to hush and said, "Mama's asleep". He threw himself at the plank-bed where Ganna lay. He tugged at her and called, but to no avail — Ganna was already dead. They both wept, Olga wailing bitterly and inconsolably, he silently choking with tears. He was let off work the next day. With undisguised irritation, the foreman granted him half a day. In that half day he had to dig a grave, knock together a coffin, and take it to the cemetery outside the village. The cemetery was new — a patch of land in the hollow recently marked out for burials — but it already contained quite a few crosses. The deportees died easily, especially the older ones who could not adapt to that wild, cold land. But the young died too — of hunger, of back breaking work, and of consumption which struck down even strong, young men. People used to say that most died of longing for their native land, from the thought of their eternal separation from it. Perhaps they were right.

Spring was approaching, the snow on the hills had begun to melt, but down behind the settlement there was still a thick, hard covering on the ground. Khvedor scraped at it with a spade for over an hour, then hollowed out the frozen earth with a pick. He dug a shallow little grave, waist-high. He hadn't the strength to dig any deeper, nor did he have the time — he was terrified of being late, of not getting it done before midday. When he had finished, he threw down the spade and the pick and hurriedly knocked together a coffin. He had carpenting skills, his hands had been familiar with the simple joining tools since childhood, but he needed planks. He had butted into the office of the deputy manager who had rummaged through his papers interminably without saying a word. Khvedor just stood quietly in the doorway, patiently awaiting an answer. Eventually the deputy manager stood up, slowly lit a cigarette and with great reluctance went into the backyard where the planks were stacked. There were a few stacks covered in snow — thick and thin, in twenties and forties, all different shapes and sizes. The dismal man nodded at some planks sticking out of the snow and said through his teeth, "Five, no more". Shovelling the snow with his feet, Khvedor dragged out five gnarled, unplaned planks and dragged them away with clenched teeth towards the hut. He felt like weeping when he looked at the coffin in which his Ganna was destined to find her last rest, but what could he do? What could he ever do in this penal slavery.

Banadysikha helped him to bury her; they would not let anyone else off work. They managed to drag the frozen coffin somehow, on the water sledge. Banadysikha and Olga found room on the side and, weak and tormented, he led the old, half-blind mare. It was a blessing he didn't have to take it far. Sitting on the sledge, Banadysikha murmured a prayer and Khvedor thought with grief in his soul, that he too must make haste to die. Living as they lived was intolerable, it would be better to die, and he gladly would have died if it hadn't been for Olga. His little daughter was nine, she was clever and serious in an un-childlike way. She never smiled, and her eyes were always wide open as though she were expecting something. He thought she might live long enough for something better, he desperately wanted her to, but nothing better came — apparently Olga had not been destined for a better fate either.

But right now he could not think what to do. His mind had strayed as he stood in the empty farmstead in the windy evening, having suddenly forgotten everything he had formerly desired. He had lost the goal which had carried him for long weeks through obstacles and adversities to his native land, to his home. He had not even considered what he would find when he got there. All he had wanted was to get there, to crawl all the way, to look at his land even with only one eye, and then die. To die here and find eternal peace in his native soil was a happiness he could only dream of.

But what should he do while he was still alive, where should he head for? He was not sure he should go to the village: he would bring people misfortune, and he feared the police. While none of the villagers knew he was there, he was free; and freedom remained his only aim. But if they spotted him and recognized him it would all be over, and what would then happen would be worse than death. Death would be better than that. Now that he had come home.

It was already completely dark, a cold wind was blowing and Khvedor was chilly. Now and again he shivered. There was nowhere to take shelter here. There might have been some little barn or shed left standing, or the little hovel where Lobatik had lived, Lobatik was a tender puppy he had brought home shortly before their deportation, but there was nothing left of it, nothing but utter ruin and desolation. He had nowhere to go from here, however, so he did not leave, loitering aimlessly in the thistles for a long while, examining the dark undergrowth and the stinging nettles. He clambered up on to the stove and sat down on the pile of bricks — he no longer had the strength to stand, his feet ached. He sat down and began to think, about the years and hardships gone by, about his silly, unfulfilled dreams, about Ganna. He remembered how, when they were erecting the frame of the house, they had put a Tsarist rouble and two scraps of their clothes wound together in the icon corner, for prosperity and harmony, so that they should never quarrel or be parted. And that was how it had turned out — they had not parted until the moment of her death. She had been a good woman, quiet and hard-working. Khvedor could not remember them ever having seriously quarrelled, although they had had plenty of trouble in their life, there had been more pain and struggle than anything else. But was that really their fault? That was just the way life had turned out. It had promised happiness, but brought them instead work, anxiety and misfortune. He had thought they could endure anything so that it might be easier for their children. They owned the land now, they would never be hired men again. His young son Mikolka had worked shoulder to shoulder with his father while still in his teens. He was a fleshy, broad-boned, muscular lad, stubborn but well-meaning. It was a pleasure to watch the boy drive a furrow with his new dark blue plough, and scythe side by side with the men at mowing time. But little by little he had begun to distance himself from the property, first at school and then when he joined the Komsomol. Meetings, gatherings, debates began to take place in the village. They organized a cell and appointed him secretary. He lost interest in the farm, but his father never argued with him. Let him go out into the world, Khvedor thought, and make his own way. He would get by without a helper. Of course it didn't get any easier on the farmstead. Especially when his son moved to town and stopped coming to Nedolishche. Mikolka was obviously a clever lad, educated, not like his father. Maybe his leaving the farm was for the best. It was certainly his salvation — where would he have ended up now if he had not left? In Kotlas, or even farther away? As it was, they had made him a boss and he had received honour and respect. Khvedor hadn't written to anyone from exile, but he had managed to send his brother-in-law Tomash a letter while Ganna was still alive and six months later he had received a reply. Tomash didn't say how he was or what the situation was in the region. He wrote a few words about his health and, at the end of the letter, perhaps the most important piece of news: Mikolka had returned from the Red Army and was now a big boss in the region. For the first time in years Ganna had smiled happily and Olga's sad face had shone for a moment, but he had frowned. He was glad, but anxiety gnawed at him. It was funny: the son of a deported kulak, the son of a supposed exploiter, had climbed up among the bosses? What if they found out?

Night after night Khvedor had thought about his son the boss and his job; he had worried and suffered. But Stalin had said that a son was not accountable for his father. He had read those words in the newspaper and heard them from people more than once. And Stalin must have been speaking the truth. If Mikolka had been made a boss, they must have known where his parents were and what kind of family he came from. Perhaps they realized that he had been unjustly dispossessed, undeservedly, and that his son had nothing to do with it, all the more so as he hadn't lived with his parents in a long time, or tended his father's land. He had worked for the Regional Party Committee and then served in the Red Army, where he had even been made a commander. What did he have to answer for?

All the same, Khvedor had never once written to his son. He could not overcome the terror and uncertainty he felt inside, although Ganna begged him to write, and even wept once. He was afraid — not for himself of course, he was afraid for his son. He thought Mikolka would write himself if there were really no danger in it. Tomash wrote that he used to see him in the regional capital. His son could have asked Tomash for the address of his exiled parents. The fact that he didn't write must have meant that something was not right.

All the same he didn't want to think bad thoughts, he had hope. When he had dreamed up his escape, and earlier on, before the escape, and then on the terrible journey, on rafts, hiding in woodpiles on railway platforms, on his long wanderings through woods and villages, night and day he had pondered and doubted, but never come to any conclusion. He didn't know how he should behave towards his son, and more to the point — how his son would behave towards him.

If Mikolka really was a high-up, he would be able to do something for sure ... high-ups were allowed to do all sorts of things. In the way of things a simple man is forbidden what a boss is allowed. Khvedor knew this well enough. He'd seen plenty of it in Tsarist times and in the army, and under the new power.

The autumn night presided as sole master over the fields and the forest. In the distance the village was hushed, lost without trace in the darkness. For a while a pair of lights shone somewhere near the other end of the street, then they went out. Khvedor raised himself to his feet. He had suddenly resolved to walk along the night-time street, to look at the familiar huts, and at the collective farm office where a wide arch bearing a faded red calico slogan had once been raised above the street. All around there lived people he knew, old and young, hard workers and idlers, good people, bad people, people who were neither one nor the other. His former fellow-villagers. He had not set eyes on any of them since the March morning when he had been driven away from the farmstead on a sleigh, looking around him at everything — all the way to the gully, from where there was no longer anything to see. And the old women of the village, gathered under the branchy willow by Savchik's hut, had looked on as he departed and wept.

The path that used to lead from the farmstead to the street was no longer there, it was overgrown with grass, so he walked straight on until he came to the road. From the grimy, bumpy road he descended, the way he always had, into a gully with an ancient bridge at the bottom. The little bridge was as rickety as it had always been. It used to rattle loudly under the wheels of carts and traps. The street began almost immediately beyond the gully. The old willow looked as if it had dried out completely, but it still bowed over the road; beyond it stood Savchik's old house, black in the gloom. Khvedor didn't know whether Savchik still lived there; in all the five years of his exile no one from the village had written to him, and he hadn't written to anybody either. He knew nothing about anybody. He and Lyoksa Savchik had once been in the same class at the parish school, then they had been called up together. Lyoksa was a calm, sober-minded fellow, and a hapless pauper like everybody else in the village. He had fathered five daughters. Where was he now?

The street lay dark and empty in the night, in the middle was soft, cattle-worn sand, by the fence it was overgrown with burdock. Khvedor walked round a pile of new wood in Widow Avdotya's courtyard. Hadn't she finished with building yet? Why should she be doing it? Her sons must be grown up by now, and marrying means building. He walked quietly past Zyrkash's front garden. He had no wish to think about him now. Zyrkash was the man who had ruined his life (and not only his). He was a wicked, envious man. He had scribbled a complaint to the regional committee about Khvedor's threshing machine and that had started everything. If it hadn't been for that complaint, everything might have been all right and Khvedor wouldn't now be roaming in the night like a thief. He might still be living here with everyone else, and he would not have experienced all the hardships that his ill-starred fate had measured out to him.

He stopped beyond Zyrkash's farmstead and stood by the fence, listening for the bark of a dog, but the dogs were quiet. Perhaps there were no dogs in the village. There had not been any dogs here before, except on the farms and in the borough town. In their poverty the villagers would rather acquire an extra suckling pig. It was probably the same now: they had evidently not grown any richer. A miserable hut stood on the ground behind the sparse cherry orchard with naked rafters hanging off the roof. It looked uninhabited, but then where was Ivan Pogorelets's huge family? He saw yet another building with gaping black windows behind the paling — another abandoned dwelling. The house next door with the cosy bench along the leaning outer wall came right down to the street; the old men had once loved to sit here, chatting away their free hours. Now the leaning wall was propped up with a row of stakes so it wouldn't collapse. Zmiter Tsyprukov, the noisiest activist on the Committee of Poor Peasants, had once lived there. Tall and thin as a bean pole, under Soviet power he would certainly have qualified for a better dwelling by now. He had been the poorest. But he obviously hadn't qualified if he had ended up living in a little hut like this, propped up with stakes.

Khvedor stepped on some fresh cow dung and moved to the side, closer to the hedge. He was constantly afraid: of stumbling on something, of someone hearing him sneaking down the street, but there was nobody in the surrounding darkness. It looked as though the whole village was asleep. Only the cows breathed sleepily behind the timber walls of the cowsheds, and on the other side of the street a door banged softly. Someone came out for a moment to relieve himself. Treading quietly on the soft earth, Khvedor passed the last houses on the street and found himself in the cemetery.

Quiet and peace reigned here as they always had. High above, the mighty pine trees rustled mournfully. Beyond the low fence posts a few new crosses gleamed dimly in the darkness, tall ones and low ones, the graves of children. He paused by the fence a moment then, finding a way in, stepped with a trembling heart into the dark settlement of the dead. A short path led from the entrance to the pine-covered hill where they had buried their dead for so long and where he remembered every grave. First in the row, the Shuliaks' oak crosses rose above the rest: a father and three sons, their family was probably the oldest in Nedolishche. It was said that the first Shuliak had come here from Lithuania, married the housemaid of a local landowner and settled on his estate. Everything had happened in a most unlikely way. One day as he was unbridling a horse, a bull had charged at the housemaid from the corner. The red shawl she was wearing must have enraged it. Shuliak the coachman valiantly stood in the bull's path, and the servant-girl caught his fancy. Her mistress, an only daughter, persuaded her father to exchange three serf families for one coachman, so she wouldn't be separated from her favourite housemaid. After they were married, the coachman and the housemaid lived on the estate a long time and brought six sons into the world, three of whom had lain for over a century under the resinous roots of the cemetery pines. Opposite, a little further down, stood a metal pavilion with beautiful columns of wrought iron, wound round with moulded vine branches. A marble slab lay on the tomb of the young nobleman, a lieutenant who had been seriously wounded in the war with the Germans and died on his estate. Now, of course, not one of the landowners remained. The neglected grave was overgrown with tall weeds. Naughty village children sometimes played in the rusty pavilion, and passers-by sheltered there from the rain. Along the other side from this grave, between two shaggy pines, was a small plot where the peasant family of Rovba rested: his grandfathers, his father and mother, his youngest sister Teklya, and two young brothers who had died of diphtheria before the war. The last was the small grave of his youngest brother Prokop, a kind, gentle lad who had not lived long enough to marry and left nobody behind him. He had died of typhoid in 1918 when Khvedor was a captive of the Germans. After he had left for the war in 1914 the brothers never met again. It would have been grand to find himself a place beside him, there was probably enough room. If not, then at least he might still fit in another grave above one of them. The person in it would surely not object. Perhaps, without even admitting it to himself, after five years of exile, Khvedor had struggled over a thousand kilometres for this more than anything else.

Taking his time, heedless of danger, he walked round the graves of his kin in the darkness, four side by side, and two a little further down, on the gentle slope of the hillside. He touched the rough, moss-clad crosses. He was afraid a new, unknown cross might turn up next to them, but there were no new graves in this part. They might, of course, have buried people farther off. There was room. Things were different nowadays. People buried their dead where they could, among strangers and even in strange lands. Like Ganna, or his little Olga. He reproached himself bitterly for burying his daughter so badly and in such haste, without a little border or even a cross. He had had nothing to make one with and he was in a terrible hurry: the raftsmen were waiting for him, and he had three miles to catch up with them along the shore.

He sat down on an old grave. There was no cross on it, but it was neatly laid about with stones. He listened to the whispering of the gigantic branching pines and brooded. The chronic fatigue of many days weighed heavily on him. In order not to collapse with weakness he had to get up and walk. But where to? He could not go and ask anyone to let him into a house, and in a barn he would be found in the morning. He could not stay here: at dawn he would be discovered immediately. So it was back into the forest again. The forests always accepted him with silent readiness. The state forest he had known since childhood would accept him all the more readily. It would rescue him now when he was homeless. It would not refuse him.

Chapter Two

Night and Peace

He had probably not gone far from the edge of the forest. Among the trees and the thick undergrowth it seemed quieter, warmer even. He reached a dense thicket and fell on the hard, crumpled stalks of bracken. He had no strength left to walk or climb. Before he fell asleep and forgot everything, he remembered that he had covered about twenty miles that day, from the first rays of dawn till nightfall. He could not have walked another twenty paces.

He was numb with cold when he awoke, his legs stiff as wood below the knees, his head heavy as though he had a hangover. For a moment he had no idea where he was. He thought he was at the peat bog in Kotlas, late for work; but when he rubbed his eyes he realized Kotlas was far away. He was home, in the morning forest, in his native land. This thought cheered him, he rose to his knees and began to warm himself, overcoming the cold with inner strength as he had done more than once in that foreign place. Up in the north he froze almost every morning, and there he had no time to warm himself up. He hardly had time to get moving so he wouldn't be late for work assignment felling trees in the taiga or working in the peat bog. What with the strict overseers and the shouting foremen, God help you if you were late. You'd go hungry all day, or they'd beat you and lock you in the cooler.

His body warmed up little by little, but his numb feet were as cold as before. They would warm up as he walked. He knew he had to be on the move. He couldn't hang around here in daylight. Near the village they would soon be driving their herds to the forest and he would be noticed. The cattle certainly passed this way: Khvedor could see traces of cows' hooves on the ground. Then he heard voices, the cowherds calling. So as not to be spotted, he got up and quietly began to make his way into the depths of the wood.

It was slowly getting warmer. The forest was quiet. Through the shaggy fir trees, beyond the yellowed tops of the birch trees, a sullen sky loured. The sad sound of the forest floated in the air all around him, rising and falling. Khvedor was very hungry. For a long time now his empty stomach had been rumbling. It was hardly surprising: not a crumb had passed his lips the day before. There had been no room for hunger: he had been so desperate to get home. He had last wolfed down a crust of bread scrounged from a woman on the road the day before yesterday. There were no potatoes anywhere. He had to journey half-starved. Yesterday he had survived without feeling hunger thanks to his anxiety about the coming meeting with his birthplace, but since early this morning his suffering had become intolerable. But what could he scrounge here? There was no way he could approach the cowherds: they might recognize him. He couldn't approach people on the road either: he'd be bound to run into someone he knew. It was easier with strangers. If they made problems Khvedor had papers saying that he was Andrei Zaitsev, a native of the Smolensk District, and that he had worked as a general labourer at the Tasmin Timber Works. Needless to say the Smolensk District was far away and Khvedor hadn't a clue where the Tasmin Timber Works was. The papers, he knew, would be useful to him anywhere in the northern lands of Komi, but not much use five hundred miles from there. But what could he do? He had no other papers and these had helped him twice. He was thankful for that.

Softly, stealthily, Khvedor walked through the forest, keeping close to the edge. He remembered the old pear tree; yesterday there had been fruit under it, but he had not wanted to eat. Now hunger stubbornly urged him on through the forest, until he saw the expanse of familiar field through the bushes.

There was no one about near the pear tree, the grass was still strewn with fruit. The ripe winter crop in the field beside it probably protected the pear tree from the cows, they were herded away along the edge of the forest. Khvedor stuffed his pockets with half-rotten pears, and began to eat them; he remembered their taste from childhood. He soon realized, however, that pears alone would not satisfy his hunger, he would have to go looking for potatoes. The winter crop was ripening all along the edge of the forest on this side, there must be potatoes just beyond the forest, as long as they hadn't already been dug. They shouldn't have been. They were never harvested before the end of September.

It was already completely light in the forest. The pines were rustling more loudly, ragged storm-clouds raced through the sky, but there was no rain and no dew on the ground. His feet in their crushed, toil-hardened boots warmed up as he walked. These boots had done him good service. What other footwear could have borne such a journey? In rain they got soaked through, but didn't come apart. When it was dry they shrank and tanned and went hard as metal, boots that would never wear out. It was all thanks to that worker with a scythe over his shoulder who met him near the transit camp and handed him a piece of stale bread and the boots. "Put them on," he said simply, "you'll walk better." Khvedor was barefoot, one of his left toes was cut and bleeding. He didn't stand on ceremony. He wound the footcloths and pulled on the boots. Sure enough, walking was much easier than when he was barefoot. He must have covered a hundred miles in them, and he could have gone as many more. The boots could take it.

With his ears pricked up, on the lookout, Khvedor walked at an easy pace through the familiar forest and a serene feeling of happiness swelled in his soul. This was his native forest, where he had once herded cattle, gathered mushrooms, and felled trees when, in winter, he had been making pit props to be sent out to the Donbass coal mines. He even recognized the half-forgotten rustle of these trees. Up there in the north the forest was different and it made a different sound, desolate, mighty, menacing. This sound was not menacing. The leaves of the reddish birch trees whispered delicately and melodiously in the wind. High above, rhythmically swaying, the tops of the firs slowly floated off somewhere. The undergrowth, however, had thinned out since Khvedor had last seen it, or maybe what had been scrub had grown up into the well-formed trees around him; and it was already autumn. Faded yellow leaves were strewn over the grass. They rustled under his boots and he feared someone might hear him but, thank God, he got past the pine-covered hill, and on the edge of the gully emerged into what used to be clearings in a remote corner of the state forest.

The abandoned plots were thickly overgrown with alder

thickets and young fir saplings, there was green juniper everywhere. A little further on began the long gully with a purling stream flowing along the bottom of it. Khvedor covered about a mile from the gully through the undergrowth and came out on the edge of the forest. Ahead of him lay the field.

Just as he had thought, the area by the forest was planted with potatoes. It had already been dug up, the ploughed furrows were black with scattered potato tops. The earth had been turned over and trampled by people and horses' hooves. Khvedor dug into the edge of a furrow close to the forest. He found a potato immediately, then another two. They're not digging well, he thought, his farmer' sensibilities suddenly aroused. They must be going to plough it over. If you dig it properly, ploughing it over's an easy job. Here it looked as though they had done as little as they could get away with. He crumbled the dry clumps of earth in his toil-hardened fingers, finding potatoes in them, cramming them into his pockets. Fairly soon he had filled three pockets. There was no room for any more and he stood up regretfully. Such riches in the earth. If only it had been like this in Kotlas, where they had eaten grass and bark from the tree. A potato there was worth more than an apple, even a raw one. Satisfied, with his pockets heavy, he made his way back into the forest. He had to choose somewhere to light a little bonfire. Making a fire was probably the most dangerous thing he could do. The smoke might be noticed in the forest. Perhaps the best thing would be to go to the glade beyond the gully where he knew that in the old days people from Nedolishche never used to poke their noses, except in the summer, when old women went there to pick berries. Mushrooms did not grow there, and sometimes there were wolves there. On St. Philip's Day you could hear their howling in the village. Children never went there. This time he had no choice but to go that way. Towards the wolves, not towards people, Khvedor thought gloomily.

He walked through the forest until he came to a clearing, and descended into the dark gully overgrown with alder. He rinsed his muddy hands in the stream. The water was ice cold and as clear as tears, and he drank enough from his cupped hand to last him a while. He crossed to the other side of the gully on slippery green stones. He did not manage to scramble up the slope at one go but stopped twice to rest. He felt very weak, just as he had two years ago doing forced labour in the peat-bogs, when he hadn't had the strength left to climb out of the pit in the evening, and his spade felt heavier than a log of wood. That's what life and the years do to a man. In his youth he had found it easy to heave pine trunks onto a sleigh or drag bags of corn along the gangways in the mill at a run. Once, fool that he was, on a bet with some lads from Kusenkovo, he had lifted Ivan's horse off the ground. She was a glorious filly with a tiny bald spot on her spine. Later on she belonged to Zavialov the policeman. And now he could hardly manage to get out of a gully he had once been able to leap across in one bound. That was what time and his wretched life as a captive had made of Khvedor. If he had known in advance would he really have let it happen this way? But how could he have made it work out any other way? Had any of it happened by his own design?

The clearings were overgrown with alder and aspen. The hard bracken stood waist-high, the large-bladed forest grasses had grown towards the sun through the summer. Walking further away from the gully, Khvedor chose a small clearing in the bushes and began to make a fire. He was very hungry again, just as before, and nothing could be more delicious than baked potato hot off the ashes. But first he needed ashes. The fire, made out of brush and twigs (of which there was no shortage here), lit at the first match but gave off a thick reddish smoke and Khvedor was afraid he might be spotted. He spread the fire out a little to thin out the smoke, but it was impossible to get rid of it altogether. He tossed more brushwood onto the fire, and went and hid in the bushes. If anyone was attracted by the smoke, at least they wouldn't find him by the fire.

He sat among the brushwood. As he watched the column of smoke he thought, "What have I come to! All right, up there, a thousand miles away, I had to be afraid of everything, hide, conceal myself. But here? In my own land? Among my own people?" When had such a thing ever happened to anybody? But it had happened to him now and there was nothing he could do but hide, or else.

Or else what? Would he die? Death was even tempting. He might be buried in his own cemetery. Would they put him in prison? How could prison be any worse than this? He would have something to eat and a roof over his head. After all he had lived through he was not particularly afraid of prison, but would they really send him to prison? More likely they would send him back to that freezing land where he could not bear to live, where he could only die. Ganna had died of consumption, and then Olga had died of fever in two days. He had sensed then that his own turn had come.

But he wanted to die at home.

And he had been lucky: he had reached home.

So why should he complain? Yesterday, when he had seen his native field and village, his whole soul had shone and sung out for joy. Of course he had been upset when he saw his nest ruined. He had thought his farmstead would still be standing. He had dreamed so many times of the garden, the farmstead, the well with the groaning windlass and the unfinished house. He had often wondered whether the people who lived there now realized that the barn needed roofing. The eaves in the left-hand corner had started to leak, especially in heavy showers. He had always meant to cover them with fresh sheaves but never managed it.

Where was it all now? Where had they taken it? Perhaps

they had let it be used as firewood for the village soviet, just like they had done to Albertovka? It had been a fine little farm, the house and the stable both nice and sturdy. The stable was especially enviable. It was made from a sawed beam, with shingles on top. They had destroyed it all, broken it all up and burned it in the village soviet and the reading room. His house had gone up in smoke and flames in the same way. Oddly enough, he felt no regret. If he were to regret everything he had suffered he would go out of his mind. He had built it all up over the years, starting out with a few kopeks, with bloody callouses and backache, he and his wife, struggling over every grain of earth, every single straw and splinter. And he had lost it all in a moment and found himself in prison.

But why?

That accursed "why" stuck in his head like a red-hot nail. He had asked himself "why" a thousand times when they were travelling northwards in stinking goods wagons, when they were driven along the frozen river in a convoy, when he was labouring in torment in the Taiga. He had asked his wife; he had asked people he knew and people he did not know; he had asked the bosses — Why? They had told him about the authorities, about the class struggle and collectivization, but nobody had been able to make it comprehensible. Why had the land the authorities had given him been taken away? Why had the property he had built up been confiscated? Why had he been sent into exile? Why? What was his crime? Was it the fact that he had trusted them and agreed to take the land? How could he have done otherwise? How could he have supported his family? His brother Mitka did not want to share his land with him because there was really nothing to share — sixteen acres apiece was nonsense. What would have been the point of dividing it up like that? And anyway, his brother was older and had more right to the property than Khvedor. For two years running Khvedor had worked as a farm labourer, then married a farm-girl who, like himself, had no land or dowry. Ganna's land was also the size of a pocket handkerchief, and she came from a family of eight, five of them boys. How could he refuse? He had taken the land.

Was it because he had earned a small profit? Summer and winter he had worked like a horse. He had put up buildings, tilled the field, tried to pay his taxes punctually, pay off his personal levy, repay his loans, his insurance. His son Mikolka had grown into a young man and begun to help him. And the government's slogan had run, "Cultivate your property". Who wants to vegetate in poverty and eat chaff for bread? Khvedor had believed the authorities were speaking the truth, but he had been deceived.

The fire had not yet burned low when he impatiently buried a dozen potatoes in the embers: there were only enough hot embers for a dozen. He went a little way off again and began to wait. All was quiet. From the gully a magpie chirred for a moment and flew away. Hunger was beginning to gnaw at him. After about ten minutes, Khvedor ran out of patience and rolled a potato out of the fire with a twig. It was still hard and slightly damp, but it would do for a hungry man. He wiped his ashy hands on his trousers and, scorching his mouth, began to eat. He raked out another one. The potatoes were surprisingly tasty and he ate them one after another until there were only a few left in the fire. These would be properly cooked by now. He shoved them into the pocket of his coat while they were still hot. Fortified, he felt much more cheerful. Now he had to think of a way of getting out of the forest. He was very eager to get a look at the field. He might recognize one of the villagers. Even from a distance he would try to guess what life was like on the collective farm. It couldn't be very good, but it would be better than the way he had lived these last years. The most important thing was to be at liberty, on your own land. No news from the village ever reached Kotlas, only occasional rumours. But the rumours were sad and he had no desire to believe them. What was it really like here?

He emerged from the undergrowth, walked round the gully, and came out on the edge of the forest where it met the damp, mossy marsh. He was already on the third side of the forest. The field here bordered on the neighbouring village of Chernoruchiye. He could just see its eaves on the hill. Far away in the field people were working, his neighbours turned collective farm workers, picking potatoes. He had not been able to work a single day on a collective farm, but he had read about collective farm work in the newspapers and expected to see the whole team engaged in amicable common work. They might even be singing. Instead of that, in the windy distance ten old women from the village were picking at the furrows in an uncoordinated fashion. From here he could see their bent backs, their big heads in thick knitted scarves, and their bare feet. They were all dragging huge sacks of potatoes behind them, which they deposited on a heap in the middle of the field. A long-legged man was running around near the heap with a paper in his hand, he was probably an accounting clerk, while three others drove ploughs along the furrows, swearing viciously at the horses every now and again. It was obvious from where Khvedor stood that the horses could hardly move from exhaustion, shaking their low, despondent heads. These were the skinny, overdriven farm horses which in their village used to belong to the most good-for-nothing farmers like Zmiter Tsyprukov and Ignalyonok. All the others had tried to look after their horses, however hard times were, because without a horse you cannot farm. These horses looked like they had been worked to death. He could only see from a distance. Maybe the work would not look so arduous from closer up. Maybe the women were more cheerful than they looked; but a strangely sad feeling oppressed him as he stood near this field. Of course the people were too far away for him to recognize any of them, much as he wanted to. He stood there a short while, then moved to the other side along the forest edge to the high road where he hoped he might recognize someone he knew. All he wanted was to recognize a face. He didn't plan to talk to anyone or ask any questions. Content yourself with something small and you will get it. That seemed to be his destiny. They had sent him away from his village, cast him out like a mangy swine so he wouldn't spoil the herd, they had flung him out and forgotten him. Would it be right to confront anyone? Wouldn't this sudden appearance just do more harm?

The high road had not changed as far as Khvedor could see. It was just as broken up and worn down, with stagnant puddles shining in the middle. Ruts showed how the traffic from both directions went round them. Two birch trees stood on the other side just as they had when he was young, one tall and straight and the other forked, old, hardened birch trees with slashed bark on their trunks. A fire had recently burned under the straight one. The flame had scorched the bark and singed the lower branches. It must have been the cowherds. Khvedor sat down lower behind the dusty roadside bushes and waited, watching both ends of the road. There was no one in sight, they were probably all out in the fields, which meant he could safely walk along the road, but he sat patiently and thought. Who did he want to see most of all? Lyoksa Savchik, perhaps. After all he was a neighbour, the same age as Khvedor, and basically a kind-hearted fellow. God grant him happiness. But God had not granted Lyoksa happiness. In the Great War he had got a shrapnel wound in his shoulder, and as far as Khvedor could remember he had always had pain in his hand and heavy work had not been easy for him. But where are you to find light work on a farm? The unfortunate Lyoksa had laboured on a small plot of land, with a pack of young kids to support. Khvedor sometimes helped him out sawing firewood or loading manure on to his cart, but he had helped out of neighbourly duty, without enthusiasm, and sometimes with irritation. At times he had lent him money. Khvedor had taken pity on him because he was a neighbour, because they were the same age and both had suffered much in the German war. If he had known how everything had turned out he would have pitied him even more, with all his soul. Lyoksa had been a good man.

But waiting for what you want is futile.

Khvedor sat by the road a long while. It was as empty as before. He wondered whether he had dragged himself all this way for nothing, but no sooner had he done so than a vehicle approached from the direction of the borough town. A skewbald horse trotted energetically down the hill pulling a cart with two people in it, a man and a woman. For some reason the horse was being driven by the woman, who was sitting in the front seat. He did not recognize her, even when the vehicle came closer. But the man! He was wearing a shaggy winter hat and a sheepskin coat with a turned-up collar. He was slumped in the back of the cart, his hands on his knees, his legs covered with a patch-work quilt. He coughed constantly, a harsh, dull cough. There was something familiar in his worn-out face, and when the cart was right in front of him, Khvedor suddenly recognized the man, as though someone had whispered the name in his ear: Zyrkash! Yes, it was Mikita Zyrkash, who had reported him for owning a threshing machine. That had been the start of everything. First one grain levy, then another, and so on until they had sent him into exile. But he could see that life was not going too well for the envious Zyrkash. He was obviously very ill. His wife must have been driving him home from the hospital or the doctor. When he looked at his pallid face, Khvedor realized that Zyrkash wasn't long for this world. One foot was already in the grave. Khvedor had an acute sense of this. He had seen enough people in this state. A vindictive feeling towards the invalid flickered involuntarily in his soul: God really does see all and punish justly. Once this would have made him rejoice, but now he could not. He bore hardly any ill thoughts towards the people who had wronged him. Those had all burned out in the long years of his suffering. He wished no ill on anyone, just as he wished none on himself. May envious Zyrkash mend his ways and live long upon this earth.

For some reason he began to feel miserable. And bitter. The day was declining towards evening. The first, long-awaited day of his homecoming was drawing to an end. Everything had turned out differently from what he had expected: it had all been so blundering. What lay ahead?

He sat a little longer hoping he might see someone else on the evening road, but no one else appeared. It was beginning to get dark. He stood up and dragged himself towards the village along the edge of the forest. Perhaps while it was still light it would have been better to plod on towards his little clearing, but he was stubbornly drawn towards the village. So he walked slowly through the forest then, daringly, he came out on the edge of the forest towards the winter crop. The autumn twilight was already thickening over the hollow and the field, a few lights shone dimly in the distance. The collective farmers were lighting their lamps. He longed to peep into one of the windows from the street and look at the people inside, maybe see faces he knew. It was risky but they might not recognize him even if they did catch sight of him. And if they greeted him he would not respond, he would just carry on walking quietly along the street as if he were deaf. He felt an irresistible yearning to see a living being he knew! But a good man rather than a wicked one, of course.

Softly, stealthily, pausing after every step, he passed his unfortunate farmstead along the edge of the field, just as he had yesterday, and slowly made his way towards the street through the vegetable plots. He came to Savchik's squat house under the crooked, branching willow tree. If he could get into the vegetable plot he would end up by the window facing Lyoksa's stove: the kitchen table used to stand right by the window sill. It was completely dark by now. Khvedor climbed over the fence, stinging his hands on the nettles, and picked his way towards the buildings. There was no light in Lyoksa's windows, yet Khvedor sensed that the people inside were not asleep. He could still hear occasional muffled sounds from the house. He waited, concealed in the nettles. Eventually he heard the dull sound of a door closing and the flickering light of a wick lamp appeared in the window. It flashed in one window, then another, and died in the far corner, by the stove. Khvedor strained to see who it was. Someone cast an indistinct shadow behind the window. It was impossible to make out who it was from here. In Lyoksa's house, which had once been full of children, there was no sound of human voices. Maybe there was nobody there but the silent shadow. But where were all the others? Where was Lyoksa? Where were his five daughters?

He could not see anything more from the nettles; so he crept back to the road through the vegetable plot and, just as he had yesterday, he wandered silently around the village. Red lamplight flickered in a few houses. In two houses the windows were curtained. Someone was loitering by the wicket gate in the yard of another. So, with his head down, Khvedor hurried past.

Chapter Three

Full Moon

Once again he spent the night in the forest. He walked further away from the village along the forest edge, found a patch of dry moss and settled under a juniper bush. The night was cold, his sleep was short-lived. Almost before the first cock crowed he was fidgetting on the moss, shuddering from the harsh cold, and pondering the absurd vagaries of his unhappy fate.

He was in a constant state of surprise at the fact that for perhaps the first time in his life he had been lucky. It was true that if he had known in advance what awaited him at home he might not have reckoned it worth the risk. But he hadn't known, and couldn't have guessed, and it was probably better that way because now he was home. When he had decided on this course he had not even considered what would happen next, and he did not think about it now that he had achieved his aim. The most important thing was that he had got what he wanted, and from now on what would be would be. This was not very intelligent, perhaps it was stupid, but he was like a drunkard straining to get hold of a bottle, not thinking about the hangover to follow. Or a hungry man who can only think about eating his fill and does not care what happens afterwards. Khvedor, it seemed, had satisfied his soul's hunger, but he was afraid to think about the day ahead.

During the night, hunger had begun to nag at him again. He had eaten two baked potatoes as he roamed about in the forest, all he had left in his pocket were three raw ones. In Kotlas or Syktyvkar people happily ate raw potatoes. Sliced up on bread like radish or swede they tasted good, and they helped keep away scurvy. He would have to start eating them raw, especially when his matches ran out. However hard he tried to make them last, there were now only six matches left in a crushed box. Where would he get any more? He would not find any in the forest, and he could not ask for any in the village. He could ask somewhere else where people would not recognize him, but here they would know him immediately. How strange, Khvedor thought. It's safer for a fugitive not to be in the place where he was born, the place he had struggled to reach day and night, the place he had never stopped thinking about, where so many of his village acquaintances and neighbours lived. He had spent his life with these people, and now he musn't get anywhere near them. He had to avoid them more than anything else. This was the absurd way things had turned out. It was so inhuman, so ungodly. Why was it like this? Like a little child he now had dozens and dozens of these unanswered questions, and he could find no answers however hard he thought. Nobody he had met had ever been able to answer them either.

The night seemed endless and passed in an unceasing battle with the cold. He fidgetted on the chilly moss, no longer able to control his shivering, his few remaining teeth chattering. He tried to keep warm, but it was impossible. A vague unease persisting on the edge of sleep held him tightly in its grip. He would lose himself in drowsy visions for a while, then wake again. All was quiet. Towards midnight the familiar sound of the forest was almost stilled, the tops of the firs were lost in the thick darkness of the sky, a lone star twinkled and disappeared between the storm clouds. It must have been after midnight when a forest owl began to hoot from the direction of the marsh, beyond the glades. It let out a last short hoot and then fell silent as though it had been choked. He may have dozed off for a while towards morning, completely exhausted by the struggle with the bitter cold, imperceptibly growing accustomed to it.

He awoke seized with a murky feeling of anxiety, almost fear. He lifted his head and saw before him the wet nose of a cow with a thread of green saliva on its lip. The cow stared at him with its large, sad eyes and chewed. There was a rustling of branches nearby and another cow with a crushed horn emerged from the bushes. It too fixed its eyes on Khvedor. He took a moment to realize, to his horror, that he had ended up near the village herd, which was gradually surrounding him, and he leapt to his feet. He was not afraid of the cows, of course, but the cowherds must be somewhere about and they might spot him. He was waving his arms at the cows and edging towards the juniper bushes when, right beside him, a little dog began to bark. Judging by its high-pitched barking the dog was not about to attack him. It was certainly not a sheepdog. But damn it, it was kicking up an almighty commotion in the forest and it was bound to make the cowherds aware of his presence. Summoning all his strength, Khvedor plunged into the depths of the forest. The little dog jumped up out of the juniper bush and darted along beside him, as though they were running a race. Cantering feebly through the trees, Khvedor swore quietly, trying to rid himself of the dog; but his swearing failed to calm it down and its frenzied barking pursued him relentlessly. "You may be small, but you're an evil pest. Why don't you drop dead!" Khvedor thought as he ran. But the dog was not about to drop dead and it kept up the chase for a long time.

Eventually the little dog began to tire, its piercing barks became less frequent, and finally ceased altogether behind him, but the running race had left Khvedor utterly worn out and he could hardly find his way between the trees. He was choking with fury and indignation. That was all he needed, a dog on top of everything else. He had been afraid he might run into a dog in the village, and one had caught up with him in the forest. He would not have minded a wolf, a wild boar or a sheepdog like he used to meet in the north, but not this tiny, shrill creature. Drop dead, damn you! He'd be lucky if the cowherds hadn't spotted him through the thin bushes after all that.

The wretched dog had chased him to the end of the wood he knew least well. On the dusky, bare earth there was not even grass or moss, only pine needles strewn everywhere. The sky could not be seen through the dense, dark fir trees. At the same time the place was quiet and peaceful, as though no human passion could ever penetrate it. The even sound of the forest floated somewhere above him, hardly reaching the ground, twigs crackled underfoot. Khvedor had only twice been on this side of the forest, both times during the winter when they were cutting down the forest for the Donbass coal mines. He remembered driving his cubic metres of timber forty kilometers to the station. To the west began the Bogovizna, notorious in these parts. It was a huge stretch of marsh without roads or villages, a wide expanse of land which stretched all the way to the Polish border. He was in a completely alien place, mysterious and unknown.

Khvedor was so tired his feet would hardly carry him. He wanted to collapse and never get up again. It took him a long time to calm down after his exhausting run, and he loped aimlessly through the fir grove, avoiding the low branches. There was nothing to be afraid of now. The herd wasn't likely to be driven this way, there was nothing here for people or cattle. He slowly calmed down, but his calm was accompanied by the familiar pangs of hunger. He automatically looked around as though searching for something to eat, but there was obviously nothing to be found here. Completely worn out, he sat down on a low branch and took his old knife out of his pocket. He had bought it in the village shop, long ago, before the collective farms, and it had served him pretty well up in the north and on his journey. Its large blade was loose and worn to a narrow feather. The smaller blade rested firmly in its metal handle. With this blade Khvedor lightly scraped a potato and began to eat it, cutting it into thin slices. He found the taste of the raw potato strange, but taste was not what he was after now. All he wanted was something to chew on, something to quiet his hunger, for he no longer had the strength to make his way through this wild, unwelcoming forest.

He ate the rest of the potatoes in the same way. There were now no more left in his pocket. They hardly relieved his hunger. He felt just as hungry as before and decided he ought to look for mushrooms. Eating raw mushrooms is risky, of course, but if he were able to start a fire. Maybe here it would be safe. Or he could go even deeper into the forest, nearer the Bogovizna. Nobody was likely to find him there.

He wandered through the fir trees for a long time in an exhausted state with no clear idea of where he was, but the fir grove never ended, and there was not a mushroom in sight. Occasionally he came across old, darkened death-caps left over from the summer, but that was all. Perhaps it's been a bad year for mushrooms, Khvedor thought, falling deeper and deeper into despondency after the day's bad luck. Then he turned towards the forest village of Chezliaky, which he imagined must be somewhere nearby. This fir grove must surely come to an end near there and he would find something in the copses. If not boletus mushrooms, then at least he would find russulas, as long as they did not graze cattle there. You never find mushrooms where cattle graze.

He had not yet reached Chezlyaky, he did not even know how far it was, when he saw cranberries on a marshy clump of moss among the firs. There, nestling in the small glossy leaves, was a wealth of berries, apparently untouched, as though waiting there just for him. Khvedor threw himself at the clumps and began to devour the berries greedily, hardly bothering to pick them out from the leaves and the stalks. Crawling on his knees along the damp moss, he gathered them up in handfuls and poured them into his pockets. Of course, the cranberries did not do much to sate his hunger, but the tart taste he remembered from childhood was pleasant. He had not forgotten it while he was in the north. Up there one might occasionally chance upon spots overgrown with cranberries or cloudberries, which often saved the exiles from hunger and illness, but rarely such an abundance of berries. Near the villages they ate the berries when they were still green. It was a pity he only had three pockets without holes in them, in his trousers and his coat, but he could get plenty into them. When his pockets were full he began to rake the berries into his cap, crawling over the moss clumps until at last he had to say to himself: that's enough! You can't eat them all, and you haven't got room in your pockets for any more. But he tried to identify the spot, beyond the huge fir grove on the way to Chezlyaky. Perhaps he would use it again.

Somewhat cheered, with his pockets and his cap stuffed full of cranberries, he walked on, not knowing where he was headed. There seemed no end to the fir grove; or perhaps Khvedor had gone the wrong way. Yes, he must have, he realized, when the fir grove came abruptly to an end. Up ahead it was light and he could see a wide band of sedge, and beyond it dense thickets of willowherb, buckthorn and alder. It looked like the edge of the Bogovizna, notorious with the local inhabitants as a peculiar, almost diabolical place. All things odd and uncanny were associated with the Bogovizna. They frightened bawling children and drunkards with it. They would curse people by wishing them through the ground in the Bogovizna. People talked of some kind of underground passage or channel connecting the marsh with other lakes and pools. When Zmitrov's cow had drowned in the Bogovizna some time before the revolution, its body had been found that autumn in the White Lake three miles away, although on the surface not even a small stream connected them. The place was cursed by God and men: miles and miles of impassable quagmire and marshy pools, scattered with clusters of stunted alders and rushes, and in some spots willow growing thick and profuse on the tussocks. From time immemorial people had avoided these parts, and if anyone did wander this way inadvertently he was haunted by dark terrors and would cry in fear in the night. In winter the Bogovizna was lightly frozen over, but its numberless marshy apertures were only covered by thin, fragile ice even in the hardest frost, too weak for the weight of a man, or even a wolf. In the frosty January nights the long drawn-out howling of wolf packs carried through the air. There had once been bears in the forests neighbouring the Bogovizna which upset the inhabitants of the local villages. Khvedor remembered from childhood one of his grandfather's stories about an encounter with a grizzly. The old man had been caught in a heavy shower and taken cover in the hollow of an old oak burnt out by the cowherds. The rain poured, it was twilight, and the hollow had become very dark when something shaggy and stinking shoved its way in. Grandfather was squashed, more dead than alive; the bear's wide, shaggy rump pressed so hard against him he could hardly breathe. The grizzly made himself at home in the cosy hollow, clearly settling in for a long stay, but grandfather had no time to hang about. He had to get home, and first he had to find and catch his horse, which he had left to graze not far off. But how could he get out without disturbing his uninvited guest? Grandfather fretted and thought, but in the end he could not think of anything better than to shout with all his might from behind the bear's back. The bear shot out of the hollow like a cork from a bottle, leaving grandfather covered in its stench. That was what the Bogovizna was like.

Khvedor stopped by the marsh, headed away from the god-forsaken place, and again wandered for a long time in the forest. Then, worn out, he sat down under a large, branching fir tree and put his capful of cranberries on his knee. He munched a few berries and thought. How wonderful to be free in the forest! Nobody making you go anywhere, nobody needing you, and you not needing anybody. If only one could live one's life like this. People did once live like this, in friendship with nature and the forest, finding nourishment in it in years of famine, and refuge in hard times. The forest gave them cover, warmth, food. It was man's best benefactor. But that was then. Now everything was different: even the forest could not save you. With people there'll always be some reason, envy or malice. They'll track you down in the forest, they'll find you under the ground. He had learned that lesson well, although he could not see where it all came from, what the cause of it was. It is almost the same in nature, though why is something of a riddle. He remembered an incident on the river in the north when he was working as a raftsman. He was once sitting in a cabin on the raft, whittling a wedge to go under a weakened joint. Suddenly a sparrow flew headlong towards him through the open window and threw itself at his head, knocking his hat off. Khvedor started in fright and waved his hands to beat off the bird, which immediately flew out to freedom. Leaping out after it, Khvedor realized what had made it throw itself at a man. Above the rafts a flock of sparrows was circling. All at once, as though to a command, they fell upon the wretched creature. In the air the evil gang of birds began to spin frenziedly and tore their unhappy fellow to pieces. Soon there was nothing left of him but a few feathers falling softly on the water. The flock wheeled sharply and disappeared behind the wooded precipice above the river. The stunned Khvedor stood and wondered, why? Birds too! Is this a primordial law of nature: all against one? But why against that one? What did that sparrow do to summon up the fury of the rest? Had he behaved differently from the others? Had he breached some bird etiquette? Maybe it was just that he was different. Could it be that it was not he who was in the wrong, but the flock? Like it is with people? Maybe it's the same with birds?

No, it's different with birds. There's more justice with birds. He had seen the incident with the sparrows just once in his life, but he had witnessed human injustice till it made him sick. Almost every day of his life.

He sat for a long time under the fir tree, relaxing a little, as though he were at home. He even dozed off briefly. Somewhere above him, in the tops of the firs, a crow was cawing noisily, and he came round from his nap. His thoughts were all a long way from this fir tree. They were there, in the village. He had thought about it in the north, he thought about it now. About its daily concerns, about his neighbours, about its fields soaked with sweat and blood. He could not simply walk into it, but in his thoughts he was always there; and he was irrepressibly drawn towards it. Regardless of the danger.

Sometime towards evening he finally gathered his resolve and dragged himself back through the forest. He walked back the same way, across the fir grove to the spot from which the dog had chased him. He walked cautiously, looking round from side to side, stopping frequently, listening to the mysterious sounds of the forest. It was quiet and empty. Towards evening the wind seemed to drop, the fir trees stood in lofty peace, as though they were deep in thought about something. Khvedor imagined the herd which had frightened him making its way back to the common pasture and the dog dutifully chasing home the lingering cows. People were also hurrying home from the field. Nobody wants to stay by the forest when night is setting in, not even an unfortunate wanderer like Khvedor.

He had not yet reached the edge of the forest by the time it began to get dark. In the forest the gloom thickened beneath the trees, the nearby bushes merged into an impenetrable mass, the grass underfoot became damp, and Khvedor began to hurry. In the twilight he had already passed the place where the dog had rushed at him and he soon emerged from the forest. Ahead the field shone in the half-light, the herd was nowhere to be seen. He had to walk towards the village along the forest edge on cattle-trampled stubble. But it was too early yet to come out on to the field; it was still not completely dark, and he sat down under a bush on the edge of the forest. He sat for a while and waited. He ate his cranberries to while away the time. At some distance in front of him lay the common pasture, the outskirts of the village, familiar in the most trivial detail: the two pear trees on Petrak's strip, the heap of stones where the boundary at the end of the common pasture used to be. His father's strip, on which he had laboured, had once been here. It was true, his elder brother Mitka had tended it longer and harder. Then at the start of collectivization he had gone to the Donbass coal mines. First he had gone himself and then he had taken his family, leaving his house, his land, and all his belongings forever. It must have been impossible to go on living there as the brother of an exiled kulak, and Mitka had chosen voluntary exile. How was he now, in the mines? He had never written to Khvedor in far-off Kotlas, just as Khvedor had never dared to write to him. He didn't even know his brother's address. Families had been torn apart, blood ties had been broken. Brothers had become strangers. That was what the times were like.

And what was true of his brother was true of his son.

Khvedor had not ceased thinking about his son Mikolka for a moment. He was his constant anxiety, his eternal pain. It was a good thing, of course, that his son had succeeded in dissociating himself from his family's shame, even managing to be made a boss, but it was all still very risky, it might all go up in a puff of smoke. His fatherly heart told him Mikolka's position was terribly precarious, terribly insecure, and he so wanted to protect him from ill. But what could he do, a deportee on the run? All he could do was behave as though he had disowned his son, never reminding him of his existence, not with an appeal, or a letter, not even a niggardly line; as though he were dead or no longer existed on the earth. Let his son Mikolka be happy, let him never reproach his father for anything. Perhaps the last of the line of Rovbas would be lucky. Good luck had passed the others by forever now.

The cold night was sinking softly over the field and the common pasture. In the sky, between the torn tatters of the clouds, the shining disc of the moon appeared, hung for a moment over the field and rolled behind the dishevelled edge of the stormclouds. It soon rolled out again and shone long and clear, pouring its transparent silver light over the field, the edge of the forest, and the man. Khvedor had never liked the full moon. Its queer light always upset him with its vague, enigmatic foreboding. Now the full moon came at a very bad time, and Khvedor waited for it to disappear. The village and the houses were barely visible from the edge of the forest. From here they were shrouded by the cemetery pines, which darkened into a tall, undifferentiated mass beyond the common pasture. Darkness reigned there and one could not pick anything out even by the light of the moon, but Khvedor stared at the distant features of the outskirts of the village, and again he was drawn more towards the cemetery. When at last the moon disappeared in the stormclouds and everything around shrivelled and darkened, he climbed out from under the bush and hurriedly set out across the field. The moon appeared again for a moment, then hid itself behind the clouds, but he did not stop again until he reached the cemetery.

The old fence between the cemetary and the field was broken down. The cattle had probably trampled it. He jumped over the low rail and stopped. The chary light of the moon silvered the disorderly assembly of crosses and graves, making them appear hoar-frosted. These were obviously new graves. There were many clustered together here and not one of them was known to Khvedor. There were large crosses, and small ones, and some were absolutely tiny. The low area beside the pasture was taken up with burial mounds without crosses. Some of the tall Catholic crosses had white cotton ribbons on them and dried-out bunches of flowers beneath them. Khvedor noticed a five-cornered star in the distance, probably cut out of plywood. Its distinct silhouette was outlined against the background of the luminous sky. He walked cautiously among the graves with a smouldering curiosity, and by the light of the moon read in amazement on a black plank, "Ivan Sokur". Below were inscribed his dates of birth and death. For a moment he stared at the inscription in bewilderment, and at the low burial mound. He noticed that there was no border round the grave. It looked as though nobody had tended it. It was overgrown with nettles and appeared utterly neglected. Indeed it was just like many of the other graves near it, but they were obviously old, forgotten graves, while this one belonged to a man they must still remember in the village. When Khvedor had been exiled to the north, Sokur had been helping the regional authorities, and at that time seemed a cheerful, perfectly healthy fellow. How had he ended up here before his time? Khvedor wondered. He had not seemed a bad man. Khvedor had no grudge against him. He might have behaved better if he had known the end was near. He could have behaved as his father would have done. He had been a peaceful, reasonable old man, never causing anyone any harm, and helping many people in their hour of need. There was the time he had sheltered the family of his brother who had been killed by lightning. His brother had taken cover under a pear tree in the field during a thunderstorm. He was found dead that evening by the cowherds and buried the next day, leaving an ailing widow and six young children. Old Sokur moved them all into his house, brought them up, and gave them a good start in life. He was a good man. But the son did not take after his father. He never caused anybody any great harm, but he was too complaisant in his duties as chairman of the village soviet, and the regional authorities had ordered him about as they pleased. The day they exiled the Rovbas he was charged with seeing that, in accordance with the order, the exiles took with them only a saw, an axe, some clothing and enough food for three days. All the rest — potatoes, grain, property accumulated over years of labour and sweat — was to be requisitioned for the use of the village soviet. He wouldn't have minded if it was to be used for public needs, but they confiscated it so the exiles would not have it with them on their long journey, so they would die more quickly from hunger and cold when they arrived. Six-year-old Olga had put on the new felt boots that had been specially made for her in the autumn in the borough town. All winter the little girl had saved them, going about in her old ones which had been patched and re-patched. They had decided that she should go on wearing them till spring before she threw them out. But when they began to prepare for the journey, her mother told her to put on the new ones: they were going out into the world and her mother did not want her little girl to look any worse than the others. To her misfortune, Olga obeyed, and just before they set off she came out on the porch in her nice black felt boots. It would have been better if she hadn't. The felt boots caught the rapacious eye of the dour authority in the black sheepskin coat, and he gave Ivan Sokur an order. Sokur hesitated, his clean-shaven face contorted, but in the end he went up to the little girl and repeated the order. Olga obediently took off her boots and stood in the snow in only her torn stockings. Seeing this Ganna burst into tears and brought the old footwarmers. Khvedor muttered reproachfully: "For heaven's sake!" at which Sokur silently shrugged his shoulders. What was he supposed to do? He didn't give the orders. He picked up the little felt boots and took them away, while the exiles loaded up their belongings and said farewell to their relatives, but all the time Khvedor thought: that was not Christian, taking away a child's boots. They weren't headed for a warm region, they were going north, to the bitter cold; but he said nothing, and Olga set out in the old footwarmers and wore them for another two winters and froze and fell ill, until she caught a chill for the last time and no longer needed anything.

At that time they were driving rafts down a wide northern river, a whole floating caravan of logs, a thousand cubic metres of timber. There were thirteen men in Kuznetsov's team. He was a bearded man in middle age who had spent all his life working on rafts. He knew the river well, all its turns, banks and shoals; he could navigate round dangerous rapids without spilling his load or running up against rocks and half-submerged sandbanks. He was stern and taciturn, and he could not abide slackers and weaklings (who to him were all one and the same). That was obviously why Rovba had ended up in his team. He had been capable of great endurance then, and he was patient and unquestioning, but something happened which almost brought his job on the float to an end. After his wife died, ten-year-old Olga was left alone, with no one to look after her and Khvedor had to take his daughter with him. But it was strictly forbidden to be on the rafts without authorization, so when Kuznetsov saw the raftsman with the child he immediately told him to go and see the boss. Perhaps he thought Rovba would become obstinate or plead with him, but instead he submissively picked up his bundle, took his daughter by the hand, said "Goodbye" and silently stepped ashore. From the shore he turned to take one last look at the river and at the team leader standing silently on the raft. Suddenly the team leader waved at him, signalling him to return. Khvedor returned as submissively as he had departed, and Kuznetsov blurted irritably, "Stay. Only watch out. You get caught, I don't know anything about it. Right?" "Understood," was Khvedor's laconic reply as he rejoiced infinitely in this turn of fate. He had become used to working on the float, he enjoyed the freedom of the river, the wooded shores around him and the high limitless sky above. He was not afraid of hard work. He could not imagine any work harder than in the peat bogs or felling trees in the taiga forests. Olga would always be with him, and his heart would not ache and he would not have to torment himself about how she was, whether she was hungry, whether any of the adults had hurt her. When her mother was alive everything had been simpler and easier, although even then Olga used to sit in the cold barrack hut for days on end while her mother worked in the wood-chopping area. Now there was no one left whom they knew and could trust, and the people there were of all sorts, gathered from the whole world. How could one leave a child without supervision? Khvedor was very grateful to the team leader for his kindness and threw himself into his work on the float with redoubled energy.

If he had only known what would come of this kindness, it would have been better to have left his daughter in the taiga, in the first forest settlement they came to, among strange, unknown people. Oh, if he had only known.

Olga was never idle on the rafts. She was a helpful, diligent little girl and she assisted the stern silent men in whatever way she could. A few days later the team leader gave her a position as helper to Kravets the cook, a quiet, obliging man, the eldest in their team. In general Kravets did not behave badly towards the little girl, he never upset her. Sometimes he would raise his voice if she did not do something quite right or dawdled, but he raised his voice without malice. Without malice, that was the most important thing. Not like his fellow-villager Rogovtsev, a loud, psychotic rogue who came out with obscenities at every step, even when there was nothing to swear about. Undoubtedly it was more because of his perpetual, ingrained bitterness than anything else. Every time Khvedor heard his foul language he felt as though his heart had been pierced by a nail. He tried to keep Olga away from him as much as he could, and as soon as Rogovtsev began to use filthy language he would deliberately strike up a conversation with her about something else or send her off to the other end of the caravan. But once, when the foul-mouthed lout was talking particularly obscenely in her presence about some women standing on the shore Khvedor lost his patience and discreetly reproached the man, telling him he shouldn't let his tongue run away with him in front of a child. Couldn't he be a little more decent? Rogovtsev immediately began to shout that he would not take orders from an exile like

Rovba, that his cussing was a small thing compared with keeping a stowaway on the raft and breaking the rules. He would report him as soon as they got to the nearest settlement and then his daughter would have to hear much worse things at the nearest transit camp where she and her straightlaced old man would be sent.

Khvedor was so taken aback by these shameless words he could not muster an answer. He thought he had witnessed every form of human baseness, but this was a new variety. That evening, when they were clear of the hazardous Ustiuzhny shoal, he told the team leader about Rogovstev's threat, thinking he would stand up for him and give the insolent fellow a dressing down, but Kuznetsov just scowled and said, "He is capable of anything." "So what can I do?" Khvedor asked perplexed. Kuznetsov glared at him severely. "If strangers show up, hide your daughter." "Where can you hide someone on the raft?" Khvedor asked, genuinely amazed. "You can hide her under the raft," the team leader remarked, and walked away along the slippery logs, towards the stern. Khvedor could not work out whether this was serious or just a jibe, but gradually it became clear: he really could hide her in the water, behind the raft. Olga swam reasonably well, she could hold on to a log so she would not drown. There was only one thing that worried him: summer was ending, the water was getting colder every day. On the rafts they had already stopped bathing, they only washed in the morning, and the mornings had become very cold.

There was no way of knowing whether Rogovstev had carried out his threat, but about that time a guard from the regional command came aboard to do a check. It was the last stop before the Usysvinsky shoal. This had happened before, but the checks were mostly for show. The guard would ask the team leader a few questions, give a cursory look round, and hurry ashore. But after he had spoken to the team leader this one, a jowly, thickset lout in a long grey coat, decided to walk down the rafts to the stern. Khvedor's heart clutched horribly. He stood on the right side of the raft with a boathook in his hands, and Olga was in the water five feet away holding on to a rope, her blond head bobbing near the timber on the surface. Then the guard stopped in the middle of the raft, rocking lazily on his fat legs, and conducted a long conversation with the team leader about the cunning of the local fish, and which spoon-bait the salmon bite in the autumn. It was not that late, but it was long past midday and a cold north wind was blowing. Khvedor was tense with impatience as he listened to their endless, pointless conversation. Just as it looked as though they were about to go ashore, when they had already turned round and begun to walk away, they stopped again. Pointing at the settlement the guard said something to the team leader, and Khvedor silently cursed: Why don't you drop dead, you self-satisfied pig. Olga had visibly begun to go numb with cold in the water behind the raft, but the guard slowly walked along the stationary rafts, stopping frequently and talking and talking, then he hung around aimlessly on the bank, his eyes never leaving the river. Khvedor stood, tensely wondering whether Rogovtsev had squealed or not. At long last the guard disappeared behind a riverside bush and with great difficulty he dragged Olga out of the water. She was blue with cold and her teeth were chattering loudly. She could not say a word. With trembling hands her father hurriedly dried her with rough sacking and rubbed her skinny little shoulders and her hollow little chest. She had to be changed into dry clothes. He took off his coat and wrapped his daughter in it. Kuznetsov arrived, understood everything at a glance and threw off his quilted coat. "There, cover her!" Kravets boiled some water and gave it to her to drink. It seemed that he had managed to warm the little girl up.

He put her in their usual place for the night, behind the

cabin on a bed of damp rags, wrapped up in sacking and the quilted coat. She warmed herself and fell asleep, and sitting beside her he thought everything might turn out all right. But it did not. The fever started before morning, his little daughter began to burn. She asked for a drink, complained that her head was aching. He gave her warm water. They had nothing else — no medicine, no herbal remedy of any kind. In the morning she began to doze lightly, but as she slept her body was fiery, and he had to go to the stern. "Up ahead," said the team leader, "is the hardest part of the river. We need everyone looking out with both eyes." But although they kept a look out, they let the last raft hit the rocks and it took until dinner time before they managed to pull it clear. During these hours he was able to steal a few minutes to go and look behind the cabin and every time his heart clenched horribly. Olga was in a bad way. To his misery, along both sides of the river the empty banks of the taiga drifted by, wild slopes stretched as far as the eye could see, and above them towered thick forest. There was no human habitation in sight. The team leader saw his grief and, as though in sympathy, said, "At the end of the week we'll get to Meza. There's a sick bay there. Maybe we can take the little girl there." Khvedor waited for Meza to appear like a deliverance. He waited two days and two nights, he did not lie down or close his eyes for a moment. When he was not manning the stern or the boathook he would run back along the slippery rafts to the cabin. Olga was getting worse all the time. On the third day she no longer recognized him; she just asked him to chase away the birds, and he was perplexed: What birds? Then it struck him: she was delirious. The next night she went quiet, became completely peaceful and silently left this world. Like a bright little bird, her pure child's soul flew away forever into eternity.

She lay there till midday on the rags behind the cabin. They did not know what to do with her. Finally the team leader pulled up three planks from the floor of the cabin and ordered Kravets to make a coffin. He knocked up a small oblong box, in which they laid Olga's cold body. But where were they to bury her? There was water all around them and the rafts would not land on the bank. What was he to do? The team leader thought up the idea of letting the hindmost raft float a little way towards the shoal on the bend (it was impossible to stop such an enormous thing completely) and taking the coffin ashore across the sandbank. Khvedor jumped off the raft, they passed him the little coffin and, standing chest-deep in the water, he took it. He fell into the water several times before he reached dry land, then, barely alive, scrambled up the steep bank and looked around. The forest stood like a wall on all sides, pines and silver firs. Just as before there was no human habitation in sight. In one place on the steeply rising bank a deep ravine yawned, and next to it was a bare, flat promontory. He carried the little coffin across to the promontory and began to dig a grave. He dug the stony earth long and hard and, unable to restrain himself, he gave in to tears. Life had taken his last joy from him, his sole consolation, and he thought: what more can I expect of it? What more can it take? After all that had happened to him his own life had lost all value, he no longer cherished it, it had become a burden to him. What could he do? Hang himself? Drown? He could run away now but he did not want to let the team leader down and, as soon as he had hurriedly buried his daughter, he rushed along the shore down to the river.

Late that evening he overtook the rafts. For a long time he could not even look at Rogovstev, shuddering at the mere sound of his voice. He could not understand how Kuznetsov and the others could get on with the man as though nothing had happened. Didn't they understand? Perhaps they were afraid of him. What else could it be? All the same they did sympathize with Khvedor. Kravets sighed softly and shook his head. The team leader kept stubbornly silent, not appearing to think about anything but his rafts. When at last they arrived in Kotlas and delivered their caravan load to the timber exchange the team leader softened a little and became more talkative. Once as they were returning to their barrack hut in the evening, he nodded discreetly at Khvedor and beckoned him to the corner of the storage building. There was nobody about and he asked quietly,"Do you need papers?". "What kind of papers?" Khvedor did not understand. "What do you mean, what kind? Take them!" Kuznetsov hissed angrily, and, glancing round furtively, he shoved a neat wad of paper into Khvedor's hands. "I was keeping them for myself, but I can see they might come in handy for you," he finished, more kindly.

Khvedor took the papers, which were in the name of some Andrei Zaitsev. They would indeed soon turn out to be useful to him. He would have been grateful to the team leader from the bottom of his soul, had it not been for the price he had paid for them. This immeasurable price stood in the way of gratitude. Compared with a dead child's soul, nothing in the world had any worth.

The moon shone cold and clear in the breaks in the storm clouds above the field, and threw the slanting broken shadows of crosses on to the graves. In the distance, under the pine trees lay an impenetrable gloom, its wide shadow reached the edge of the cemetery above the common pasture. But close up he could see everything distinctly, every cross and every mound. Then, when the moon hid itself behind the clouds again, everything was plunged back into darkness. Khvedor covered his eyes and stood unseeing among the graves. He felt peace and joy here. It was as though he had renewed an interrupted communion with people and was conducting a silent conversation with them about everything, arguing, questioning, complaining. It was a pity he received no answer, but he was well used to his mute questions going unanswered, as if he had gone deaf over the years of his wanderings. As he moved around the graveyard in a state of sleepy pensiveness he came upon a fresh grave, on the slope, near the pine-covered hill. Even by night the well-cared-for appearance of the little grave and the neatness of the lovingly laid turf caught his eye. It was strewn around with fresh clean sand, pure white in the moonlight. It bore two eight-pointed crosses, one large one and a smaller one in front of it, both painted white. Near it was a small bench, like a toy bench; Khvedor sank on to it. He had no idea who was buried here. It didn't look like an old man or woman: old people's graves aren't so well looked after. Could it be a wife taking such pains for her beloved husband? But a woman would hardly have done it all so expertly and neatly. So was it a husband doing it for his wife? It was probably parents who had done it for their child. Yes, that was the most likely guess, but there was no marking anywhere. It was an anonymous tomb engraved forever only in the hearts of those who loved the deceased.

Probably not even a tiny mound remained of his Olga's grave.

The quiet moonlit night wore on. Towards morning it became quite cold out in the cemetery, as though frosts were on the way, Khvedor thought, sitting dejectedly by the grave of this unknown person. He did not want to leave this place. He felt safe here as nowhere else, he was at peace here. As morning approached the moon set and it became dark all around, like a crypt. Khvedor had long grown used to the gloom of night; it did not frighten him. So he sat, remembering, thinking. He munched on the sour cranberries, taking two or three out of his pocket at a time to make them last longer. Without realizing it he dozed off. As always the cold of night began to torment him. He could never get used to the cold, especially as he grew older, and his miserable diet didn't help. He had suffered from it in the war and in exile, and now he was suffering from it at home too. In his life he had felt the cold more than anyone else; he had never managed to warm himself up the way others did, by clapping their hands together, or crouching down and stamping their feet. In the cold he lost his mobility and became like a block of wood, his whole body became tense and twisted into contortions. He would simply have to endure it, the way he had endured hunger, humiliation, despair. For many years all his strength had been directed towards one thing alone, endurance. He did not crack, like some people, when he felt he could no longer go on. He did not curse the disgusting slops, the back-breaking work, the injustice. He gritted his teeth while he still had some, and endured. There was probably no labour in the world so hard he would not have learned to endure it in silence, but there was one thing he could not endure: the longing for his birthplace, the forest, the humble forest glades. He had lost the power to overcome this yearning: his whole being had strained homewards, first in his thoughts, now in deed. The first time he had not succeeded; he had been unlucky the second; but he had succeeded the third time and now all he wanted was peace for his soul. What was cold to him!

It was time to go back into the forest so nobody would spot him when morning came, but way-worn and drowsy, he lingered, dragging out the time, in no hurry to leave the dark night time graveyard. A little while later he noticed it had become lighter. The pines, the nearby graves and the crosses were emerging through the gloom, and he realized it was getting light. The edge of the sky over the forest was already brightening with the beginnings of the day. Khvedor rose from the bench. An insane idea suddenly came to him: to walk quietly down the street at this early hour before the village awoke. Who knows, he might never get another chance, and at this hour he might not be noticed.

He walked down the narrow path between the graves through the thinning darkness under the pines and descended into the village street. The eaves of the houses, the tops of the trees along the street and in the gardens were just floating out of the darkness, the streets and courtyards lay in the twilight, the houses drooped in the sleepy peace before morning. The grey twilight huddled under their sagging eaves, among the cattle-sheds and the courtyard buildings. A light morning breeze fluttered a colourful red-striped rag on a fencepost, and Khvedor thought, "It's getting light fast. Maybe I'm too late." Quickening his pace, he walked along the side of the road, his boots rustling softly in the grass, looking from side to side with a watchful, avid eye. He wanted to take in and recognize as much as possible. Then in sudden bewilderment his glance was frozen by a motionless female face behind a paling: the eyes looking at him were also rounded with mute, astonished fright. The expression, which he could not quite catch, struck him all of sudden: Lyubka. He stopped. Next door, two paces away, was a wicket-gate. He pushed it abruptly without knowing why and it opened. The woman looked at him silently for a moment. He could not make out whether she recognized him or not. Then she uttered a strangled cry and rushed towards the house. Dumb with fright, he stood in front of the wicket-gate until he heard the bang of a door and the rumble of a metal bolt.

Fearing that they might now run out on to the porch or see him through the window, Khvedor ran into the courtyard and set out along the dewy beetroot tops in the vegetable plot towards the field. Nobody chased him or shouted after him. His whole body was shaking after the unexpected meeting with Lyubka. He had grown up with her in the village and worked side by side with her on their fathers' strips. He had even been in love with her before he was conscripted. He felt indignant and bitter. The woman had probably taken fright, but she'd almost been the undoing of him. Perhaps she hadn't recognized him and had taken him for a night intruder, a burglar? And it wasn't surprising. Would he even recognize himself?

What was left in him of the former naive, silent Khvedor Rovba? He was more ghost than man, a night-time, incorporeal apparition which people shy away from in terror, whose only place is with the wolves in the forest.

Chapter Four

The Joy of the Land

By the time it was light, he was already in the forest. He made his confused way along a cattle-trampled path, looking for a spot where he would be able to tuck himself away for the day. They were sure to drive the cattle this way again, there was no place for him here. So where could he go, further away from dwellings and people? The corn field and hay-field of course. That meant he would have to drag himself back to the glade or the distant, gloomy fir grove and the marshy moss clumps. When he had thought it over he decided, better go to the glade. It was true it was more dangerous than in the fir grove, but there were potatoes over there. It was time to pay them a visit. As always, since morning his stomach had been rumbling. He was hungry. He had eaten almost all the cranberries during the night. They don't do much for your hunger, but you're not thirsty after them. He had to go and look for potatoes.

At least at that early hour he did not have to fear any chance meetings in the forest. He walked half a mile or more on a well-trampled little path intricately looping its way through the young birch wood. The path turned in the direction of the winter plots. He went towards the long gully. On the other side of a sparse fir glade he climbed wearily up a gentle slope. Visibility in the forest was already much better. It was daylight. All around, the firs nodded softly, not a leaf stirred on the yellowy birch trees. The weather seemed to have settled, soon it was bound to freeze. Then all the alders would blacken, the birch trees would shine with gold, and the falling leaves would rustle amiably. A little more time would pass, and the leafy forest would become transparent, every living thing in it would be visible from a long way off. Then things would get bad for him. But Khvedor did not want to think about what lay ahead, he lived from day to day, never looking beyond the approaching evening. In the evening things are calmer, but by day you stay on your guard.

In what looked like the same place as last time, he cautiously descended through the bushes to the wide gully, had a good drink in the brook and washed his face and hands. He took a long time climbing the opposite slope, stopping to rest, feeling again how much his strength was reduced. Quite recently, on the journey, he had not noticed his weakness. He had probably been impelled by the great force of his goal. But now his goal was behind him. During his long wanderings he had grown weaker without bread, and berries would not satisfy him. So what then. Should he walk into the village again, beg for a crust of bread? How would this end? The recent encounter with Lyubka worried him. She might trumpet it around the village. But perhaps she hadn't recognized him when she let out that ominous cry.

Once out of the gully it took him a long time to get his breath back. Then he went deeper into the wood and found a little spot for himself between two hazelnut bushes, sheltered by their bowing tops. Before lying down, he rummaged through the branches. No, it was too bad, there were no hazels, he wouldn't find anything here. There were mushrooms in the clearings in the grass, russulas and milky caps. Occasionally he glimpsed the red hats of death-caps. By the look of it the turn of the real mushrooms would come soon, but while there were still some left in the field, he was more interested in potatoes.

Potatoes were linked in his mind with an unpleasant incident that had taken place when he had been a captive of the Germans. Now it was funny to look back on. He remembered it from time to time, because the bitter and the funny often sit side by side in our experience. For the first six months of captivity Rovba had barely survived on the steamed swede which the half-starving prisoners were fed in the iron foundry in the Ruhr. Then fate took pity on him and he found himself working for a farmer, an elderly German by the name of Egan who had two sons fighting on the Russian front. His daughter-in-law and two grandsons had remained at home. Egan had fifty acres of land and the farmer took on six Russian prisoners as farm-labourers, soldiers of General Samsonov, to cultivate it. Overall, life on the farm was not at all bad for Khvedor. He was fed decently, although he was made to work long hours without days off or holidays. They worked like devils, like oxen, coping with all the work in the field, on the threshing-floor, and even around the house. Egan instituted a firm, barracks-like order, which was supervised by the master of the estate himself, who had once served as a sergeant-major, a fact he used to remind the prisoners of endlessly. But in the fields his daughter-in-law gave the orders. She rode about on a fine light bay filly, overseeing, checking where something was not quite right, deciding whom to punish and whom to praise. The master took care of them and trained them in his own peculiar fashion. It was a military regime. Once he fined the cook: she had put too much meat in the pot with the soup. For careless work you had to go without lunch: you had breakfast in the morning, and that was all you got. Once when Belosheyev, a prisoner from Tula, complained to the master that another prisoner had stolen a cigarette case from him, Herr Egan, without giving the matter any scrutiny, punished them both. He ordered the farm-labourers to join their left hands as though they were shaking hands and slap one another round the ear with their right hands, saying to each other, "Guten Morgen — Guten Tag". All the farm-labourers, the cook, the children, the master and his daughter-in-law sat on the porch and watched. At the beginning it was funny, watching the two Russians lazily giving each other feeble slaps, but soon they had to be pulled apart to avoid bloodshed.

They were woken at five every morning by the ringing of the overseer's bell. They smoothed the blankets on their trestle-beds, drank coffee with bread and jam, and got ready for work. For lunch they were given a bowl of soup and porridge with a piece of meat and a pound of bread each. They slept on clean linen, which the old cook changed every Saturday, and on Saturdays they washed under a warm shower in an outhouse. Belosheyev, with whom Khvedor had made friends, could not get over his luck for, as he used to say, at home he didn't sleep in such cleanliness or eat as well as he did in captivity, and as for the work, he was used to it. Perhaps everything would not have been too bad if it hadn't been for Rudi, Egan's fourteen year old grandson.

The vile Rudi thought of nothing but playing dirty tricks on the Russians. He would block the door of the privy with a pitchfork while someone was using it, hide the saddle when a horse had to be harnessed, or stand the kvass pitcher under the horse's tail. Once he surreptitiously took the pintle out of a wagon loaded with potatoes, and when Khvedor moved it the wagon fell off its detachable front and spilled all the potatoes. While Khvedor, cursing, gathered up the potatoes, Rudi impudently let out a coarse laugh in the kitchen garden. Khvedor lost his temper and dealt him a lash of his whip across the fence, fixed the wagon, and without saying a word to anybody, drove off to the field. When he returned to the courtyard in the evening, he saw Herda, red with anger, and that vile little Rudi, with a bloody scar across his cheek, standing on the old master's porch. Old Egan immediately set up an investigation. Khvedor tried to justify himself but nobody listened to him. The daughter-in-law shrieked something about the cooler, but her father-in-law immediately said no to that. He couldn't allow one of his workers to sit in the lock-up sponging food at this busy time or lie around on a trestle-bed with his backside thrashed with birch twigs. He would punish him with shame: tomorrow Fedor would go out to work without his trousers on ("Ohne Hosen").

At first Khvedor did not understand. What a weird punishment, without his trousers on? In just his underpants, or what? But it turned out not to mean in his underpants, but with the lower part of his body completely exposed. It was not particularly cold, the spring sun warmed him, but Khvedor's suffering had no limit. He kept pulling and straightening the short hem of his shirt, vainly trying to cover his shame, but covering it was impossible. He had to work, load potatoes onto the waggon, drag the sacks in the field. And all around him there were people, German men and women, their children, adolescents, young girls. They all looked at him in laughter or bewilderment, and he could have howled with humiliation. He could hardly wait for the evening of that endless day and when he got to his warm bed, he lay down under the blanket without eating supper. What bliss it was to feel his body hidden from others' eyes! He was thirty, he was married, and he thought he could not imagine a worse humiliation. But time passed, other humiliations rained down on him, in comparison with which Herr Egan's weird invention seemed an absurd joke, nothing more.

Swallowing his hungry saliva, Khvedor curled up under the bushes on the sparse, low grass, tucked his head into his crumpled collar, slipped his hands into his breast and lay still. He closed his eyes from time to time, not fearing he would miss anything. From under the bushes he couldn't see much, but his hearing, as always, was straining acutely. Even asleep

Khvedor was listening. How would he be secure in that position otherwise? The trees made a slight noise nearby, but the noise did not disturb the quiet of the forest that Khvedor knew so well. From time to time a tiny bird fluttered in the bushes, but that did not disturb his peace either. Gradually and imperceptibly he felt he had shut himself out of the forest, slipped out of his own time, as if he was falling asleep, and seeing himself from the outside perhaps for the first time he realized the whole hopelessness of his predicament. He looked at himself as if from a distance and involuntarily started in somnolent surprise. What was the matter with him? Why was he lying about here without a place to rest, a mile from the place where he had first come into the world, where he had lived his adult life, where his children had been born? Why had he become a despised stranger, a hated outcast. Whose fault was it? Was it his own or someone else's? Or nobody's? But how had all this been possible then? Why on earth, after being given land, did he have to lose everything, become an exile, a convict on the run, a man without rights, an outlaw? What had started it all? However much he thought about it he could find no intelligible answer. No doubt because it had all begun so imperceptibly, so absurdly and unexpectedly. Could he have foreseen everything that frosty winter evening when he had been sitting in the village soviet and the chairman Sokur had raised for discussion the puzzling question: who should get the three grain levies he had brought back from the District Executive Committee? This had not been an easy business for the members of the village soviet, whose number then included Rovba. In those years he was considered a "middle" peasant. He had thirty acres of land. There were a few richer farmers in the village, some had thirty five or more, but what kind of acres were they? Zmitrok Beduta, for example, owned forty acres, but remained the poorest of the poor because there was nobody to work the land. His two sons had not returned from the war, and he was old and infirm. At the time of the revolution and the civil war, his strip in the faraway water meadow by the river had been covered with bushes and only counted as arable land on paper, but it was counted all the same, and Zmitrok was the first in the village to receive a kulak's grain levy. Khvedor did not even admit the thought that the same fate might one day befall him. Even if he did live no worse than the others, how could he be a kulak? One horse, two cows, sheep, a pig: just like everybody else in Nedolishche. It's true he had geese. They swam in the pond at the end of the vegetable plots. The stream flowed from the marsh. One spring he and his son had managed to lay a log path on the river-bed near the little bridge and channelled a shallow pool, and it had stayed like that. But it wasn't because of the geese that he was considered a kulak and his life ruined.

It was the threshing machine that ruined his life. That damned threshing machine, why had he ever had anything to do with it! He could have kept threshing as before, with flails, there wasn't so much corn then that they could not have got it threshed in the course of the winter on the threshing-floor with three flails. But no, he had wanted it to be done the sophisticated way, with a threshing-machine.

His son Mikolka had given him the idea. At that time he was already a smart, tall lad. He was expecting the call-up to the Red Army in the autumn, and he had become secretary of the local Komsomol group. When he started work as the secretary, newspapers, pamphlets and all kinds of interesting journals began to appear in the house. Like *The Atheist*. Usually his son was occupied with business all day, but he used to read at night by lamplight, and the next morning he would push the most interesting pieces under his father's nose: an article about taxes and self-taxation in the *Byelorussian News*, or Comrade Stalin's speech against the opposition, or a pamphlet by Commissar Prishchepov about the management of the village economy. Khvedor read, not understanding everything but nonetheless grasping the most important things, and he could see for himself: they really were living badly, poorly, in an uncultured way. They were managing the economy wrongly; but how were they to manage it correctly? Certainly, to manage an economy well, knowledge alone is not enough. You need money, machinery, fertilizers. With the specific aim of getting more fertilizer for his acres he had acquired a second cow. He had reared a calf though there was plenty of milk for the family from just one. About four years before that, he was the first person in the village to buy a new factory-made plough in Polotsk. It was painted a pretty cornflower blue with finely moulded oak handles. The little plough turned out to be good, it was a pleasure to plough with. Even the neighbours asked to have a go. Then a few other farmers bought ploughs like it. Everybody liked the new ploughs.

Late one autumn evening Mikolka arrived home. He was tired, hungry, up to his knees in mud. He had been at some important meeting in town. His mother hurriedly put a bowl of soup on the table. He ate a little and said, "Papa, let's buy a threshing machine. There's a chance to through the Consumer's Co-operative Society, with payment in instalments." Khvedor did not answer immediately, he thought about it. Of course, there was no harm at all in a threshing machine. He had already seen one in a neighbouring village where a few farmers had pooled their resources and bought one. They said it threshed well, the farmers were satisfied. It was better than flails, and faster. However, it was as if his heart could sense what would come of this. He already knew from experience that the new and the unprecedented in peasant life often go hand in hand with idiocy and deceit, and you have to think carefully to avoid putting your foot in it. He said all this to his son, who burst out laughing. What kind of deceit do you expect from a threshing-machine? In a week everything would be threshed, they would not have to spend all winter waving flails. That's true, thought Khvedor, but he kept silent, harbouring his doubts. In the morning when Mikolka had rushed out on Komsomol business he carefully discussed the matter with Ganna, and they decided to buy it, before someone from another village beat them to it.

They brought out the threshing machine the day after the Feast of Our Lady's Veil. His brother-in-law Tomash helped. They spent a long time adjusting the gear under the awning with the wooden connecting rods and the iron-toothed lever. Mikolka laid aside his work and helped too. He understood something about new farming technology. At last they had adjusted and tested the machine; and of course there was no comparison with the flails. It was fast and it threshed differently. It did need more people than the threshing floor: one to untie the bundles, one to lay them on the table. Then there was the operator, the most important person on the threshing machine, and two more to throw away the chaff and gather the wheat. It also required one person to lead the horses around. The threshing machine demanded at least six people, no fewer, but it was worth it. They threshed for two or three families at a time when they could. Khvedor never refused anyone. People could come in on it as they wished, and pay as much as they could, depending on how much they threshed of course. Everything was by agreement. Was he going to exploit his fellow villagers? He would have been prepared to thresh for free if he hadn't needed the money, but the threshing machine had not been cheap, and because they had taken it on credit, he had to pay up every quarter. Before Christmas he had done all the threshing for all his neighbours and several of his relatives. People even came from the neighbouring villages. Rovba did everyone's threshing.

But the red threshing machine did not roar on the threshing floor for long. At the beginning of the following autumn Sokur arrived as chairman of the village soviet, accompanied by a conceited, moustached official from the regional soviet, and they sealed up the threshing machine. It turned out that Rovba had allowed exploitation and received unearned income. "But what now? What will happen?'" asked Khvedor. "What will be will be," the man with the moustache replied darkly, buttoning up his shabby briefcase. Both of them left the courtyard without a backward glance, and Khvedor lingered by the gate, already sensing that this was more than just the loss of a threshing machine. It was the beginning of far worse trouble, trouble which was circling above his farm like a clawed crow. Mikolka had already left home by then. He had been called up to the army two months earlier, and posted to the Far Eastern border. He had sent his first letter home from there in raptures about serving "in such close contact with the Japanese samurai". Khvedor wrote sparingly about his health, and that was all. Not a word about the threshing machine. Let his son do his military service in peace.

But problems were brewing in Nedolishche. There were envious people like Zyrkash who sent in a complaint to Polotsk about how Khvedor was fleecing the peasants. But was he really? He didn't even set the wage rate. He was never asked any questions, but when the grain levy was being imposed they remembered that threshing machine, and Sokur said that in fairness they should impose a heavy one on Rovba, who had made some money from the threshing. Khvedor did not know what to say. He could not explain it simply, and there was no opportunity to go into it in depth. So they said that, whether Rovba had made money out of it or not, there was no other threshing machine in the village, and a levy was imposed on him by law. There had been no provision in the law to come to his defence.

How many times had Khvedor repeated the question to himself since then: why the devil had he got that threshing machine? It would have been better to have carried on threshing with flails like everyone else, he would have made his living somehow, and he would have been spared the misfortunes which, with diabolical inventiveness, had begun to dog his life.

But there was probably nothing that could have saved him by then. The threshing machine was only a snag. Like when a heavily loaded cart starts to keel over on a hillside, however much you try to hold it down it will topple over, one side will tip. The threshing machine was the weight that toppled the keeling cart of Rovba's life. Because he was already marked, like a bad sheep in the flock, a special mark had appeared by his name in the village soviet or maybe in the regional centre. The levy, two and a half thousand pounds of corn, he paid somehow, but he had to clear out the granary to do it. He delivered everything before the first of March, like the paper prescribed. They began to go hungry on the farmstead. There was nothing left for sowing the winter crop. About seventy pounds of barley and a half sack of oats were all that was left. He did not know whether he should buy the rest or borrow it from someone, but to buy he needed money and he had no money. He had not thought of anything when they imposed another even harsher levy: three thousand pounds of grain and one hundred roubles in cash. Then he said to himself, have they gone mad over there? Where the devil was he going to find such an amount? He went to the village soviet, travelled to the borough town to see secretary Terebilnikov whom he knew — he had worked in the Komsomol with Mikolka until recently — he complained, grovelled, pleaded. It was no use. They told him, if you don't pay on time, we'll distrain the property, "including the outbuildings and the cattle". He was downcast for a couple of days, then he began to run from one relative to another, and to his wife's and to some of the well-to-do people in his and the neighbouring villages asking for money. But it was as if everyone had turned to stone, gone deaf. Nobody wanted to understand his miseries, and no one gave him anything. Of course, at that time everyone was desperate to clear his own debts, the papers with the severe levies had already started to appear in other villages. He tried desperately to sell the threshing machine, he advertised it among his acquaintances and even at the market in the borough town, but nobody bought it, or showed any interest. He had to sell off the cattle, both cows, all the sheep and the pig. Of course, he was a fool. He did not realize that it was all futile, that not even paying the full amount would save him. Nothing could save Rovba now that he was marked out with the villainous, terrible word "kulak".

During those hectic days, running around the borough town in search of money, he had met Nahum, an old Jew whom he had once done business with. He had paid a visit to his little house under the lime tree when he was buying the threshing machine. They had never been great friends but Nahum used to lend money and was even prepared to wait if the debt could not be repaid in time, or accept eggs, butter or a couple of bags of potatoes instead of cash. Always busy and active, Nahum was dragging along the street in bewilderment as though he saw nothing around him. Khvedor delicately asked after his health. They got talking, and it turned out that Nahum had also had serious run-ins with the authorities. When Khvedor complained of his misery the old Jew took him by the buttonhole and pulled him hard towards him: "Let me tell you, drop everything. Take your children in your arms and run away. Where to? It doesn't matter where: where your nose leads you. Later it will be too late. That's what Nahum is telling you! I've got rid of everything and now, with this knapsack, I'm going to the station. I don't have a home here anymore! I'm a refugee! You listen to me, Khvedor!"

No, Khvedor did not listen then. How could he abandon all this, his land, his property? And where would he go? His roots, his people, the villagers were here — how could he go somewhere else, out into a shelterless, unfamiliar world?

He lived on in Nedolishche about ten more months. His life was joyless, famine and starvation settled into his poverty-stricken house. Khvedor gritted his teeth and hardened himself, but Ganna often wept, especially in the mornings when she began to cook and needed to put something in the pot or the frying pan. To get milk for Olga, they went to the village to Lyoksa or to the Grechikhins. These people had compassion, they experienced his hardship like their own and helped as much as they could. He remembered one occasion when he had called on Zmiter Tsyprukov who had owed him thirty roubles for three years. He had borrowed it for the threshing and never repaid it, and for a long time Khvedor could not make up his mind to remind him. He felt awkward about it as though he were demanding someone else's property. He should have listened to Ganna. When she saw him getting ready to go to Zmiter's one evening she said, "Don't go! Let them burn, those thirty roubles, if he has so little." He must be shameless, thought Khvedor. In fact I know he is, but how can I not go, when I'm so hard up? So he went and, of course, received nothing for his pains. Whether Zmiter had no money, or had made up his mind not to give him any, who could say; but their conversation turned nasty, and after he returned home Khvedor stayed moodily silent until the next morning. It would not have mattered, they would have managed without those thirty roubles, had Zmiter not been active on the Committee of Poor Peasants. When the most terrible time began, the "dekulakization", it was he who suggested that Khvedor Rovba be dispossessed as an exploiter. They listened to him, and Khvedor was sent into exile. They waged class war in the village, and Zmiter kept the thirty roubles. Khvedor did not begrudge him the money; it was just that everything on earth had become so much worse because of it.

Somewhere in the sky the tepid autumn sun was shining, the tops of the pine trees shone softly in its slanting rays. On the upper branches of the trees crows were warming themselves, occasionally flying off somewhere, perhaps to other trees nearby. Down below, beneath the hazels, there was a humid shade. It was damp, and Khvedor turned from side to side so as not to get too cold from the ground. He dozed off for a while, an hour or more, then hunger began to gnaw at him again. He was tempted to go to the field and look for potatoes, but he kept on sitting there under the bush, thinking. Maybe it's all been dug up already and the people have left the field. He might find something there, a dozen potatoes that had not been picked. That wouldn't count as theft; and if it was theft, it wasn't bad theft. The collective farmers would forgive him. Anyway, they'd taken far more from him, whatever a farmstead is worth, and a threshing machine. All he needed from them was a few potatoes. It wasn't all that much.

He got up, wandered through the hazelbushes, and made his way to a young aspen grove, so thick with brushwood he hardly managed to get through it. He tarried a while in the undergrowth of a raspberry cane as tall as a man with a few dry, black berries on its wands which the birds had pecked. He picked them one by one and ate them. The berries crunched in his teeth in a disgusting way, and tasted of nothing now that they had lost their summer sweetness. Towards the end of the day he went out to the edge of the forest some way beyond the potato field and realized he had gone too far to the right. He would have to go back along the edge of the forest. He must have gone half a mile or so when he heard a low grumbling voice nearby.

Concealing himself in the bushes, he looked around stealthily. A little way off, holding a black cow on a rope, a hunched old man in a faded peasant coat was wandering slowly along the edge of the forest. The cow was tugging to get at the grass in the bushes, and the cowherd grumbled at it gently from time to time. Khvedor stared out from the undergrowth, trying to tell whether he knew the man. No, the old man did not look familiar. He must be from a far away village. Khvedor could have bypassed him through the wood, but he suddenly had a thought. What about asking him for some bread? If the old man had been tending the cow since morning he must have brought some bread in his pocket, and maybe he'd give him a piece. He so craved a morsel of bread.

Summoning up his courage, he crawled out of the bushes on the edge of the winter crop and approached the cowherd. The man could already hear his footsteps but, busy with the cow, did not appear to pay him any attention. Fronting right up to him, Khvedor greeted him with reserve. The man looked at him with faded eyes. His face was grey with stubble, like Khvedor's own must be. The old man blinked, weak-sightedly looking the stranger up and down without replying. Khvedor greeted him again.

"Yes, I heard you, I heard you," the old cowherd said at last, mumbling with his toothless mouth. "And good day to you."

"You're tending the cow?"

"What does it look like? It's not a horse. I don't look after horses any more. I'm all finished with that."

"Where are you from?" asked Khvedor, and fell silent. It was the most crucial question: would the old man know him or not?

"From Ushaty, over that way," said the cowherd, looking attentively at Khvedor for the first time. It seemed Khvedor's miserable appearance didn't surprise the old man. He was not dressed any better himself. Khvedor sighed with relief. In faraway Ushaty very few people knew him.

"Might you have something to smoke?" Khvedor asked unexpectedly, not recognizing his own voice. It had become so plaintive and weak. He did not want a smoke at all. He had lost the habit long ago, but lacked the resolve to ask for bread immediately.

"Oh yes," said the old man and rummaged about in the deep pocket of his coat. "I've got some homegrown stuff, but I don't have anything to light it with."

"Maybe we'll find something," Khvedor said, regretting having turned the conversation to smoking: he had to save his matches.

They silently twisted a scrap of yellow newspaper into a cigar shape for each, and with trembling fingers Khvedor carefully struck a match. With equal care he lit up, then with more confidence gave the old man a light.

"Would you be from a collective farm?" asked Khvedor, after they had inhaled. It made his head spin and he tottered slightly. The old man eyed him suspiciously again.

"Yes, of course. Where else would I be from? Now everybody is on a collective farm, of course."

"So are there no smallholders left?"

"Smallholders?" said the old man, squinting with one eye. "And where are you from? Far away?"

"Yes, I'm not from these parts," replied Khvedor, lying. "I'm visiting relatives."

The black cow moved forward towards a bush, giving the rope a good tug and pulling the old man with it. Khvedor followed.

"And in your area, are there any smallholders left?"

"No, you know."

"And there are none left where I'm from," remarked the old man miserably. "The ones who didn't want to join the collective farm were taken away. The ones who wanted to later on were dispossessed too and sent away. Kulaks, sub-kulaks," muttered the old herdsman in a plaintive tone, as he followed the cow.

"And what's it like on the collective farm? Is life good?"

"Good? From Easter to St Elijah's Day we ate grass. After St Elijah's Day we began digging potatoes, but what sort of potatoes can you have so early? Nuts."

"Is that how it is?"

"U-huh. Don't you know? Or didn't you have a famine down your way?" The old man stared at him with a look of curiosity and reproach.

"Yes, of course we did."

"Well, the cow's been our only salvation. Milk! But you have to give some away — two hundred litres, and also some meat and eggs, wool and sheep. In the winter we slaughtered a pig. They gave a fifty rouble fine for it."

"For a pig?"

"For the skin. You have to give away the skin. Are there different regulations where you are?"

"Where I live? What can I tell you? It's strict, but maybe not as strict as where you are?" Khvedor was getting utterly confused, trying to think of something to say. He had no idea what things were like in other parts, whether it was like here or different. The old man took his evasive answer in his own way.

"It can't be as rotten anywhere as it is here. Worthless authorities, worthless people. How can it be like this? They requisition your cow for the slightest delay in paying taxes. And what about the youngsters? How are they supposed to do without milk? They just die. So many of them died this summer. Old and young. So I just trudge about in the forest with this old girl." He gave the string an expressive tug. "So they won't take her away. And I've nothing to pay them with. And three little ones at home. It's misery..."

"Misery," Khvedor said distractedly. Until now he had not spoken to anyone about life here, to find out what life was like for his countrymen; the old man was the first. Khvedor wanted to ask him more detailed questions, but was afraid he might become suspicious. After all he was an outsider here.

"Misery, yes."

"Shouldn't you make a complaint? Write a letter to someone?" Khvedor suggested delicately. The old man's stubbled face cracked into a crooked smirk.

"So who am I supposed to complain to? The bosses? They're like beasts to us. They'll send someone along like that Rovba. He's a holy terror. He threatens you with Siberia..."

Khvedor suddenly felt as though the earth had quaked under him and the field tipped on its side.

"Rovba?"

"Yes, Rovba. He's the Party Secretary here. He's young, but what a terror! He's disowned his own father. His father was dispossessed in Nedolishche and he refused to help. He's going to change his last name so he can keep the whole thing hushed up."

Khvedor felt as though he was falling slowly to the ground, the ground was swimming, being pulled out from under his feet. He could hardly hear the old man speak, no doubt carrying on with his complaints about life and the regime in the region. Khvedor was not listening. He was too stunned by the sudden news about his son, the information had struck him with such heartache that he had ceased to feel. He could no longer ask about anything, he just looked with detachment at the wide expanse of winter crop and beyond it the eaves of the next village on the hill. He wandered along the edge of the forest in silence. He did not ask for any bread. He could no longer ask for anything. He plodded along like a beaten dog, thinking, why have I dragged myself here, why did I talk to that old man? It would have been better not to have known anything about life here or about his son. He would have lived as he had before with the troubles he had borne inside for years. Why should he add new ones? Where would he find room for them in a soul exhausted by suffering, how could he live with them?

But what kind of life had it been?

Utterly indifferent to the forest and the field, forgetting caution, not looking about him even once, he walked away from the old man and the cow, deep into the forest and, drained of strength, wandered into some tall, sparse ferns. What he had heard about his son Mikolka seemed nonsensical. It would not settle in his head. He struggled to understand it. Okay, he had cut himself off from his father — but why be so cruel to people? And to change his name too. What was wrong with his name? What would remain of what had been lived through? And what would he live with? What would he say to his children, if he had any? It was not easy for Khvedor to understand how his son lived and what he thought about things. He had not seen him in seven years. What he had just heard was incomprehensible and unthinkable.

Mikolka had been a gentle, obedient little boy who loved animals. He had kept a grey hen, which had broken its foot, in a cage under his bed for a whole winter. He was devoted to his mother. He was beside himself when she caught scarlet fever. As a young man he obviously loved the Komsomol with the same devotion. Maybe not so much the Komsomol as the loud, busy bustle which the young people threw themselves into with such excitement in those dark, snow-muffled villages, so lonely and uneventful for months on end. They were always thinking up something, holding meetings and discussions and passing resolutions. Mikolka and Shurka had been particularly active in their Komsomol group. Shurka, who was the same age as Mikolka, was the only son of poor Widow Mikhalina. One day they passed a resolution to take down everyone's icons. Of course thinking up the resolution was easier than putting it into practice. So, as a start, they decided to remove the icons in their parents' houses. That was an easier task, but not all of them succeeded immediately. Some parents simply threatened to beat the godless Komsomol boys. Khvedor was quite calm about the lads' intention. Icons? What of it! It's true they hang in the corner and don't bother anyone, but they're no use to anyone either. But Ganna put her foot down. She would not take theirs down for any price, and from Christmas till spring Mikolka tried to persuade her. In the end he got his way. Before Lady Day he took down the icons and the oil lamp, and hung a huge portrait of Karl Marx in their place. From then on the bearded man hung in the corner, serving no purpose, doing no harm. Mikolka was pleased, and that was enough for them.

But that spring it came to the Komsomol secretary's attention by chance that there was still one icon hanging in his friend Shurka's hut. Mikolka convened a commission of three people and they went to Shurka's to investigate. It turned out to be true. An icon of the Archangel Gabriel was peacefully hanging where it had always hung. Shurka's mother Mikhalina was crying. She would not let them take it down, and Shurka could not get anywhere with her. He showed himself up as a spineless person. Mikolka carried it off impressively. They all thought he would throw the icon to the floor, but he did not touch it. He called a Komsomol meeting and, notwithstanding his long friendship with Shurka, put his membership in question. Khvedor was a little surprised by his son's conduct, and in the evening he rebuked him mildly. He said he thought maybe they had treated their village pal a little too harshly by throwing him out. Mikolka responded to this with a ferocity that had never before appeared in his voice.

"The Komsomol grinds double-dealers like that to dust!"

"Oh, come on," Khvedor muttered indulgently and carried on with the household chores. He looked on Mikolka's mischief with the icons as a childish eccentricity. He consoled himself that his son was just fooling around and that he would grow up and grow out of it.

But he had grown up his own way.

In the forest Khvedor calmed down a little and began to

reason differently. Maybe that kind of thing is necessary. At home and in exile he had seen all sorts of people and bosses. Their severity extended to absurd cruelty, and they had one sole object: to scorn you. He already understood that you find goodness where you find justice and truth. And where there was class struggle, that unreconciled state where everyone on top does what he wants with the people beneath him, where was goodness? With time goodness had obviously sunk into oblivion and something had come to take its place — something cruel and merciless. His clever Mikolka had obviously grasped this a long time ago, and if he had now become so intolerant, that must be how one had to be. Especially if it was not through his own ill will, but in the interests of the state. It must mean there was no alternative. And the fact that he had disowned his father, well, that was very hurtful, of course, and painful, but what was to be done? Maybe he had disowned him because his father had somehow died for him and would never find out about anything. It certainly looked that way. He had died for his son, he had not sent a letter in so many years or passed on any word about himself.

But it was painful and upsetting all the same.

It had begun to get dark in the forest, and he got up from the bracken. His body was weighed down by the weariness of many days, his numbed feet felt fat and swollen like logs. Overcoming his weakness, he wandered through the thick of the forest again to the edge, then he turned towards the potato field along the wedge of winter crop.

The sun had set in the meantime. It was hidden behind the forest, but the sky above the field was still filled with its dusky light, and fluffy white clouds floated freely in the light evening sky. As Khvedor had anticipated, the potatoes had already been dug in the field, no woman or horse could be seen. In the distance stood a solitary pile covered in straw, but he had no need for that. He went a little way from the edge of the enclosure and scratched in the fresh furrow with his fingers, digging into the crumbly earth. No, there was nothing left, it had all been dug. He went further in, shovelled the ground in two or three places and found half a potato that had been cut by the plough. He looked up and glanced around: there was nobody about. He went a little way to the side, where potato tops lay thickly in the furrows; maybe there was something left there. He burrowed in several spots and found four potatoes. Of course he could just go over to the pile and stuff a few into his pockets, but he did not want to let himself get too far from the forest. And would it be right to steal collective farm produce? He did not want to steal, he would only allow himself to take what was left over, what belonged to nobody, this had never counted as a sin, and it was all the less sinful now. Scrabbling hurriedly in the ground, he found three more small potatoes and looked around him in terror. There were two people walking straight towards him across the field from the edge of the forest. He realized what was happening immediately, dropped the potatoes and fled diagonally across the field towards the sanctuary of the forest. The two men turned to intercept him at once. One was middle aged, wearing boots and a quilted jacket, the other was younger, thin and long-legged, with his cap pulled down over his forehead. Khvedor realized he was in for it, that he would not get away. With all his strength he made a dash for the edge of the forest, moving diagonally all the time to stay ahead of his pursuers. His boots kept catching on the potato tops, his exhausted legs would hardly carry him. The four potatoes in his pocket banged against his hip. Fatigue was shortening his stride and he was terrified he would not get away, that they would run him down. But would the two of them really trap him like a hare in the field, surely they would stop? He managed to get a little way ahead of them, he had nearly reached the birch coppice at the edge of the forest, a saving hope had appeared.

It seemed as though they were lagging behind, then behind him he heard a malicious cry:

"Stop, you kulak pig! Stop right where you are!"

Khvedor tripped over in amazement, he had not foreseen them recognizing him from a distance. But if they were shouting like that, they must have. When they shouted a third time, Khvedor guessed it was Zmiter Tsyprukov. Oh my God, all I need is to fall into the hands of that malicious creature, thought Khvedor. The indignation suffusing him gave him renewed strength, he strained with his last hope and without looking round, ran into the birch saplings on the edge of the forest. In the forest he carried on running, picking up his feet more and more slowly, then he walked a little way with an unsteady, tired gait and jogged along again exhaustedly, trying to get as far from that ill-fated field as he could. His pursuers did not seem to have entered the forest. He wandered a long time among the sparse, squat firs, breathing hoarsely and thinking that today he had been really unlucky. There had not been a single ray of hope for him in the whole fine, sunny day. It would have been bad enough finding out about his son, but then Zmiter on top of everything. He had tracked him down, just about seized him red-handed. He must be a watchman or some sort of boss if he's strolling about in the field after working hours. He's most probably a foreman at least, guessed Khvedor. Zmiter Tsyprukov a foreman — that was a joke! The most good-for-nothing farmer in the village, a man whose mare had died of malnutrition. She had eaten straw eaves all winter, and they hadn't been enough. Zmiter, who in his whole life had never learned to make bast shoes, working here as a foreman, supervising the growth of agriculture. It was true, he had always had a loud voice, he could yell at anyone. That was probably more important than anything nowadays. Just as it was in exile, so it was on the collective farm. It was just the same.

Chapter Five

The Manhunt

That night the wind picked up, the forest began to moan, the firs and the pines droned deeply and agitatedly under the weight of the wind, the tiny leaves of the birch trees muttered interminably and, with a sense of doom, Khvedor waited for the rain to start pouring. That night he did not go to the village, he did not emerge again from the forest in which, for so long now, he had found refuge. It was not a secure refuge, but there was none other left him on this earth. Every night he tried to find a new place for his overnight stay, trying to get further away from people into the depths of the forest. That evening, after shaking off his pursuers when it was already dark, he ended up on prickly ground in a young fir grove and lay motionless for a long time. There was no sense in going on, ahead was the marsh, and anyway, he no longer possessed the strength. After he had rested awhile he sat up, cut his four potatoes into slices and munched them without appetite. He had no more food, and he sat through the night in the fir grove and thought.

"Why has all this fallen on my head? Have I really sinned so greatly before God or man? Have I ever killed anybody or robbed or insulted anybody?" He had always tried as best he could, God help him, not to give offence to anybody or to deserve a reproach. He had behaved respectfully towards the authorities. He was grateful to them for the land he had been given, for their generosity to an erstwhile farm-labourer. How could it be otherwise? He had genuinely considered Soviet power to be his own power. Sometimes at meetings people had complained there wasn't any of this, too little of that, no manufactured goods, no nails, not enough paraffin, you couldn't buy sugar. He would say to the impatient people: wait, don't demand everything all at once. Soviet power will not hurt the poor man, because the poor man and the worker are Soviet power. Had he thought that up himself? He had read it in newspapers, heard it at meetings from the representatives of that power. And he had believed it. He had been prepared to believe everyone who spoke well of the Soviet power because he had received confirmation of its greatest truth, the greatest truth that could ever exist, the name of which was — land.

Who had deceived him? And deceived him so cruelly, so pitilessly for the rest of his life thereafter? Deceit was nothing new to him. He had become accustomed to it in the course of his life. Sometimes his neighbours deceived him, his relatives and co-villagers. The bosses had deceived him more than once at home and in exile. Comrades-in-misfortune had deceived him. He was even grateful to some of them for their barefaced deceit.

People usually escaped from the north in the spring when the snow melted and the taiga came back to life. Although the taiga in spring was a stingy provider and there was nothing to eat except berries, in spring the sun rose higher in the sky, the frosts ended, the floods subsided, and the most important thing was the green grass, paths without footprints. You could go where you pleased. In springtime there were few exiles in the camps and settlements who did not pine with the dream of that sacred hope, of returning to the places where they had been born, where they had lived their lives, from which they had been torn by force. But the thousands of trackless, uninhabited kilometers of the taiga drained the courage of most of them. Even more than courage, you needed an iron constitution, animal strength, and a supply of food, and towards spring the exiles could scarcely put one foot in front of the other. All the same the dream beckoned and excited and intoxicated them and, as everyone knows, when a man is intoxicated he is capable of anything, good or bad, depending on his character and circumstances.

Running away from the riverside lumber camp was simple enough, but conquering the taiga was hard. Many were caught nearby on the rivers and roads, others were seized hundreds of kilometers away on railway stations and wharves. They took them from the roofs and brake platforms of railway carriages and searched them out with dogs in stacks of sawed timber by the railway lines. While Khvedor had a sick wife and a little daughter on his hands, he did not even admit the timid thought of finding freedom at the price of separation from them. Even later, when he was left alone, he only thought about it occasionally, to forget it immediately. He lacked sufficient resolve, and he told nobody of his inmost dreams. He was usually silent and reserved, the people in that place were not his kind, and with strangers he had to be careful. Didn't he just! He didn't like many people. They were all cruel, raucous, shameless. Many of them scorned him openly, a downtrodden, barely literate Byelorussian. He saw this and did not take offence. What was he to them? To whom could he be useful? He was accustomed to his insignificance, his lack of distinction, he never thrust himself upon anybody in friendship and nobody was particularly friendly towards him. Khvedor was even surprised when one day a man beckoned him over for a few words.

One damp, foggy morning the team was beginning to prepare timber on the floating barrier. There was a big float ahead of them, the whole section was strenuously preparing for it. Khvedor was sliding logs along the squared timber lying on the platform, then rolling them up to the top of the stacks. A man nicknamed Eel quietly approached him. He was an exile like the rest, but not one of the dispossessed. He was in some other category. He had arrived in exile from the Vorkuta mines, risen up the ranks and become one of the bosses, but he had quickly slipped up. He behaved with circumspection and refused to fawn on the bosses. He knew his own worth. From time to time he even used to take liberties: he would allow himself an extra minute for a smoke, or arrive late for a work allocation. He always had his own tobacco, and the bosses never found much fault with him. They even seemed to indulge him. They doubtless had their reasons. Near the stack Eel glanced around and listened out. There was no-one around.

"Want to go home?" he asked quietly. Khvedor was confused, not grasping what this was about right away, so Eel explained briefly. "There's a chance. You'll be the third, get it?"

Understanding little, Khvedor stood silently, as though crestfallen. Of course he would gladly fly home on wings, crawl on his belly, but how? What chance had cropped up? But one must have: a good man had suggested it.

"Does that mean you're in?" asked Eel. "Tomorrow, be at the last stack."

The next morning Khvedor did just that. He started work near the furthest stack. This was not difficult. The workers usually tried to avoid standing at the end of the platform: it meant rolling the timber further; but this time Khvedor bravely stood in front of the foreman and ended up in the foursome ordered to work in the appointed place. Eel was there too. They began to roll the thick logs with ostentatious zeal. Then as soon as the foreman was out of sight, Eel nodded to Khvedor and sidled off the platform. Khvedor hurried after him with a sinking heart.

Their escape was successful. Nobody intercepted them near the settlement, maybe they hadn't yet noticed their absence. In a nearby coomb they were joined by a third man, a lanky, one-eyed fellow named Skakun. As far as Khvedor could understand he was an old pal of Eel's. On the first day they covered about thirty miles through the taiga. Usually in these parts one travelled along the frozen river in winter and along the riverbank in summer, but now that would not do. The banks swarmed with police and military guards. Instead they traced a roundabout route through the forest. Eel and his pal had stored up a small quantity of grub for the escape, a few pounds of flour and about three dozen rusks which they carried in turns in a stamped regulation pillow-case. Eel organized everything on the journey. Khvedor was grateful to him, well aware of the fact that Eel could have chosen someone younger and stronger. It was as though he had grown in his own eyes as a result of this unexpected faith in him, and he tried to oblige Eel in every way. He would carry the food further than the others, tend the fire when the pals went to sleep beside it, gather twigs and go to fetch water. Once, near a stream in a coomb where they were drying off after a rainshower, Khvedor, deeply moved, thanked Eel for his kindness. Eel just winked cunningly:

"I could tell that you wanted to go home in a bad way."

"Thank you so much, I will remember it forever."

"You can thank me later, with a little something," grinned Eel, but his grin was cordial. In general he treated Khvedor as an equal, slightly condescendingly perhaps, but for the most part in an entirely comradely way. He seemed to be a good companion. He divided their scanty supplies fairly into three, he had the matches and kindled the fire in the morning, planned the route and always walked in front. As far as Khvedor could tell this was not Eel's first time in the taiga, and he oriented himself excellently in its frightening dense forests. Where they were heading Eel did not say and Khvedor never asked, trusting implicitly in the knowledge and experience of his comrade. If he had been on his own would he really have covered about 150 miles in a week through unfamiliar forests without roads? It was only later, taught by bitter experience, that he began to understand something of the complex secrets of flight through the taiga, but on this first escape he was an abject fool, like a rookie soldier.

They were caught by chance, stupidly. It wasn't Eel's fault nor anyone else's. One evening near an icy taiga rivulet they stumbled upon an empty hunting hut and went in, hoping to find something to eat, but there was nothing. They decided not to spend the night there and carried on for another half a mile. In the dark, without bothering to light a fire, they lay down wearily in a fir grove, side by side on the soft moss. At dawn they were woken under the barrels of two rifles. It turned out that the night before, near the hut, a local huntsman had spotted them and run around the neighbourhood to fetch his brother, then the two of them had tracked down the fugitives. It all happened unexpectedly, suddenly. If they had had a little more time perhaps they might have got out of this scrape, but they had not had time to come to their senses when a cart arrived and they were taken, tied up, to a forestry, from there to a landing-stage, the headquarters of the local military guard. The hunting brothers must have received a reward for their non-hunting labour. Their position became worse than before their escape. Khvedor took the failure badly. He kept silent, even refusing the bread he was thrown every evening in the lock-up. Eel dropped his usual imperturbable front, and one day he growled malevolently,

"What are you moping for? You should be glad!"

"Why should I be glad?" Khvedor did not understand.

"You didn't turn into a pig, that's why."

"What do you mean, a pig?" Khvedor asked in puzzlement.

"You should be glad you'll never find out."

Khvedor still did not understand. What pig? Why should he be glad? Only later, when he had fallen into a worse hell, in the peat bogs near Syktyvkar, he was talking one day with common criminals and asked what a "pig" was. Their eyes darkened. It turned out that was what they called the simpletons who were incited to flight and then eaten when the food ran out. That was a "pig".

And all that time he had been grateful to Eel. In his simplicity he had loved him for his loyalty and his kindness. Eel had looked after his pig so carefully! When Khvedor learned the truth he thought he would hate his accomplice, but strangely enough hatred never came. It was a different feeling, something like pity. That shattering failure changed Khvedor. He had experienced freedom. This tiny gulp had not satisfied his hunger, but it had excited his hope, and wherever Khvedor ended up from then on, whatever circumstances he fell into, he hungrily sized up the situation and the people, pondered, estimated everything with a sole aim: escape.

And now he had achieved what he had strained so hard for, he had accomplished the impossible. He was home. What now? Where could he run from here? Or would he die of starvation in the forest?

Perhaps this was a punishment from God? For the icons he had silently allowed Mikolka to remove from the house? First of all Ganna had hidden them behind the chimney in the garret, but Mikolka had found them, dragged them out and smashed them on the corner of the barn. His mother had burst into tears, but Khvedor had not known how to react. He felt a little sorry for the saints who had shared the life of generations, still, if his son was doing it not out of malice, but following orders. At that time Khvedor believed the authorities could never make mistakes, that in Moscow and Minsk sat clever, educated men who knew for certain whether God existed or not and how to act towards Him in the interests of the people. Behind him were only two winters of parish school. He had reflected little on questions of religion and assumed that his son, who had completed the seventh grade, had gained a better understanding of it than he.

But God was punishing him and not his son. It looked as though He was rewarding his son. But what if God were to punish his son too?

It was well past midnight when it began to rain in the forest. The wind drove the sleety drizzle through the trees in waves, drenching the fir grove every now and then. There was nowhere to hide from its wetness. He wanted to seek out old fir trees, but an impenetrable gloom reigned in the forest, and he would get nowhere. The rain died down from time to time and almost stopped, having wet the grass, the fir branches, and Khvedor's head and shoulders. Then it began again. Khvedor did not get up from his long-occupied spot and did not lie down on the wet ground. He sat warming himself, shivering from the biting cold. It was damp and uncomfortable, but he cheered up a little. At night, in the rain, it was possible not to be afraid. He awaited the dawn with growing anxiety, not knowing where he would get to during the day and where he would find something to eat; and his soul sensed that this day would bring still more trouble. If not disaster.

The rain stopped before morning, but the wind did not die down, from time to time it blew up and shook the moisture off the wet branches, so that in the forest it felt as though it was still raining. Above the tops of the trees the grey storm clouds were being blown off, the sky had risen above the fir grove — the joyless sky of a rainy autumn day. At this dawn hour somewhere nearby, startling the morning quiet of the forest, crows began to caw. There was a vague anxiety in their incessant cries and Khvedor, hearing them, thought irritably, what the devil has set them off? He wanted to stand up and frighten them away, but hadn't the strength. After his miserable night he was drowsy and he sat in a dismal half-doze. Little by little it became light, a thicket of fir branches stood out nearby, dry twigs protruded from the trunks, the wet ground was thickly strewn with pine needles. Suddenly a hare appeared in the fir grove. It turned its lop-eared head this way and that and perched on its hind legs rubbing its whiskered snout furiously with the front ones. It did not notice Khvedor and he stood stock still for a moment trying not to frighten the little grey fellow. The hare calmly jumped past and disappeared in the juniper bushes.

The crows kept up the noise above him. Were they pursuing something or simply quarrelling among themselves? They probably have their disagreements just like people, thought Khvedor. Except that the kind of enmity that exists among people can hardly exist anywhere else on earth. The crows will have a fight and a scream and fly apart, but in a moment they will have forgotten their quarrel. Man never forgets an affront, he can remain an enemy all his life. He's a cruel creature, man.

He could have sat there all day in the fir grove. It was peaceful, despite the lack of shelter and the damp. If it had not been for his hunger. His belly gave great spasms of hungry cramp, the pit of his stomach ached with it, and he was anxious. Where would he find something to eat? He knew he would find nothing except mushrooms in the forest: there were a few, particularly on the mossy bank near the marsh, but you can't eat raw mushrooms, and he did not want to make a fire. So his thoughts turned increasingly to the village, to the pear tree on the edge of the forest. Its rotting fruit was now the only accessible food. He wouldn't manage to find anything else around here.

He was soaked to the skin as he dragged himself out of the fir grove. Every branch he brushed against showered him with cold drops of water. It was cold in the forest and it made him shiver, but what could he do? He had to bear it. He was used to bearing the cold and the wet. If only he could learn to withstand hunger. But no one is blessed with the ability to overcome hunger, neither man nor beast. Hunger is a cruel master over everyone.

Khvedor slowly made his way through the forest, keeping to the bare patches without undergrowth, avoiding the wet thickets. For some reason he wondered what day it was. He had long ago lost track of the days and could no longer distinguish Sunday from a weekday. What was Sunday to him anyway? The recent excitement of seeing his home had passed irretrievably, he was overcome with an ever more weighty presentiment of doom. He could not account for it. Was it yesterday's bad news about his son, or had he been alarmed by the encounter in the potato field? Or was it something else? Perhaps it was just the harsh noise of the crows ringing out in the wet forest morning? The crows must be fighting over something, he thought, as he listened to the muffled sounds of the forest.

Once again his ear, which had become sharper as he wandered through the forest, did not mislead him. Before he reached the forest edge where the pear tree grew, he caught some indistinct sounds in the distance. There was someone there. He went on the alert, slowed his step. Through the shrubs he could already see green patches of winter crop, the posts on the path, the grey boundary between plots of land overgrown with weeds. Right by the boundary, near the pear tree stood two men: one, carefully cupping his hands, was lighting the other's cigarette. When the one who was giving the light looked up, Khvedor recognized Shurka, Widow Mikhalina's son, who had been thrown out of the Komsomol. His mate stood with his back to the forest: Khvedor could not make out who it was. When they had lit up they both turned away. Khvedor could hear a mumbled conversation and he looked in the same direction from his position in the shrubs. Along the field stretched the long curve of the edge of the forest, and on it he saw about half a dozen men, standing twenty paces apart. They were stepping from one foot to the other, waiting for something. And they were his fellow-villagers, two old and four younger ones. He knew them all. The closest Khvedor recognized as Mikhas Maistrenok, whose farm had stood opposite Khvedor's pond. They had argued a couple of times about the geese which had damaged Mikhas's vegetable plot. A little way from Maistrenok, on the boundary, stood Lyoksa Savchik, thin, looking older, with white locks under the black rim of his hat, dressed in a long peasant coat with a shepherd's whip under his arm. Good God, we've finally met again, Khvedor thought with anguish. But why were they standing there, what were they waiting for? Then it dawned on him: they had come together to catch the fugitive. They had spread out in a chain as though they were in battle or on a winter wolf hunt; only they wouldn't circle him down with red flags when they came for him, because he was not a wolf, he was a man. With him it would be easier.

Khvedor slunk into the depths of the forest on his weak legs. He was shuddering with hurt, with hopelessness, with the presentiment of impending disaster, and he could do or say nothing in his own defence. All he could do was run, seek refuge, like an animal. A human being should not run away from people, flight is always a humiliation, but apart from this last humiliation there was nothing left for him. He was no longer a human being.

In the mixed coppice on the gentle slope he turned to the right, in the direction of the high road and the flood lands from which he had so joyfully run three days earlier. He had to get out of the forest while he still could. The forest was no longer a sanctuary for him. It belonged to them, and they would try to capture him in it. But he would never surrender to them. While he still had the strength, he would get away from them. He would never let them send him back to the place he had left at such cost. He would never go back there.

Khvedor ran with difficulty, hardly knowing which way. He ran straight through the alder grove, getting soaked from head to toe. Behind him it was quiet, as though they were no longer chasing him, but he hurried. He could still make it out of the forest into the water meadow. Along the river was another territory, the region beyond the river, maybe nobody had heard of him there. There was hardly any distance left to cover in the forest and from the edge he would get an open view of the wide hollow and the high road; but he was out of breath, utterly exhausted and hardly able to drag himself to the edge of the forest. Before coming out of the forest he glanced at the hollow. There was nobody there. Then he looked at the pine-covered hill, and sank down on the ground. Beneath the pine trees on the high road there were vehicles, three heavy lorries, and to the side of them, fanning out towards the forest, there were people, thirty, if not more. At their head, across the overgrown aftermath in the hollow, strode a tall man with his black coat flung open. He was saying something to the others, pointing with a broad gesture towards the forest. Perhaps he was signalling them to spread out in a chain.

Understanding everything in an instant, Khvedor turned straight round and ran back into the forest. He still had a small chance of escaping. They were only just crossing the hollow. By the time they had climbed the slope and come into the forest... No, he would get away from them, he wouldn't let them overtake him. But where could he run? To his left was Nedolishche and the chain of people from the village, behind him were those others, from the town. They were all dressed in dark clothes, not village clothes, so they must be from the town: party activists probably. They were behind him. To his right was the fir grove, and the Bogovizna marsh. He'd never get across it. Maybe the way out lay ahead, through the forest near the potato field and the village, where he had met the old man and the cow yesterday? There might not be anyone there. Just reaching it would be an achievement. He was lucky they hadn't spotted him, he had seen them first. That gave him hope, providing his legs held up. He ran with difficulty, he was desperately short of breath. Bitter saliva filled his mouth, he could not get rid of its bitter taste even by spitting it out. His shoulders and his chest were covered in hot sweat under his heavy wet clothing, his face broke out in perspiration, he gave it an occasional wipe with his sleeve. Looking from side to side he would run, then slow to an unsteady, rickety walk as he gradually moved away from the high road and the village. But it was no easy business keeping the right direction in the forest. It looked as though he had gone too far to the right. He was heading straight for the Bogovizna. Realizing this, he turned slightly to the left, trying to get out of the forest towards the potato field. All that mattered was to leap from the pincers that were tightening around him before they snapped shut. He had a sudden hope that he would somehow elude his pursuers. It looked as though he had got clean away from the ones from the town, and as for the villagers, they were only just entering the forest. Maybe they wouldn't even come in. They might just wait for him on the edge. If only he could get to the potato field.

But his strength was failing, he stumbled feverishly through the undergrowth on the wet grass. He looked round constantly, to see if they were on his tail. He couldn't see anyone yet, but behind him he could hear voices coming from the high road. They must have spread out in a huge chain. The shouts grew louder; he heard the sound of barking. It was not the bark of the cowherd's shaggy mongrel: this was a larger dog. Khvedor started into a run again, a heavy, doom-laden jog, looking around him all the time. He was completely preoccupied with what was going on behind him. He must have let slip the moment when he should have looked ahead of him, and he almost ran straight into a hare behind the juniper bush. The hare was bounding towards him in wide leaps; when it saw him it leapt off and ran back the way it had come. He has no rest either, Khvedor thought grimly and stopped. A loud vicious clamour rang out from the place where the hare had disappeared.

"Stop, or I'll shoot!"

"What do you mean, shoot! It's a hare!"

And they burst into a young, carefree laugh.

Khvedor stretched out his neck, on the alert. Up ahead, through the yellow foliage of the young trees, he glimpsed two green caps. Some way off someone gave a quiet shout and they disappeared. Khvedor realized that his path in that direction had been cut off, the border guards were coming towards him from the potato field. Their post was a mile beyond the forest. But why border guards? Was he a spy, a saboteur, an infiltrator? Was he a convicted criminal escaped from prison? All he had done was come home, to the place where he was born, where he had grown up; where, in their day, his ancestors had been born and grown up. Why border guards?

But apparently he was worse than a spy. Only border guards come after a spy and he was surrounded by three chains of huntsmen to beat him out: in addition to the border guards, there were the party activists from the town, and the villagers. He was a wolf! A wild animal!

Fortunately, nobody in the manhunt had spotted him yet. He had seen the danger first. For the moment he was in luck, but how long could his luck last? In the end they would spot him: he was not like the invisible woodcutter in the fairy tale. True, he knew this part of the state forest well, but they knew it just as well, especially his fellow villagers. Now he was running randomly he had no idea in what direction. He had lost his way and was gradually veering towards the fourth side, from where there was no escape. On the fourth side was a dead end, the Bogovizna marsh, quagmire all the way — you couldn't enter it in summer. No animals even put their feet in there, let alone people. Right up until the frosts it was sodden: you'd sink and die.

But where else could he go?

He was no longer able to run, he could hardly drag himself along the edge of the dark fir grove, his boots kept getting tangled in the soft wet grass. He kept his ears pricked up, trying to follow what was going on behind him. He could hear shouting all around him, and the dog's loud bark. The chains must have met and missed him. Maybe they'll turn back towards the high road and the village, Khvedor thought with a slim hope, and he hid behind a fir tree. If only they'd let him catch his breath. A bitter lump was sticking in his burning chest.

But they did not let him catch his breath.

They were already very close, he could not see them only because of the trees. The trees gave him cover too, but now he could hear their animated shouts, someone's muffled voice, "Over here, there's a trail!" — and he realized there was no escaping them. There were several dozen of them, peasants and Red Army soldiers, they had closed round the forest from three sides, and there was only one of him. He was completely exhausted and didn't know where to run, how to save himself. He had run the last few metres pointlessly. Up ahead in the fir grove something stirred in the grass: that hare again. First it had run away from the soldiers, and now it was running away from him. But why was it running away from him? He was like a hare himself, even worse, because the hare would probably escape.

"My people, why are you doing this to me?" a desperate groan burst from him. "What wrong have I done you? Was it that threshing machine? What harm did it do? It helped you too. Did I take too much for myself? But I gave it all to you. It's all yours! Is that why you've turned against me? Think again!"

None of them even considered thinking again. They were chasing him the way a wolf is chased on a crowded hunt, but still he kept expecting one of them to stop and shout, "Stop, brothers! What are we doing?!"

Nobody stopped or said it, they just carried on the chase.

"Rovba, stop!"

Here it was at last.

From the first steps of his absurd flight he had been expecting this cry night and day. All the same it came suddenly and terribly. Khvedor did not look round immediately. Among the firs the dark forms of men flitted, the villagers or Red Army soldiers, he could not even tell. But he understood the most important thing: they had spotted him. There was nowhere else for him to run. His long journey had come to its inevitable end. His improbable, senseless journey, over thousands of miles to his native land. It had met its native son untenderly, his homeland! But God be with it, it could not do otherwise. That was fate! Accursed fate, which had made him a peasant in these times.

The dark fir grove came to an end. A strip of wet, marshy moss began. Khvedor ran into it without stopping. A thick layer of moss sank menacingly under his feet and he was in up to the knees in black, squelching mud. To go in any further was madness, but what was not madness at this point? Ahead clusters of overgrown reeds stirred in the wind, behind them towered luxuriantly wild-grown groups of willowherb and alder bushes. Among the green tussocks the windows of the bog flashed wanly. Tearing his heavy boots out of the marsh with desperate strength, Khvedor went still further in. Soon he was in up to the waist and, dispersing a layer of duckweed with his body, he reached the closest tussocks. For a while there was a foothold, matted roots at the bottom, but the bottom fell away into the deep abruptly and he felt he had dropped off a precipice. He steered with his head into the cold, muddy chasm. He surfaced immediately, having lost his cap, and in order not to choke in the stinking bilge, clung to a clammy root sticking out from the tussock. This kept him from going under. His head remained on the surface, and he took convulsive, greedy breaths.

On the other side of the mossy swamp muffled voices were audible in the forest. A dog barked in a bass voice. His pursuers must have gathered in one place and stopped. They seemed to have lost him, or maybe they just didn't want to climb after him into the cold stinking marsh. A distinct sound reached his hearing:

"He ran this way."

"There he is, in the marsh."

"Look how far he's got!"

"If he climbs out he won't get anywhere, the kulak scum!"

"I won't climb out!" Khvedor said to himself in bitter despair, swinging the torn duckweed with an involuntary movement of his body. He sat, up to his neck in water, hidden from the shore by rushes and tussocks, and the men stood on the shore, afraid of the quagmire. In the past he had sometimes looked with terror at this marsh, planted around with mounds, overgrown with willowherb, feeling an almost superstitious terror whenever he came close to it. Now he sat in it calmly and waited. His extremities were stiff with cold, his insides clenched in a tight, sick knot. Everything would soon be at an end. His heavy, clumsy coat was dragging him down, his heavy boots pulled him towards the bottomless depths of the bog, but he did not have the will to let go of the clammy root and quietly leave for the next world. As though he still hoped for something, he gasped like a fish washed up on the shore.

"Rovba, come out of there!" he heard nearby, behind the rushes.

"Come out quietly!"

"Citizen Rovba, in the name of Soviet power I'm asking you to give yourself up."

They were shouting but he hardly heard them. He had not the strength or the will to come out.

"It looks like he isn't there..."

"Yes there he is! Over there, there's a trace in the reeds..."

"Oh people, people! Why are you like this! Oh people..." Khvedor's soul cried out. To whom was he appealing?

They were already climbing in. Khvedor moved towards the water a little, swaying the duckweed again, and turned his head. Lifting their feet high in the sedge by the shore, two men cautiously approached the bog he was in. One of them was carrying a long, thin pole. Were they planning to poke in the bushes? Khvedor wondered. From here he could see them well. He didn't know these lads, Komsomol kids from the region no doubt. Somewhere behind the bushes, not far away, a dog barked lazily, but they did not seem to have let it loose in the marsh.

"We can't go any further!"

"Go on! You can go a bit further," he heard a little way off, and at these words Khvedor's heart stood still. He recognized that voice. He would have recognized it even from the next world. It was the voice of his son. Poor Mikolka, Khvedor thought suddenly, he's come here too! It can't be of his own free will. They must have made him come.

The two with the pole seemed to have lost the fugitive, they turned away towards a clump of willowherb, having made up their minds he was there. But he was not there, or here. He hardly existed at all any more. There was one small thing left to do: to see, and to say goodbye. As soon as he had seen his son he would be on his way. There was nothing more for him to do in this world.

The lads were beating back the thick bushes with the pole, but Mikolka did not appear. Poor Mikolka, what he must be going through now, thought Khvedor. This can't be through his own choice. He's been made to do it. Maybe he was ordered to, by someone higher up. There must be someone above him, and they've sent him out to hunt down the father he disowned. If he's disowned him, he can go out and catch him can't he? But if that was possible, how could he go on living? What should he live for? No, he couldn't go on living.

"Leschuk, poke over there!"

It was Mikolka again. His authoritative hard voice, which Khvedor had not known before, came from somewhere far off. Khvedor was hearing that voice for the first time, and every sound it made struck his heart a painful blow. Lucky Ganna, she would never have to see this, or hear it.

There was a rustling in the neighbouring bush. The end of the narrow pole ripped through the thick leaves. Now it was the turn of the tussocks where he was hiding; but they would not be able to get to him. He would beat them to it. Khvedor breathed in as deeply as he could and let go of the knotty root. His heavy feet, in boots that would now never wear out, pulled him straight down into the chasm and he choked. His ears were struck painfully from inside, everything darkened in his eyes.

He had not been granted a quiet life, but he could still have a quiet death.

They searched for him a long time, they poked their poles into the bushes and tussocks, they rummaged in the rushes near the shore. But they did not find him.

Vasil BYKOV (1924-2003), a major Byelorussian author writing in Russian as well as Byelorussian. In June 1941, as a seventeen year-old boy, he abandoned his studies at the Vitebsk art college to volunteer for the frontline of the Second World War which became the dominant theme of his writing in the subsequent decades.

His best known works include *Obelisk*, *To Live Till Dawn*, *The Dead Feel No Pain*, *Sotnikov*, *His Battalion*, to name but a few. Amidst the flow of bombastic paeans to war heroism he was the first in Russian literature to look at the unheroic aspects of the war and to investigate the problem of moral choice and personal safety in the war.

More recently Bykov turned to Russia's post-revolutionary history, marked by the dispossession of well-to-do peasants (kulaks) and the Cheka's ruthless repressions of innocent people when, moreover, victims and executioners often changed places.

This theme figures in *The Manhunt*, published here, as well as in *The Frost*, shortlisted for the Booker Russian Novel Prize in 1994.

Whatever his theme, Bykov invariably touches on the subject of betrayal. "Betrayal has always been a fascinating theme for literature and art," says Bykov. It is well known that on Nazi-occupied territory the local police was recruited from voluntary collaborators among the local population. The history of the Civil War in Russia abounds in cases when children denounced their parents, and vice versa, to the Cheka, when close relatives were fighting on opposite sides, and when on the strength of neighbours' or colleagues' denunciations whole families were dispossessed and exiled to Siberia to die of cold, hunger and back-breaking toil.

Bykov has always been preoccupied with the problem of retaining humanity in inhuman conditions. Among his characters there is always one who, faced with a moral choice, prefers death to infamy.

Boris
YAMPOLSKY

THE OLD ARBAT

Translated by John Dewey

What really did happen then? What took place in that office — clean and of lofty proportions, like the hall of a crematorium — when my name was mentioned?

"Arrest him!"

The young lieutenant just out of a KGB college wrote out the warrant, admiring as he did so his own self-assured handwriting, the elegance and legibility of which had landed him this particular posting. Then this neat product of the art of calligraphy, endorsed by the section commander with a signature resembling an express train hurtling along at full speed, was recorded in the book and despatched through the appropriate channels.

The day before a 'fitter' came to the courtyard.

"How's that old tart Fortunatovna? Still up to her tricks?" he asked to get the conversation started.

"Now and again," came the guarded reply of Ovid, the janitor, who had received a half-litre replenishment of meths from her the day before.

"And what about that bloke?" asked the 'fitter' as if in passing, nonchalantly, and with a somehow brooding and distracted air. "The long-haired one..."

Ovid appeared puzzled. "Which one's that, then?" he asked, looking away from the 'fitter'.

"You know the one: full of himself, an egghead," said the 'fitter', sidling closer and also looking away.

"Oh, him," remembered Ovid. "Hasn't been seen for three days."

"Hasn't been home at night?"

"Maybe his job's taken him away somewhere," surmised Ovid.

The 'fitter' reported back: "Not present at address."

And the lieutenant-colonel or major, or perhaps just captain, without thinking, almost without looking, drew a line through the authorization, cancelling it for the time being.

Then everyone was inundated by a new campaign, with new enemies; in this new political configuration yesterday's enemies ceased to be of any significance whatsoever, and there were no medals to be won for taking them out, no commendations and no bonuses.

Or perhaps it was like this:

"Everything's taken: we've been given extra numbers, transports to organize — and no vehicles."

Then the man in the steel-blue military blouse (of that style, cut from steel-blue covert cloth, that was exclusive to higher ranks, and scented with 'Chypre', the eau de Cologne used by MVD top brass), as if letting fall a casual remark, with studied indifference, gave his order:

"Cut the numbers!"

And it was this word 'cut', harsh and short, one of two hundred and twenty thousand in the contemporary Russian language, that for a second time gave me the gift of life.

The Arbat

Now that Moscow has had the broad and towering New Arbat Avenue driven through it, the Old Arbat has been left as a tranquil, narrow side-street, lying forgotten and out of the way. Although pedestrians now cross it at will, it was at one time a street subject to the strictest discipline, along which, they say, Stalin was in the habit of driving to and from his dacha outside Moscow.

With all its aristocratic stone mansions, blackened barrack-like buildings from the first Five-Year Plans and square concrete blocks of flats, with its entrenched smells, its little old women in antiquated coats and hats and Young Pioneers in their red kerchiefs, the old Arbat lived a life that was hidden from view, secret, classified, in which each building, each entrance, each window was listed in an inventory, and in which everyone was followed and kept under close scrutiny.

From the famous 'Prague', with its securely boarded-up front entrance and desolate flat roof, which had long since ceased to be the 'Prague' and was now jam-packed with offices large and small, where long after the war there were still shell cases from the anti-aircraft battery lying around, and where a generation had been born and grown up not even knowing that this had once been a renowned restaurant, — anyway, from the 'Prague' as far as the 'Gastronom' food store on Smolensk Street, the Arbat exhibited as it were a second face. There was the cheerful hat shop in the 'Prague', on the corner; the stationer's on the corner of Silver Lane redolent of school, geometry sets and virginal lined paper; 'Children's World' with its pot-bellied, multi-coloured Russian stacking dolls; the pet shop with orange fish in aquaria and odours of droppings and down from suffering birds; the antique shop with golden vases bearing depictions of Egyptian pharaohs and Roman legionaries; the Vakhtangov Theatre, rebuilt after the bombing raids, with a poster for *The Two Gentlemen of Verona*; and the 'Young Filmgoer' cinema with its advertisement for the film *The Vow*. But above all this, like a shadowy silhouette imposed on the street, or a shifting mask, there stretched along the whole street a stern, mysterious and unspeaking human chain, wearing identical beaver coats and overshoes in winter, and in summer smock shirts and open sandals. In blizzards, rain or fog, when the lilacs and jasmine were in blossom, and when the leaves were falling, at dawn when the first trolleybuses emerged, in the rush hour, at the hour when theatres emptied, and at the hour of the cash collectors, on New Year's and Easter night, and May Day, yesterday, today and tomorrow — always — there was this silent human chain on the Arbat.

They lined the whole street, avoiding the light of street lamps, standing at intersections or the entrances to blocks of flats, pretending to be residents, and stared at the road. They stood looking somehow alone, separate and self-sufficient, and seemed to be trying to remember something they had forgotten; all day and all night they stood like this, trying to remember something forgotten. But suddenly they would be seized by a frenzy. The traffic lights turned red at all crossroads simultaneously, and the police telephones howled in their large metallic boxes; the human chain would surge forward to the edge of the pavement, and it was as if a bare electric cable had opened up in the middle of the street and the whole Arbat, with all its shop windows, tailor's dummies, permed heads, alarm clocks, plaster casts, goldfish and canaries in cages, had a high-voltage current passing through it.

Communal Living

It was one of those patrician apartments so frequently found in the old mansions on the Arbat. Occupying a whole floor of the building, it had large Venetian windows and two entrances: the front door, leading to a wide stairway of white marble once carpeted, but now long since worn down, filthy and dilapidated; and a back door into the kitchen, with a narrow iron staircase reeking of kitchen slops and thieves, not to mention the frisky rats that scampered around there.

There were many such communal apartments with the servants' staircase at the back, clattering and grimy, the walls where the plaster had come away, revealing laths beneath, the economy light bulb, dusty, wretched and bare, its crimson element scarcely glowing, the doors covered with graffiti expressing either love or abuse, the common kitchen with its cement floor, its ceiling blackened with soot, so that the cupids and grandees depicted thereon looked like sinners in hell, the bathroom, where cabbages and potatoes were stored, and where later a young artist slept, and the carbolic toilet like those at railway stations, in front of which a queue formed on those dark winter mornings when everyone had overslept and was in a hurry to get to work, with all the concomitant brawling and scheming, so that for some time now the house management committee had started handing out numbered tickets the night before.

For many a long year — possibly since the owner of the house, a tea merchant, had fled to Paris to escape the revolution — neither painters, nor carpenters, nor roofers had touched the walls of the building. The stucco had long since fallen off, and the Empire figures stood covered in a pink typhoid rash, while in places even the ceilings had collapsed, laying bare the wooden joists. If people were invited round and there was dancing, the whole house would shake, and the hosts would plead with their guests: "Please keep the noise down, or we'll have the people from downstairs up here, throwing a fit." When it rained, the residents carried buckets, basins and cooking pots up into the attic, there was flooding in the rooms and corridors, and fungi grew on the drainpipe.

It was only during the preparations for the May Day that housepainters would arrive with their long brushes and, suspended in cradles attached to the roof and singing songs, paint the facade a pre-revolutionary pistachio: not, it must be admitted, the pure, noble pistachio of the eighteenth century, but one that was just a touch too crude, too blatantly bright and tasteless; yet at least they refrained from painting it with red lead or ochre, or in anti-aircraft camouflage colours. The rain soon washed away this rouge, and the house stood there like an old, faded beauty who has suddenly taken it into her head to rouge her cheeks; the tears had run down, leaving grimy blotches like age marks. But then another May Day came, or suddenly some famous guest from overseas was visiting the country, and once more a painter would be heard singing outside the windows. Then a van would arrive, and an electrician would change the opalescent globes shattered during the icy cold of winter and unscrew the dud, burnt-out bulbs, and at night the outside light shone brightly again, and it seemed as if a new life were beginning.

Yet nothing really changed. The communal apartment carried on shouting, brawling, marrying and divorcing, giving birth and dying, just as before.

On the tall, massive oak doors dating from pre-revolutionary times, once graced by a single, zealously polished brass plate, there was now a multitude of bell-pushes and buttons, with detailed written instructions on the number of long and short rings for each resident.

If you opened the door, you found cardboard visiting cards hanging on strings inside: "Chernomordikov at home", "Tsulukidze at home", "Svizlyak at work", "Leibson at home", "Knunyants away on business".

And then came a wide, dark passageway permeated with odours of moth balls, candle-ends and mouse droppings, and chock-a-block with old, disintegrating cupboards holding unwanted books; with iron-bound trunks against which you always banged your knees; bales and baskets crammed with all kinds of rags and trash; and perhaps even stones — no matter what, as long as there was something standing there, something to get in people's way and make life difficult. There were zinc wash-tubs like children's coffins; huge orange and blue carboys used for storing God knows what; an old samovar, glinting and hump-backed; a woman's bicycle, invariably with sharp spokes protruding from the wheels; a desiccated rubber plant; there was even — goodness knows where it had come from — a stuffed bear, ancient and moth-eaten, who would touch you with a fatherly paw and make you start, as though he had been waiting just for you in this communal forest.

In general, everything that was of no use to anyone was left out here; and yet just try touching anything or moving it even a fraction... Often there would be washing hanging on a line overhead, and your face would be struck by the wet straps of long johns.

Tall, wide doors with oak patterning opened on to the passageway, and from racks there hung old army greatcoats dating from the Civil War; antiquated men's winter coats, long and gathered at the waist; pre-revolutionary ladies' pelisses; and women's peasant-style jerkins; and it looked as if standing pressed to the wall and awaiting their hour were commissars, Cheka officers and aged witches from Russian fairy tales.

Behind the doors a radio blared, a gramophone played, people wept, or sang, or smashed crockery; or it was so quiet as to be ominous; while the smells varied from fried fish to joiner's glue, medicine, rough vodka, greasepaint, or terrible, irreversible emptiness.

Communal life tuned everybody to the same wavelength. Sometimes there would be deathly silence in the flat, yet it needed only one person to start shouting for rows to break out in all the rooms, as everyone remembered past affronts, insults and suffering...

Such large, clamorous, chaotic Moscow communal apartments differed, it must be said, in no way from those in Leningrad, Kiev or Odessa; except perhaps that here the conditions were even more cramped, the space more populated and the odours of fumes, laundry and the latrine more pungent, because having been converted from former offices, shops or prisons, they were less well-equipped and suitable for human life, for bringing children into the world, for illnesses, weddings and deaths. And here, as in any other communal apartment, there lived the most variegated, mixed and motley assembly of individuals, completely lacking in any mutual understanding or sympathy.

It was not they who had chosen this place of residence, nor had anyone specifically allocated it to them; in fact it was through the chaos and muddle of the tempestuous years of revolution and civil war that they had ended up living in this place, driven here by ruin, conflagrations, expropriations, looting and mobilizations. And having moved in and become securely attached to this alien location, they went hungry, knew poverty, and procreated like rabbits.

Some had lived here for ages, since the time when there were no housing warrants yet, only class rights and class intuition. None were left of those who had moved in under the law on requisition and capacity utilization, but their descendants lived here and had multiplied, sending for their relatives from villages and small towns to join them. There were, however, some who had no connection at all with those who had originally moved in under class law and taken over accommodation befitting the ruling class; these were the ones who had entered into bogus marriages to obtain residence permits, and then had not even bothered to get divorced, but had simply shown their blushing brides the door, or had waited for old women to die, doing all in their power to hasten the final outcome. But there were also others who had not even found a bogus marriage to be necessary. Goodness knows how and why and on what basis they had acquired a residence permit, yet their names had gone into the register of tenants, and all the rubber stamps were there, all the required duty stamps had been stuck on. Everything pertaining to them was in apple-pie order.

Then there were those who were not even registered, but just lived here: they had quite simply wormed their way in and then lived here for years on end. They never played lotto or backgammon together, never gathered for sessions of shelling sunflower seeds; and never, never visited each other's rooms for a spread of preserves, pickles, marinated mushrooms or home-made fruit liqueur. When there was a wedding or name-day celebration, or any sort of party, although visitors came from the other end of the city, the people behind the plywood partition in the next room would not look in at all; indeed, if there was too much noise, they banged on the wall with a brush, belabouring the partition until plaster started flaking off and the wallpaper came unstuck; or sometimes they would come out into the passageway and issue a final warning, or even just go and fetch the local policeman without any warning at all.

Yes, all kinds of people lived here... Everyone had their own separate table in the communal kitchen; some were larger, some smaller, and all stood edge to edge, so that whenever the housewives were chopping meat or shredding cabbage, bits would fly onto the next table.

There was only one old woman, a cleaner in a public lavatory, who did not have a table, but only a shelf on the wall, right by the door, and she would stand there, quietly getting on with her work. Her modest frying pan, cooking pot and washing-up bowl were not kept locked away in a cupboard with a big padlock like everybody else's for the simple reason that she had no cupboard; they hung in the same place, above the shelf, always painstakingly washed and scoured, and actually gleaming. All the other neighbours used to avoid these utensils, and would try to put their own as far away as possible.

When she fell ill and was bedridden for a long time, alone in her little cubicle of a room and living on goodness knows what, a whole delegation arrived one day bearing a cake in a box tied with coloured ribbon. There was the chairman of some local committee in charge of public lavatories, and two women, one of them old, an exact copy of ours, and the other very young, with her hair in curls. They knocked on her tiny little door for some time, and it was strange to hear the way the committee chairman addressed her: "Comrade Soroka! We're here on behalf of the trade union, Comrade Soroka."

In reply there came, first a choking cough that seemed to re-echo from somewhere far away, almost from the next world, and then something hoarse and indistinguishable that could have been a curse, a plea for forgiveness or some sort of appeal to the author-ities.

"Comrade Kukhtenkova," said the chairman to the old woman who had come with him, "I can't quite make out what she wants."

"She doesn't want anything, she's dying," replied the old woman calmly.

"Then some action must be taken!" he shouted.

"What action?" rejoined the old woman as calmly as before, and wearily. Whereupon the young woman, her curls quivering, burst into tears.

But then old Mrs Soroka suddenly appeared in the doorway, took her presentation gift and disappeared into her room again, shutting the door behind her.

On the ground floor there also lived an old retired performer who in her time had been an operetta diva.

At night — and only ever then, in the deadest hours of the night — I would hear her singing, practising light arias in a cracked and tremulous voice, and this would make me feel like crying.

Once my telephone was out of order, and I went to her room to ring the faults department.

The door was opened by a boy who for some reason was wearing an astrakhan hat and fur coat with a scarf.

"May I use the phone, young fellow?" I asked.

Clearly offended, he replied in a squeaky, petulant voice "I'm not a young fellow."

"I'm terribly sorry," I said, recognizing that he was in fact an elderly dwarf.

"No need to apologize, " he snapped.

With his yellow face that was as wrinkled as a dried date, the dwarf contrived in spite of his stunted growth to look at me as if from a height, with an aloof and haughty expression — just how he achieved this remains a mystery to me.

"Only keep it short: I'm in a hurry."

On the wall above the telephone hung a list of numbers:

'First Aid Hospital'

'Kashchenko Mental Hospital'.

'Medicinal leeches'.

'Fire'.

'Theatre Repertoire Committee'.

'Dulev'.

Who was this Dulev? Why did he find himself included in this list of emergency telephone numbers? When was he called, and how was he able to help?

While I was dialling the faults department and explaining what was wrong, the dwarf in his astrakhan hat, fur coat and scarf stood some way off, in a corner, fixing me with a contemptuous gaze that seemed not even to acknowledge my right to exist.

Well, not long after, the dwarf, Pyotr Petrovich, died of a heart attack.

His little, child-sized coffin stood near the entrance to the apartment.

And it was quiet.

In a communal apartment too everyone ponders briefly on the vanity and futility of life when somebody (even a dwarf) dies, and for a while everyone is very good and pure. In our communal kitchen that day people spoke in respectful, sad voices.

The Never-ending Day

It was the era of commercial restaurants, Stalin Prizes, whitewash propaganda novels that were all of a pattern, courts of honour, which have gone down in history as courts of dishonour, an era when mediocrity was synonymous with reliability, impotence trampled strength underfoot, and the vilest, most dishonourable and perfidious elements made the running, when the lowest forms of life were taking over, and winter reigned in my country.

Those confused, dark, icy days of terror, those dead days of my life when I was thirty-five years old and at the height of my powers.

There were many achievements that year: in agriculture, public catering, socialist realism, in the struggle against Weissmanism-Morganism and against cosmopolitanism and revisionism, and in nationalities policy.

And the constant flow of meetings: lengthy, turbulent, involved meetings held into the night, when nobody knew exactly what it was all about, what was required of them, what they should do, think or say, how they should vote... Lord God almighty!

Nobody had any idea yet, nobody even dreamed what the consequences would be, how all this might end — how it must inevitably end.

Nothing actually happened. There was no fatal epidemic, no plague of rats or locusts; nobody died of a terrible, unknown, mysterious disease; there was no fire, earthquake or flood in this or any other city, or anywhere else in the country.

And nevertheless, like a thunderbolt on a sunny, bright, serene day, a spark of madness suddenly flew past, piercing its way through all hearts, all institutions, editorial boards, ministries, workers' collectives, schools and kindergartens; and at once everything was electrified, the whole atmosphere became stifling and laden with fear, and there were universal demands for sacrificial victims, for an unceasing and insatiable orgy of sacrifice.

Waves of paranoid suspicion alternated with periods of relative calm and even periods of a certain half-hearted mercy and forgiveness; and usually at the height of the storm, when the situation seemed at its most desperate, there would begin a new campaign to rectify errors and excesses. The sun rose, people suddenly looked at each other with half-sober eyes, were ashamed at what they had so recently said and, shuddering at the deeds their silence had condoned, felt themselves to be human beings — even those whose souls had been corroded and completely enveloped by fear, those in whom all pride, honour, faith and conscience had been supplanted with fear. Yet even during these major periods of transition one could already sense, as in the calm before a storm, the approach of a new, even more virulent attack of paranoia, crude, blind and merciless, when, as from a stone cast into water, ever widening circles dragged more and more people into the whirlpool, sucking them down into the deadly vortex — people who were without the slightest shadow of guilt and had never in their waking or sleeping hours spoken a word out of place.

All this was like the changing seasons, annual rings on the cross-section of a tree, or the phases of schizophrenia, and people were beginning to live with it. Life moved on from one meeting to the next, from one campaign to the next, and each new campaign was more total, merciless and grotesque than all the rest put together. And all the time the atmosphere of guilt was being intensified, collective guilt and the guilt of each separate individual, which could never be redeemed in any way. One had continually to feel guilty, guilty, guilty, and meekly accept all punishments, all criticisms and all sentences.

Gradually this feeling of constant, inexhaustible, frenzied guilt and the fear of shadowy powers-that-be became your alter ego, your second nature and character. The moment you woke up you already felt guilty of something, although as yet you had no idea what it was. Somebody had not fulfilled the plan, somewhere there had been a crop failure, derailment, landslide, some festering sore in the body politic, double-dealing... Reading about this, you felt as if you yourself had been guilty of neglect, had failed to notice it, had been caught napping and had allowed it to happen, and, to add insult to injury, had aided and abetted the perpetrators. You were under constant pressure, in a constant state of vigilance, of eagerness to expiate this feeling of guilt, to prove yourself worthy of trust. But such trust, whether complete or partial, never existed and never could exist in any case, and you never felt at ease, in a state of secure well-being, for always, at any moment night or day, you could meet with the greatest, most terrible disaster, which when it happened would be irremediable and irreversible. And so you lived, trembling at each suspicious glance, expecting the worst to happen at each turn, zigzag or new rumour.

Nobody knew what it was all for; everybody was drawn into this atmosphere, suffocating in it as in the oppressive sultriness preceding a storm, and they all thought that this was a normal state of affairs. As always there were some who rapidly and skilfully acclimatised themselves, who shot ahead and rose to the top faster than anybody else; these were actually in their element and found all this to their advantage. They had already learned how to turn things to good account, to be the first to respond, the first to shout "Infamy!", and they were already the drummers, the buglers, the gleaners of rich pickings.

Tomorrow or the day after, during the next campaign, the latest conflagration, they would be the ones to be strung up; but they did not know this yet, nor did they want to know. They had no foreboding of it and did not think or even want to think about it; while for today they bent all their efforts to securing the noose around the necks of others as tightly, as meticulously, as conscientiously as possible.

Each time some idea would appear on the scene unannounced, like a tsunami, for example a new interpretation of the character of Kutuzov in War and Peace, or the assertion that Russian science had discovered everything first, or something else. Why did these ideas appear precisely when they did — in March or August, in this year and on this day — and not at any other time? Where was an explanation for this to be found: in economics, the international situation, sunspots, or in the ghastly nightmares and phantom visions of just one man?

Nor was there any shortage of academic stooges and phoney scholars, selected at various times according to their position: professors, lecturers and research students who thundered from the pulpit or led hymns of praise, who battened onto Hegel and Plekhanov, Aristotle and Karl Kautsky like bed bugs, and who wrote commentaries on His every word, His every comma; even if a comma was used incorrectly or at-random they would find a hidden, brilliant significance in the error. Moreover, this would all immediately become not just a great discovery but also the law of the land and an article in the Criminal Code.

And however tenuous a connection it might have had with the events of everyday life in the here-and-now, with the interests and concerns of the state and its subjects, with their vital interests in matters of family, love, overcrowding, or child-rearing, nevertheless it would immediately become the most important, significant and decisive affair of state, overriding and demoting to the lowest order of priority questions of bread, school or family, filling pages of newspapers and journals, of learned treatises and dissertations — those dissertations gathering dust on the book-stacks in their handsome hard covers with gold lettering, which research students copied from each other complete with quotations, mistakes and distortions.

It was subjected to prolonged exegesis at all conferences and meetings, and on every platform; dissenters, and sometimes even non-dissenters, would leave lecture halls and laboratories to be put straight on transports to penal servitude in distant, fearsome places such as Magadan and Kolyma, while their wives were sent into exile and their children put into orphanages. Whole academic schools were banned and anathematized, lists were compiled of books and treatises of past centuries to be removed from libraries forever and destroyed, manuscripts disappeared from archives and were burned, with all due legal authorization, so that nobody was ever able to find them again. Learned disputes would begin with bootlickers and hangers-on in lecture rooms, continue with the examining magistrate, and be concluded with screws in the camps.

I learned all this the hard way, from experience. I myself attended those meetings, sat through them from beginning to end, listening to and absorbing everything, transfixed with terror lest I too should be named; and when I joined in informal discussions outside the main hall, I was startled to hear the sound of my own glutinous voice, as if there were a dwarf speaking from inside me. But nobody bothered about me as long as I didn't disturb them or get in their way, and wasn't a beam or even a mote in anyone's eye, and the speechmakers, those big shots who laid into each other until the sparks flew, forgot all about me. I was granted a temporary indulgence for as long as I stayed outside the field of fire.

But on that winter's day all my capacity to achieve melted away, and I did not have the strength to build it up again from scratch.

The day began strangely, grotesquely.

I was woken by the telephone ringing, and a high woman's voice, edgy and debilitated, asked "Is this the Orphanage? How is the Clumel child?"

Before I could doze off, the telephone rang again: "I queued for a whole two hours, but when I got home and unwrapped it, they'd given me nothing but bones."

I did not have the strength to explain, so I said wearily "All right, bring it back."

"You'll authorize it then, will you?" the woman shouted into the telephone. "I'd been queuing since the early hours."

"I will, I will," I said.

And it seemed as though I could hear filtering through into my room the clearly audible sounds of a queue forming in the gateway: that pre-dawn, circumspect, surreptitious rustling, as though people were queuing not for legs of mutton but for cocaine, their numbers in the queue scrawled with indelible pencil on palms calloused and wrinkled or pink and youthfully soft, as yet untouched and unmarked by the ominous lines of fate. And the queue taut as a spring, murmuring, the people back in the darkness of the gateway clinging to each other like links in a chain — what chain can be more dogged, more unbreakable than a line of people queuing for food? — clinging together, emerging into the noise and light of the street, guided by a police sergeant, stepping as in a slow-motion film; this tangled mass flowed along next to the wall in meanders, grey, grey quilted jackets, toile de nord, women's outsize tarpaulin boots, swarms of shopping bags — string, oilcloth, leatherette. As though the din, sweat, commotion and convulsive torment of all the queues massing in this morning gloom for fish, for kvas, for trousers had burst into my room.

I looked out of the window. In the grey, lifeless half-light of a winter dawn dark figures were moving at speed, almost running, along the pavements, and they all had shopping bags. Some carried their children, still asleep, or else dragged them along behind them, wrapped up in their little coats and downy shawls, and shod in felt boots. Some of the children were grizzling at this unearthly hour, while others remained impassively silent, which was an even more disturbing sight.

Lit from afar by approaching headlights, solitary black little figures were running across the still empty street. Then all of a sudden there burst out of the darkness a huge van, its roof white with fresh snow (somewhere outside the city, where the slaughterhouses and storehouses were, it was snowing), and, speeding past, disappeared. Yet more diminutive figures ran across, and again there were headlights approaching, this time several together; and then all at once it was as though a dam had burst: as a fiery herd they came, impatient, thundering, filling the whole street, and light from the headlamps swept fitfully across the ceiling of my dark room like waves of an ever-flowing river.

Heard as if through a fog of sleep, the radio was droning on about the luxuriant wheat, the luxuriant wheat, which would now never grow to full height; then the radio voice grew hoarse and died away, and suddenly, from all directions and in all the rooms at once, there was music playing and an energetic voice saying: "One, two! One, two!" As though the broadcast were coming from some Elysian scene of eternal sunshine.

Yet in the voice of this presenter, ordering children, old women and lunatics in all the rooms to "One, two! One, two!" there was a hint of artificiality and futility, a fast-dying intonation, a note of immense uncertainty as to whether you would follow his instructions and become idiotically jolly in the twinkling of an eye.

The telephone rang again, with a shrill, penetrating sound, and a flippant voice said, "Open the top window, get ready for your exercises, place your legs apart, breathe in deeply."

"Who is this?" I asked sleepily, stupidly and hoarsely.

"A well-wisher who wants you to develop your figure, so you get brawny shoulders and a rippling torso..."

Suddenly this voice was cut off, and a different one, distinct, gruff and from a completely different ball game, announced: "1556 reporting."

I dropped the receiver as if it were red-hot.

There was something at once bizarre and menacing in these telephone calls, and I was reminded of the account I had once heard, given by an old Bolshevik in a sanatorium outside Moscow, of his arrest in 1937. It had all started with telephone calls: "Is it you that's got a deaf and dumb child?" "Has Aunt Luta arrived?"

A few days after telling this he was arrested for the second time, at night, and led away, straight from his ward, the day before he was due to be discharged. The matron had come silently, on tiptoe, and woken him up; he got dressed, and woke up the others who looked out of the window, watching him leave, followed by two men in plainclothes. All three got into a Pobeda limousine, the vehicle swung round, and they drove away along the avenue, past snow-laden trees, forever.

The thick, grey depression oozed ceaselessly, permeating my sleep. Again I was having confused, grotesque dreams, and my mind was constantly haunted by a quivering, entangled terror. In my dreams I was running through streets blocked by German motorcyclists on their heavy green machines, trying to break out through gunfire and exploding grenades; or I would be stopped by a policeman in a new peaked cap who would look me straight in the eye without saying a word; another time I was squeezing through dark, airless attics smelling of felt and cobwebs and, unable to breathe, woke up to open the top window, only to find the room freezing cold.

The buildings on the other side of the street loomed up like a smudge of ink on blotting paper, and the whole of life seemed like a dreary negative.

And I thought of what a prodigious effort it would take to get up once more and start the whole business all over again.

I was also oppressed by a smarting sensation of disaster. At first, still half asleep, I could not exactly recall what calamity had struck the day before. As soon as I was fully awake, I remembered: "Of course, the telephone calls!" I was shaken by the uncertainty in which I had been living recently, and by the vague awareness of a guilt that I had never committed.

The wick of my makeshift lamp was floating in sunflower oil in an old shoe-polish tin; the house management committee regularly switched off the electricity after midnight on the grounds that the quota had been used up.

I lit the lamp and saw my room as if for the first time: the smoke-blackened, sooty ceiling; the hundred-candle-power naked bulb hanging forlornly on its long flex; the yellowed newspapers on the table in place of a tablecloth; the frying-pan and tin teapot; my winter coat and army greatcoat hanging on nails, as though someone were standing by the wall, waiting for me.

Like everybody else I had not chosen to live here, had not come here because I liked the street, its tranquillity, greenery or peaceful atmosphere. It was in fact the most noisy, cacophonous and ravening of streets, reminiscent of a wind tunnel used to test aero engines, with nowhere to hide from their deafening roar; and it was in this wind tunnel that you slept, ate your frugal meal of potatoes, read newspapers and novels, quarrelled and kissed, went down with flu and suffered from depression.

I am inclined to think that of all the millions of rooms in old Moscow there was none more awkward, odd and uncomfortable; it was like a prison cell with a narrow window looking onto the noisiest square in the city, right next to a traffic junction, so that all the vehicles moving along the Ring Road that had to turn onto the Arbat came round just here, wailing and snarling.

At night, when the thundering of this incessant flow abated to some extent and only solitary ambulances drove past, their sirens wailing, those huge, clumsy water-carts used for sprinkling the streets would converge from all over the borough to fill up with water from the hydrant situated immediately under my window. They stood in line with their engines running, snorting and siphoning, and water gushed noisily through the hoses; and while the vehicles were filling up, drivers and janitors would chat about injustice, the vindictiveness of their bosses, the price of buckwheat on the black market, their girl-friends, their grub. It was here too, of course, that the brass bands of the Moscow Military District rehearsed 'The Holy War' before May Day and the Revolution holiday; trumpets blared, drums rolled, and window-panes rattled and shook.

The question of accommodation, like everything else in life, was determined by bizarre, blind chance.

I arrived here with a temporary residence permit one day in spring during the war; it was a cold spring, and I was wearing summer overalls and a tall Caucasian-style sheepskin hat with a red ribbon, and carrying an old TT pistol in a home-made holster fashioned in the partisan camp near Bobruysk by the local curriers.

The house manageress gave me the kind of stony reception I would have expected from a secret police interrogator.

She was a woman with the figure of a Venus and the face of an army recruit, wearing a padded jacket and tarpaulin boots, and sporting a ginger perm and lipstick: half guerrilla and half courtesan.

She read my document three times, cursorily examined the back of it, then looked at me and said, "So, you think you've struck lucky, eh?"

I did not reply. After all, she had seen the water marks in the paper.

What had happened was that a certain old bachelor, a former tax inspector, had had the good fortune to marry into a separate apartment and, having to give up his old vacant room in any case, had agreed to let me have it, leaving me to face the neighbours, who had long hankered after this accommodation, the janitor, who also had his eye on it, the bribe-taking manageress, the Moscow City Council, the police, the office issuing residence permits, every law and regulation and the Supreme Soviet itself. And by various means fair and foul, by pulling countless strings, and as the result of intercessions and telephone calls up and down the chain of command, slowly but surely, snowed under with application forms, letters of denunciation and court orders, I transformed my temporary residence permit into a permanent one.

But this was all later.

Back then, this frozen, almost icy old veteran of a house received us in silence. We walked down a long, empty corridor; someone appeared to be moving about inside the rooms, keeping busy. This turned out to be the scrabbling of mice.

At length there appeared something tall, emaciated and despondent in a shaggy dressing-gown, a downy shawl fastened crosswise and oriental slippers with turned-up toes: something resembling a cross between Don Quixote and Oblomov. It peered at us and said in an unexpected falsetto, "Why, pray, is the water-closet not functioning?"

I spread my hands to indicate my ignorance on the subject, while the manageress just laughed.

"Comrade Tsulukidze, aren't you ashamed of pestering people with such trivial matters when there's a war on?"

"I beg your pardon," said the cross between Don Quixote and Oblomov, "but what has the war got to do with it?"

"What it's got to do with it is that no funds've been allocated, that's what!" exploded the manageress.

"But one water-closet!" he pleaded, hands on heart in supplication.

The manageress gave him short shrift. "There's no point talking: it just encourages him," she snapped. "Come with me, comrade soldier." And she strode off in her tarpaulin boots as though she were the one who had returned from behind the German lines.

"There are all sorts living here," said the manageress. "If it were up to me, I'd deport the lot of them from the capital. They're no use to man or beast."

We went on and entered an empty communal kitchen with a huge range the size of a volleyball pitch. The manageress shouldered open a door into a tiny corridor that was dark and musty, and then a further door that appeared to open into a wall cupboard. We entered a narrow room that stretched out like a tunnel, grey and forlorn and exuding a stony chill and mouldiness from all the winters of wartime.

In the room there were: a nickel-plated double bed with a burst mattress and protruding springs; a home-made china cabinet of crude construction, holding chipped cups full of dust; and a bookcase that stood at an angle and contained — apart from old books and brochures on matters of taxation — spiders, whose source of sustenance in this dead, God-forsaken room was a mystery.

I had the sensation of entering a freezing morgue where the corpse of time was laid out: time that had been the stuff of other lives, a time unknown and alien to me and now forever past, which had yet known its own childhood and youth, its own happiness, radiant sunlit mornings and tranquil evenings, and nights, and pain, and partings, and an unwavering faith in immortality.

And this time — with its mice, its shadows, its irreversibility — was something I could tangibly perceive. It was no ordinary dust that covered everything, but funereal remains: a thick layer of the grey, appalling remains of decomposed papers, clothes, summer moths, perhaps even the finger-nails and skin of people who had once lived here.

Alien stone walls that spoke of the unknown lives lived within them. Mine was just beginning within these freezing cold, damp-sodden stone walls, on that eerie, icy day in wartime, in the empty, narrow street with no cars and hardly any male pedestrians, to the wail of an air-raid siren and the whispering of the radio that had not been switched off since its owner had left before the war. It was awful to contemplate how every day for all those years the radio had started speaking in this empty room early each morning, had broadcast the Department of Information news summary, sung folk

ditties, played Bach fugues, jangled to the thrumming of the
Osipov Balalaika Orchestra, wailed with the sound of air-
raid sirens, crashed out salutes to honour the Oryol, Kharkov,
Gomel divisions; and that every morning and at midnight, after
talking and talking until it was hoarse, it had played the Kremlin
chimes.

There had been a thaw; with clamouring bell, scattering water
from puddles of melted snow and striking sparks from the rails,
a tram was hurtling down from Plyushchikha towards Borodino
Bridge. At the Kiev Station a disabled ex-serviceman entered
the carriage from the front platform; he was wearing a worn
padded jacket and a soldier's beaver-lamb hat that had turned
black with age, and had a red star cut from tinplate. Taking up
position in the doorway, he doggedly scrutinized the passengers,
then removed his hat and suddenly, hysterically, burst into song:

"Ho-o-ow great is this epoch, bequeathed us by Marx..."

I did not hear any more than this; reducing speed, the tram
started clanking and squealing as it slowly negotiated the curve
by the Kiev market, and while it was still moving I jumped off,
heading for the stalls where women and old men from the
suburbs stood with bundles of chopped firewood and kindling.
A loaf of bread, already mouldy and stone-hard, which I had
obtained on a military warrant, was traded in for a bundle of
firewood, and then I made for my new home on foot through
the back streets, carrying the firewood on my back, all the
while relishing the joke: "Ho-o-ow great is this epoch,
bequeathed us by Marx..."

Each morning now I was waking up with a feeling of
oppression and despair at a life irretrievably lost and spent to
no purpose, when everything is endlessly repeated and seems

long since played out. And then I would experience a strange, quite otherworldly sense of non-existence.

Looking out of the window, I saw a snow-laden poplar, and just for a second, for one magic instant, there fluttered past, brushing against me and gently breathing on me, that celebratory feeling known of old, from childhood, of a winter daybreak, of the miracle of snow, of festive purity and whiteness.

No doubt there was somebody for whom this morning too was miraculous, serene, unique — perhaps the happiest morning of their life — and for whom even this gloomy, rust-coloured sky seemed like happiness. Yet I could not imagine this: to me it seemed that the whole world must be feeling sombre and wretched, and that this blind, stillborn day could bring nobody any good.

There was also the clear recognition, sharply focussed at this hour of the morning, that everything would be repeated once more, and that in spite of all one's expectations, one's eternal, stupid, undying hope and illusions, nothing would ever change: not today, not tomorrow, never. And that really there was no point in living.

And yet one had to live.

I turned to my bookshelves.

On the dusty shelves stood a cheap edition of Tolstoi, single-volume selections of Lermontov and Gogol, slim volumes by Babel and Andrey Platonov. Bunin and Khodasevich were there too, brought back from Harbin, from the Manchurian campaign, also Hemingway, borrowed from the library and never returned, and the diary of Jules Renard, withdrawn from library stocks in the same way. Apart from the rest stood those books which I turned to daily, which I never tired of re-reading, and which I attuned myself to each morning, as if to a tuning-fork. These were Hamsun's *Hunger and Pan*, the tales of Hans Christian Andersen, and a volume of selected stories by

Chekhov: 'The House with a Mezzanine', 'Ariadne', 'In the Ravine'; and recently these had been joined by *The Life of Arsenyev*. They were not just my tuning-fork, they were as air, as hope, as the meaning of life; they were models showing that you could achieve something if you really wanted to, and that to this end life was worth living.

And finally, on the bottom shelf, were the dark-blue volumes of Stalin, and speeches by Molotov, Malenkov and Kaganovich in thin brochures published by Politizdat in mass editions for the Party education seminar. These grey pamphlets were much-perused and well-studied; the texts had been underlined with red and blue pencil, and quotations had been duly copied out for notes.

I took out one of the books by Hamsun, *Pan*.

'Here I sit, in the mountains; sea and air are alive with sounds.

'You people, birds and beasts! I raise my glass to night and solitude deep in the forest — the forest! To leaves that are green and leaves that are yellow!'

In thousands upon thousands of such communal apartments, in the same cramped little rooms, people just like myself, some single, some with families, were waking up. There were those soldiers who had gone through the whole war and emerged miraculously unscathed; the wounded and shell-shocked ones, who were having a hard time of it in the snow and slush and feeling dreadful on this dark winter morning; and also brawny-faced deserters and dodgers, some with reserved occupations and some without, some who had been safely evacuated and some who stayed behind, who now, as soon as they were awake, were on the phone, trying to grab a slice of the action as soon as possible, before somebody else snatched it from under their nose. There were the people who would be hauled over the coals and expelled at meetings today, at thousands upon thousands of meetings, and those who would persecute them, who would take the chair and compose resolutions, or else just vote for their expulsion without really wanting to. There were the hounded and defenceless who awaited the next campaign in fear and trembling, and those who were making the running for the time being. They were all of them waking up now, and for each of them this grey morning was something different; they did not — could not, would not — understand one another.

Thrusting my legs into my tall goatskin boots (a memento of my days as a partisan), I went out stripped to the waist and entered the cold kitchen, where the cement floor was spattered with streaks of frozen water, to wash at the sink. Usually nobody looked up, but stood at their individual tables (their precious kitchen tables), peeling potatoes, chopping cabbage or cooking rissoles. They begrudged me my academic ration card — they couldn't stomach that, and would mutter as if to themselves, "What a turn-up — a research worker!"

I would pretend not to hear.

This morning, however, everything was alarmingly different. Nobody was standing at the tables. Not a primus was sputtering, not a paraffin stove burning, nor was there smoke rising from any of the strange antediluvian devices used for boiling, baking, heating and browning.

The kitchen was full of women young and old, some from the ground floor, and all were dressed warmly, with their headscarves on and their coats done up.

At first I thought there must be fresh fish on sale somewhere, or else duck or even Caspian roach, or perhaps Chinese woollen cardigans.

Although all the apartment's parties and warring factions were represented, on this occasion nobody was yelling or hissing; on the contrary, they all stood together, waiting for something: animated, laughing, somehow more mellow, somehow even (a pleasant surprise) more kindly than their usual selves, as if — "Christ is risen!" — some kind of universal Easter had broken out in the communal kitchen. They looked at me and cheerfully said "Good morning," which I had certainly never heard before and had not expected to hear until my dying day. And no doubt I gave them a strange look and replied "Good morning" in such a perplexed, startled and piteous tone of voice that to a woman they burst into playful laughter. I did not know whether they were pulling my leg or whether I was dreaming; or perhaps it was some kind of amateur drama production — or had the whole world been turned upside down, and I wasn't in the know, having slept through it all? But soon everything became clear.

"Who's got the tickets?" asked some of the women who were becoming impatient.

"Voronchikhina's got them."

At this moment Voronchikhina swept in, swarthy of complexion and buzzing like a hornet. She was wearing a short sheepskin coat, and her eyes were gleaming.

"Hi, girls!"

"What seats have you got?" asked some of the women.

"In the stalls," said Voronchikhina.

"Is it Tarzan?"

"It certainly is."

They all laughed contentedly and, pushing and jostling, poured out of the kitchen and down the stairs, talking loudly as they went.

I returned to my Hamsun.

'Summer nights, the tranquil water, and the endlessly tranquil forest! Not a cry, not a footstep heard from the road. My heart was filled as with dark-hued wine.'

I knew very well that if I did not write anything — actually get something down on paper — in the morning, the rest of the day would seem empty and worthless. It would be as if I had lost that day somewhere in the street, or as if it had fallen down a well. All the time I had this helpless sensation of days lost, days idly wasted away.

Never did I give myself any quarter, show myself mercy, slacken the tension; and with time the tension remained taut of its own accord and became part of my nature.

What was all this: vanity and ambition, overwrought nerves, the natural urge to work? Or was it a sense of responsibility, a hungering after truth and justice, a contempt for all that was base and vile? Most likely it was a combination of all these things: ambition, nervous tension, the urge to work and an insatiable hunger for truth. Apart from which, work was my only salvation. When I was alone with myself, even in this bedlam, this stifling atmosphere, memories came to me in the waves of fear; what I had seen and heard only that day or the day before merged with what I had seen and heard in earliest childhood, and all this was like a dream, unfolding and forming a mosaic of its own accord. As if somebody were whispering in my ear, as if a magnetic tape were unwinding by itself, all I had to do was write to the dictation of this whispering voice.

Then one could crush and overpower this blind, grey day, the despondency, pain and resentment, and even hopelessness itself; one could melt them down within oneself, as in a crucible, reducing them to words, to a cry.

It would come unannounced, like a whirlwind. Perpetual and unending, borne along on breathing free and untrammelled, a sentence filled with colours, sounds and resonance would unfurl calmly and majestically, with its distant and closer echoes, drawing into itself the flow of life and fusing beauty and ugliness, hesitation and fluency, infancy and old age, stupidity and wisdom, the past and the future.

Then the feeling of being humiliated and oppressed would disappear completely, and everything was possible, everything was within my grasp.

I looked out of the window. Over the road a new block of flats for generals was being built. One section had already been let; the other was still covered in scaffolding.

At nine o'clock exactly a general came out, buttoning up his greatcoat as he walked, and then got into a black car and drove off. After this another chauffeur in a coffee-coloured car reversed up to the entrance, at which precise moment a man in a coat of thick woollen cloth and a deerskin cap emerged from the entrance and, lighting a cigarette, got into the car and drove off.

Next two sisters ran out of the entrance, hastily powdering their faces as they went, and ran off in different directions. All I could hear was the clatter of their high heels on the builders' wooden paving.

Then labourers appeared on the scaffolding; they conferred, had a smoke, and started work. Next the bosses arrived. Work stopped again, and now everybody had a smoke, workers and bosses together.

I heard that the postman had come, as he rattled the lids of the mailboxes.

I went out.

The wide door was completely cluttered with mailboxes, giving it an armour-plated appearance, and each mailbox had its own padlock. Once again the postman had got it wrong: my mailbox was empty, and my Pravda showed up through the holes of the one next to it. This mailbox was old and buckled, dating from before the war, perhaps even from before the revolution; yet it was freshly painted, and soldered where it needed it, and even had some flowers on it, painted on a blue background. It was constructed of such thick tinplate that it looked like a steel fireproof safe, and instead of a common-or-garden padlock it was secured with such a massive one as though treasury notes were deposited in it, rather than letters and newspapers. Even so I eventually managed to extract the now torn and tattered newspaper, and skimmed through its grey, monotonous columns, which looked just like those from yesterday, and the day before yesterday, and last year, and the year before that. Right at the end of the paper, where the most important, depressing and hopeful news items were always to be found, one made me flinch as if a knife had slashed me: "Latest news. Arrest of gang of saboteur doctors."

I began to read avidly, feeling at once as if somebody or something had me by the throat. I read and read, at one moment understanding everything, at the next feeling completely befogged. In disbelief and with a sense of disgust and abiding horror I read it again and again, unable to put the newspaper down — something had snapped inside me.

Grey light, doleful and drained of colour, seeped despairingly through the tiny window. It had never really been a window, had never been designed as such by that far-off architect, working in the heat of inspiration on his sketch of a patrician residence; it was simply a hole in a blank wall, knocked through by somebody who had lived here before me, who then, as an act of blind volition, had just as gratuitously and incongruously filled the hole with glass.

It was one of those short, grey, uncanny days so typical of December and January: hardly a day at all, just a wisp of daylight, as though the sun and the sky had grown tired of shining, rejoicing and exulting, and as though time itself had closed its eyes momentarily, leaving people in the fond belief that they were still alive.

The usual morning set was assembled at the skating rink. Valery Valeryanovich, the manager of a flower shop, was there, of course; a sly old fellow with greying hair, kitted out in a knitted hat and white boots laced to the knee, with special figure-skating blades, he was executing various figures-of-eight and other patterns, raising first one leg and then the other in a whimsical and affected manner. Behind him came a dental technician, tall and thin as a candle and with a small head like that of a daffodil, followed by a diminutive old man who was already showing signs of shrivelling and shrinking. Together they formed a little club, and I felt completely reassured as I observed their Olympian gliding.

The Romanov and Hohenzollern dynasties had fallen, political parties and classes had disappeared, of Hitler there remained no more than dust, and yet this uncommitted, informal little club of figure-skaters had proved to be more adamantine, more indestructible.

That is indeed the way of things: revolutions and wars, uprisings and purges may come and go, yet the same old members still attend the sessions of urological and stomatological associations, while philatelists and numismatists carry on meeting to exchange coins, pencils or matchbox labels.

I pulled on my woollen socks and the stiff skating boots I had hired, lacing them firmly and then securing them further by swathing them criss-cross with white tape. When I stood up I felt endowed with a kind of additional iron strength as keen as steel.

Next to me on the bench was a tiny little girl wearing a hat that was bright yellow like a dandelion, an orange scarf and tall, tightly laced white boots with silver figure-skating blades. She sat like everybody else with legs wearily stretched out and eyes half-shut, and her face too bore a serious, reposeful expression.

"How old are you?" I asked.

"Four," she replied, without altering her tranquil demeanour.

Four! Could this really be so? It was quite alarming, quite terrifying to think of how much living she still had to do, how much she still had to see.

"Goody! " she said suddenly, jumping up on her tiny little skates and heading for the frosty door that led to the ice, diminutive and skinny in her little dandelion hat. She did not so much run as skip down the ice-covered steps, like a grasshopper, and in a flash her skates were humming over the ice.

At once she began to circle, entering into the rhythm of the routine, and her movements were light and natural, like a flower opening. And I felt that I loved her, this little girl who was a stranger to me. It was not even that I envied her, I simply loved her.

When I came out of the dark cloakroom, the low-lying winter clouds, grey and tattered, opened up, and I was dazzled by the sun and by joy.

The snow-covered avenue, red bullfinches in the bushes — all swept past; and as I leaped out onto the icy expanse of the embankment, with the Sparrow Hills and the scarlet, icy sun in the distance, at once everything evaporated, everything was dispersed, as if the wind had blown away the dark morning and the fumes and commotion of the communal apartment in the Arbat, now living its own life somewhere out there; as if the Great Epoch had sunk into oblivion and all had been a dream, and childhood had returned, all the fun of Church Hill — skate down it, down, spin like a top, fly through the whirling snow! — and stars were flying, bursting, and everything was within my powers, everything was possible there, ahead, under cover of night, under the stars, the stars where angels lived.

A girl wheeled past me with a flash of her black-and-white sweater, looking just like a swallow. She glanced round. I caught up with her and skated behind her for a while, examining her thighs and legs, then overtook her and looked her in the face. For a long time I skated at her side, keeping in step, hearing the hiss of our racing skates on the ice. We unexpectedly struck up a conversation, and she turned off into a quiet avenue; we continued alone, descending to the mirror-like ice of Tsaritsyn Pond, where snow-laden willows lined the banks, and where, filling our lungs with air, we made several circuits; and wind, sun and freedom blew away all that was dark and depressing: once again there was life, youth, hope, and everyone was beautiful, happy and young. How simple, how good life is when the world is covered with snow!

I had just come out into the snowy avenue from the light and glitter of the rink and, stepping clumsily in my skates, had started walking, as if on pins, along the scrunching frozen path. It was then that I saw them: two men in dark beaver coats standing at the end of the avenue, clearly delineated against the freshly fallen snow. And at once I knew what was happening, knew with my whole being, with my tattered nerves and instantaneously pounding blood, that they were mine, that from this moment on we were bound by a thread stronger than anything in the world. And that this was my fate, my pit of darkness: finito, curtains.

And that day: the bright winter sun that had glowed red since morning; pink striations on the snow; dazzlingly white birch-trees; the light, fluffy, sparkling snow; the sweet sounds — all had now taken on a grey, lacklustre, nauseous colour of fear and apprehension, the colour of loneliness.

I had immediately recognized them beyond all shadow of doubt from their dark beaver coats and dark cloth overboots, from the preoccupied way in which they were standing, and even from the fact that they were not looking at me, but chatting to each other with a show of animation, as if they were just a pair of good companions enjoying the fresh air on this sunny winter's day.

The sun-filled world of snow, sky and wind, free and flung open wide to every quarter, which only a moment before, bathed in its light, I had still experienced, and which even now permeated me and quickened my pulse — this ecstatic world had suddenly shrunk to the tiny patch of ground covered with dark, trampled slush where I now stood on my skates, unsure of what to do: whether to go on ahead to the cloakroom or run back into the world I had left behind me, the world of snow. They appeared to have noticed my indecision and were observing me with interest.

It was as if I had walked into a concave mirror and come out on the other side. The living objective world had become silent and invisible, and I had split into two: as I walked, I could see myself, and this person whom I was watching as if from the sidelines walked straight ahead firmly and meticulously on his skates, as though on stilts, while the person who was myself could feel his legs giving way under him.

Their muddy-brown beaver coats, utterly identical (or co-substantial, as philosophers would say) to the last button and thread, like their caps of imitation sealskin were twins in every detail; while their overboots, which had come off the same conveyor belt, even seemed to me to be the same size, although the men were of dissimilar build and must have had different feet. Because of this their faces, which in fact were quite unalike — the one puffy, impassive and pale, like an over-cooked potato; the other sharp-featured, voluble and mercurial — also seemed identical.

They did not move from the path, but continued their conversation, without looking at me. As I squeezed past, I could smell the pungent mouldering dampness of their imitation fur caps, and the high-voltage current of their attention seemed to make contact with me, binding me more closely to them. Suddenly I felt as if I had been hit. I had registered an attentive glance directed at me — at me alone and nobody else — like a crow's black eye piercing me as I passed.

I looked round before entering the cloakroom. One of them was standing with his legs apart, gaping at the clouds, and the other had gone into a telephone kiosk and was hastily dialling a number. He said something, speaking rapidly and with agitation, at the same time looking at me through the glass, openly and without any attempt at concealment, scrutinizing me at leisure and evidently describing me from what he saw to whoever was at the other end of the line. And suddenly I thought (or perhaps imagined) that I could read his lips clearly articulating my name, spelling it out syllable by syllable, and I felt as if I were suffocating.

The dark cloakroom felt like a mousetrap. The attendants appeared to be in the know, colluding with the two men: they took a suspiciously long time to find my coat, mixing up the numbered tokens in the process, and they seemed to be surreptitiously glancing at me from a distance, watching me take off the skates.

Was this the beginning or the end? Was it just the start of things — had they only just got me in their sights? Or was everything already sewn up, all the evidence collected and collated in a file, with a document attached that summarised everything and bore at its head the hieroglyphic squiggle signifying 'arrest'? And were they now just checking the lie of the land so as to be able to arrest me as efficiently, straightforwardly and neatly as possible and to make sure I would not leave the area, whether on business, to stay with friends, or to attend a wedding?

How dark it was in the cloakroom, how terribly dark and bleak! And while going from one counter to the next — one to get my coat, another for my shoes — and then sitting on the narrow bench to take off my skates, I was continually thinking about them.

Many years of trepidation, fear and apprehension had made me highly proficient in recognizing them, perhaps not so much by sight as instantaneously with all five senses. From a thousand people I could soon pick them out, find them, sniff them out amongst all the others, recognizing them by their silhouette, by their faces — grey, inexpressive, as if condemned to this greyness — and by their eyes, which seemed to avoid you but in reality were looking at you and no-one else.

They would suddenly pop up at the entrance to your block

of flats, as if waiting for a date with a girl friend; or you would find them next to you in a tram, holding up a newspaper, and their eyes, while scanning the latest news from Indonesia, would be taking in nothing but you over the top of those turbulent events; or they would be sitting relaxed and distant at the next table in a restaurant, with a bottle of Narzan mineral water and a packet of 'Prima' cigarettes. No matter whether they were there for you or somebody else, you would recognize them and feel afraid.

Recently I had started recognizing them even when they were not there, in the bath-house, at the theatre, or at somebody's dacha. They took on various guises, pretending to be a postman, a waiter, or a porter at a railway station; their gaze — strange, startling and penetrating — would make me tremble with terror, and I would find it difficult to breathe, difficult to live.

Slowly I unlaced my boots, slowly and meticulously I dried the blades of my skates, then took off my sweater in leisurely fashion, wrapped it slowly in newspaper, put it in my briefcase, and remained seated on the bench for a while, resting.

The whole of my being, every fibre of my separate identity, had been expecting them daily, hourly, unable ever to put them out of mind. If there was an unexpected knock at the door, my first thought would be: "It's them." I would ask, "Who's there?" to hear: "Telegram," or "Gas Board," or a plaintive, contrite voice piping: "Excuse me, would you have any matches?"

When you thought of nothing else but this, when you had seen it so many times, how could you do other than expect the same for yourself? It became ingrown, was the stuff of your dreams and of your waking hours, became the hub around which everything else revolved. Except that you kept brushing it aside, shutting your eyes to it, setting it apart from yourself, trying not to think about it, not to believe it. You simply went on deceiving yourself in the same stupid, paltry fashion.

But eventually you hit the deadline, and your reprieve, however permanent it may have seemed, was over.

When I left the cloakroom, the two black twins had gone; the sun was sparkling on the snow, and there was the sound of melting snow dripping from roofs. I laughed out loud, and my heart overflowed with joy and relief as I walked along the snowy avenue with a sense of freedom and exhilaration.

But as I passed through the archway (that massive, grey concrete archway that stands like a Roman colonnaded entrance, but on its own, without any palace, a frozen waif abandoned in the snow) I saw that my two black friends were already standing there, chatting away to each other in the sunshine.

A tram was approaching the stop, and for some reason its driver was ringing his bell like one possessed. Not until the front carriage was so close that I could see the driver at the window in his sheepskin coat, did I realize that I was the one standing too close to the rails. As I stepped back, the tram enveloped me in a ringing cloud of powdered snow. The first carriage went past; I boarded the tram via the rear platform and held out my fare for the conductor, whose coarse red hands were clad in knitted cotton gloves with the finger-tips cut away.

As the tram was just about to move off, the twins started running, the two of them side by side like a pair of circus performers, and jumped onto the rear platform of the end carriage.

With a clattering and rumbling the tram began to cross the bridge. The vibration of the suspension bridge was transmitted to the carriage, and I could feel the tremors passing through me, while from the white, gleaming expanse of river came a brighter light and a spacious, resonant quality of sound.

The twins stood on the rear platform in their imitation fur caps, chatting amicably.

I got off at the Gorky Park metro station and sensed without looking round that they had done likewise. Still not looking round, I made for the trolleybus stop by the former Provision Stores, walking slowly as if suspecting nothing, all the time sensing with my back, shoulders and the back of my head that I was being followed.

The red winter sun — sturdy, small and hard, as if frozen solid — was struggling to emerge from swirling dark clouds heavy with snow; but the clouds gained the upper hand, veiling the sun with black smoke, and soon covered it completely. Then heavy, wet flakes of snow began to fall thick and fast. The weather was changing, and the wind appeared to be blowing from various directions, which made me feel apprehensive and uneasy.

I stopped by a fence and stood there in the falling snow, studiously reading all the posters on it in turn: *The Great Emperor*, *Ivan Susanin*, *Sadko*, *The Road to Calvary*, *The Resourceful Woman in Love*, *The Four Suitors*.

When I had concluded my thorough examination of these posters, I turned to a showcase displaying the latest newspapers and in a routine and indifferent manner skimmed through the grey pages that were closely packed from top to bottom with monotonous type unrelieved by even a single picture.

It was said that Stalin had once for some reason expressed his displeasure on the subject of photographs in newspapers, saying that it would be better to replace the pictures with text; so editors had sacked all their photographers, and zincographers had also found themselves unemployed.

Again my eye was arrested by the 'Latest News' item; once again I set about reading and re-reading it. One of them was watching me from somewhere on the side.

"How's tricks, Hippo?" enquired a cheerful voice.

I had known her for a long time. She had started out wanting to be a film star, then an artist, then a translator, and had finally settled down to working as a retoucher for a fashion house.

"I want to make a suit trimmed with grey astrakhan," she

rattled on: "a narrow, comfortable skirt with two pleats — it won't look right under a coat, but what the hell. And then on the chest a brooch with an abstract design — interwoven patterns in the old Armenian style. How does that sound?" She screwed up her eyes. "More restrained colours suit me best. Raspberry-and-milk is in fashion now — or over-ripe cherry tones."

"Natasha, listen to what I'm going to say," I interrupted her. "I'm being followed, do you understand?"

"Who's following you?"

She stared intently along the street.

"Don't look round — whatever you do, don't look round."

"But what's happened? What's this all about?"

"I don't know — I found out just now that there were these two characters following me..."

"But who are they?" she asked, as innocent as a daisy.

I gave a sardonic laugh.

"I know what: come with me, and then perhaps they'll leave you alone," she continued.

"No, we won't lose them."

"Well, then, get on the trolleybus and go. I'll give you a ring to see you've got home all right," she said, like a mother talking to her little boy.

"Don't do that. I expect they've already bugged my phone."

"Who has?"

"Those who have their reasons."

She shook her head.

"So what's going to happen now?"

"I don't know."

"But this is terrible — like a bad dream. I don't think I could live with it; I'd go mad."

"I expect what happens is that it's hard to begin with but then with time you get used to it, as if there was nothing unusual about it."

"How do you know?"

"Somebody who's been through it himself told me. He said that when it stopped he even missed it. Can you imagine that? Something was lacking — there was a certain emptiness in his life."

"Pull the other one," she laughed. "Ooh, I couldn't stand it, I really couldn't. Look at the cheek of him, staring straight at us — he couldn't care less."

"It's his job."

"I wouldn't like to do it."

"It's no better or worse than any other job," I said weakly.

"You can't be serious."

"You're right: one couldn't imagine a worse job. It's a killer."

"Perhaps you could report them to someone to make them stop doing it?"

"Who could I report them to?"

"I don't know, but there must be somebody in authority who deals with these things. You just can't live like this, being followed all the time. You know, you could end up in deep trouble."

"I'm afraid I'm in deep trouble already."

"What is it that you've done, then?"

"If only I knew..."

"But it just can't happen like that, without any reason."

"It can."

"But look, they don't follow everybody, do they?"

"Yes they do," I decided suddenly.

She opened her mouth in disbelief.

"Now they've started following everybody," I said with conviction.

At that moment a trolleybus arrived at the stop next to the Provision Stores.

"Right, I'm off."

"Give me a ring," she called. "I'll wait to hear from you."

I nodded and jumped onto the trolleybus, registering that the door had closed behind me immediately.

The trolleybus moved off, then almost at once stopped again, and one of the black twins boarded the vehicle through the front door, which had suddenly opened for him. Where he had appeared from, and how, was a mystery.

I turned away from him and looked through the rear window. There I saw, as if on a cinema screen, the second twin appear round a corner and calmly follow Natasha towards the metro station, walking at some distance behind her.

So this was how it would be from now on, this was the precise pattern of events. I should only have to say hello to someone or start a conversation with them, for the black one to split into two, and for his shadow to separate from him and follow that person's tracks as if hunting a hare. All the people around me would turn into hares. Nothing but hares as far the eye could see.

He stood there at the front among the other passengers, holding on to a strap and swaying in time with the fast-moving trolleybus, just one passenger among all the others going about their business, on their way to the health centre, to a compulsory interview at the military enlistment office, or to friends for a booze-up.

Then, getting bored, he took a newspaper from his pocket and began reading.

I sized him up out of the corner of my eye. He had a pale, pasty face, care-worn from the worries and intrigues of his secret and exacting work.

"This stop Kiev District council offices. Next stop Smolensk Street, Food Store No.2, wine and snacks," announced the wag of a conductor.

The trolleybus stopped, and I quickly pushed past the other passengers, making an unheralded exit via the rear platform. The trolleybus moved off. I was alone as if I were in a vacuum.

The trolleybus was in motion, carrying him away with his newspaper. Now I could see him at the window like a fish in an aquarium. Then, quite suddenly, he flung the newspaper down and started thrashing about, pushing his way to the front. Whatever it was he said to the driver, the trolleybus slammed on its brakes and stopped at a crossroad. A car following behind it screeched to a halt. The doors opened; my guardian angel jumped or rather just tumbled out of the trolleybus, and without looking ran between the cars to cross to the other side of the street. Only when he was there did he look across at me through the stream of traffic. Then he suddenly lost interest and began to stroll along the pavement as if nothing out of the ordinary had happened.

I walked on.

And once again everything receded and seemed far away, as if reflected in a concave mirror. In that displaced other world there were cold, empty buildings standing in the falling snow; cars flashing past; midget people like chess figures running to and fro, indifferent, alien and uninvolved.

He was walking along somewhere over there on the other side of the street, looking at me through the stream of traffic.

It was essential that I walk past the gateway to my building, walk past it as if I didn't know it, and then hide somewhere, disappear somewhere, cover my tracks.

All the same, when I reached the familiar gates painted with red lead, I obediently turned into my courtyard as if propelled by a rough push from behind.

We have never learned how to run away or hide: it was just not in our blood. We were citizens of a state which we considered to be our own, and we trusted unquestioningly — for far too long we trusted.

I shut the door, slamming it hard, and was hurled, against the wall, concussed, as if by the shock wave from an explosion. Everything became confused, and I had difficulty in breathing.

My life, chopped in half, had receded and seemed distant

and strange, as if seen through the wrong end of a pair of binoculars.

Twilight filtered down, dim, grey and uneven. Quietly, without breathing, I crept on tiptoe along the wall towards the window.

Snow-capped trolleybuses were gliding past like wound-up toys; people were walking to their various destinations, some carrying string shopping bags or briefcases, and some just with their hands behind their backs; and all this was taking place in utter silence, as in a film with the sound turned off, or in a vacuum, and there was no sense to it, no intelligible purpose.

I was immersed in chronic gloom, dissolving in it, as if somebody had placed a cloth soaked in chloroform over my face.

There was a time during the war when I had stood like this, huddled in the corner of a ruined peasant house with my heart in my mouth, looking through a smashed window. It was in the Poltava region. A small tank with a white cross on its turret was snarling its way up a hillock, accompanied by the staccato tut-tutting of some grey motorcyclists with black sub-machine guns slung across their chests. Then some figures in green coats passed by very close. Although minus boots and cap, I was filled with strength, resistance and concentrated energy to the exclusion of everything else. I knew that there was only room for me or them in the world, that we could not co-exist. I was prepared to die; I had told myself in advance that I was a goner, and now I was no longer afraid of anything. Eventually I managed to break out of that encirclement. And now here I was filled with weakness and fear to the exclusion of everything else.

If I had been guilty, if there had actually been something to be guilty of, then I should have felt the urge to resist. I should have tried to manoeuvre, to escape, to disappear; I should have fought, drawing strength from my ideas and beliefs. But now I was like a fly in a spider's web.

What did I have to hope for now? I could not even see my executioner. Perhaps he lived somewhere nearby, in the same street, and walked past my window every morning, smoking a cigarette. Perhaps I sat next to him in the cinema, laughing and weeping together with him. And now he would torment me, torture me, break my spine. In the name of what, I had no idea, nor did he: it was simply because the plan required somebody to have his spine broken, otherwise the rest would get out of hand and start playing up.

And nobody would ever know about it. That was what made things so terrible, so hopeless.

I was alone in that room, quite alone with those grey walls, the bare electric light bulb on its long flex and the still silent black telephone. It was as if the telephone was bewitched, the way it kept silent. It already knew about the trouble I was in — our telephones know everything in advance. Or perhaps it had already been disconnected. If my friends found out what had happened, they would rather put their hand in the fire than dial my number.

Then suddenly the telephone came to life and started ringing. It rang insistently, hysterically, with a tone that was unusually shrill, and then just as suddenly stopped again. I looked at it, my head spinning.

How good life had been only the day before, and the day before that, and how little I had ever appreciated it! I had been continually disgruntled, wandering the streets in a dejected state and considering myself the unhappiest of men as I observed the faces of people walking arm in arm, waiting for taxis, laughing. They were all happy, were in a hurry to get somewhere, had a purpose.

It seemed that I alone was a misfit, inept and ill-starred, that I alone had been born with this eternal restlessness; with this eternal need to do something — anything — immediately, to squander and fritter away my energies; and with this eternal expectation of something different, something better.

Few and far between were the days in my life when I had known peace.

Why did I always think that if I got through the day in question, all my troubles, suffering and cares would pass, and that next day things would be better? Wasn't this really just self-deception?

When it came down to it, all my misfortunes and illnesses up to then had been only imaginary, spectral; they had been some sort of optical illusion, or waves produced by fear. It was only now that genuine misfortune had struck for the first time.

It was also perhaps the first time I had seen so clearly that life was passing, slipping away, constantly flowing; that it was implacable and in a way unreflecting. This actual minute, this moment of being — the grey sky; snowflakes flickering, glittering; two women in hats and rubber overboots standing talking on the other side of the road — this moment would pass, would never be repeated. It felt as if the fear which enveloped me clingingly like uncooked dough had begun to melt away and evaporate, that it was ridiculous, puny and absurd, compared with that eternal and obvious truth. But this feeling lasted only for a moment.

Suddenly I saw him. He calmly walked past in his sealskin cap and (quietly, unobtrusively, unassertively) took up a position right next to the gates. After standing there for a while, he produced a packet of cigarettes from his pocket, tapped one out, replaced the packet and began twisting the cigarette slowly round and round in his fingers. Then he took out his matches, turned towards the gates, struck a match, using his upturned collar as a screen, and lit up, as I could see from the puff of smoke. Putting the matches away, he stood there by the gates smoking, studiously blowing the smoke somewhere out of sight — one could almost imagine it going up his sleeve.

Who was he? What was his name? Somehow it seemed

impossible that he should have a straightforward, everyday name like Yuri, Boris or Victor, or that apart from this first, essential existence he should have his own private life and would that evening return to his home, where he had aged parents who did not even know where he worked; that he possibly had a wife, and even children who went off to school with their exercise books; or that some friends would drop in that evening for drinks and a game of dominoes.

"Have you got your hotplate switched on?" someone yelled in a shrill voice just outside the door.

"What hotplate?"

It was the manicurist Zoya Fortunatovna, her hair turbaned with a towel, looking as if she had been catapulted in from a lunatic asylum, so crazed was the expression in her eyes.

"Look at how the meter's spinning round!"

She seized my arm and dragged me towards the meter. It was humming, and from time to time emitted a squeal as though begging for mercy.

"Aha! The Pishchiks must have switched on!"

And she ran off in her turban.

First of all I tore up my notebook containing telephone numbers, then removed letters and photographs from a drawer and began tearing them up too.

This had happened before, in 1937.

On that bright, baking hot June day with sunlight flooding into the room, a day so full of the promise of happiness, I had burned a diary in my black stove. This diary, an album made up from reject newspaper galley-proofs, had been kept by three sailors. It contained an amusing and dangerous description of lower-deck life, an irreverent portrait of their petty officer, verses and epigrams, caricatures of each other and of everything under the sun, and photographs of the three musketeers themselves in naval blouses, bell-bottoms and bulldog boots, taken of them together and separately, full-face and in profile, or with girl friends: heads of curly hair, perms, cotton print dresses...

Then the war had intervened, bringing with it fervour and enthusiasm as well as pain and unimagined suffering, and somehow all of this had been forgotten, had evaporated, smouldered to ashes.

And now it had all started up again with renewed, incredible, brutal vigour, on that autumnal October day when the word 'cosmopolitan' had suddenly appeared on the scene and the meetings had started: those prolonged, smoke-filled meetings that went on into the night and were like a dream or delirium, and after which one had no desire or reason to go on living.

The small circular hall with its oak beams and antique panelling was hotly, dazzlingly illuminated by the powerful light of a chandelier. From my elevated position in the dark gallery where, enduring torments of fear, I always sat throughout those meetings, I looked down in bewilderment at the mass of suffocating humanity below, at a profusion of grey and balding heads. At that moment a misproportioned little man was standing on the rostrum, swaying, his face marked by illness and as pale as a clown's mask. He spoke haltingly, yet nevertheless in a strong and mellifluous voice with a distinct Polish burr to it, striving to maintain his dignity, striving to preserve his faith in his own existence, in his right to defend himself, to reason; warming to his theme, and even (old habits die hard) with a hint of intellectual superiority, with an implicit appeal to principle which struck many as insolent, he said "Lenin taught us..." At this, slowly turning red, a man with an early hint of steel-grey in his hair shouted from the presidium, "Don't blaspheme, you pigmy!"

The assembly responded with a roar of approval.

And there was nothing left: childhood, honour, the moon, self-sacrifice... nothing; and I was filled with an awareness of the utter vulnerability and senselessness of the life that still lay before me. (I did not know then, nor could I know, that at another time and on another occasion this self-same assembly, made up of almost the same people, except for those who had died in the meantime of heart-attacks, strokes, drinking or cancer, would applaud that same bow-legged little man, would respond to his witticisms with hearty, carefree laughter, completely forgetting what it — they — had done to him... and that he would forgive them. Or that the day would come when in this same hall, but now with the chandelier draped in black muslin and the mirrors covered with sheets, sombre, eloquent speeches would be made, proclaiming what a remarkable man he had been. And in his red coffin, set in a commanding position on the long presidium table, with his massive, proud head, his lilac-tinged face that was so gaunt and aloof, he would seem to be saying "Ah, this is all of no importance whatsoever.")

On that muddy, slushy December night I had been scared to go back to my room, scared to be alone, and I had gone straight from the meeting to the Kursk station. The next morning in Belgorod the carriage was lit by a wintry brightness from the snow, while in the dawn of the following day Lake Sivash could already be seen gleaming with a dull, muted light. In Dzhankoi it was as warm as April, misty and damp, and slowly my heart began to thaw; in the Crimea there was sun, there were yellow autumnal trees, the vivid colours of the mountains, the very breathing of the resort itself. I managed to buy an unclaimed reservation at the spa administration office.

The days passed one by one, night yielding to day and day to night, dead, fruitless days filled with rumours and expectation: the expectation from one day to the next, from one night to the next, of the inevitable.

For the second time in my life I was preparing for that. I was saying goodbye.

And as on the previous occasion, in 1937, I thought that if that didn't happen, I would go away to Nizhny Novgorod on the Volga, work as a stevedore. Why it should be Volga, I don't know, but of all places it was the Volga that came to mind, and Nizhny Novgorod rather than Gorky. So now, as I destroyed my papers, I thought that (provided they didn't come for me that night) I would walk out of the house, leave Moscow and go to ground. Then I would live with my thoughts and my insights, and one day I would write about it.

I lay down on the bed, and the man standing in the street was watching me through the walls.

There was the constant sensation of it all being a dream. After all, how many times had I had this dream, this same dream, yet each time I had woken up and everything had been all right. Perhaps now too I was dreaming and just couldn't wake up.

There was a mild-mannered, ingratiating fellow from the personnel department who, as he passed me one day, had uttered the enigmatic words: "Choose your close friends most carefully." Now I began sifting through memory for all my friends and even people whom I had seen only once in my life, glimpsed somewhere in the street, in some chance cluster of people; I even remembered a man in a cloth cap and ear-muffs who had a strange nose with large pores, like a sponge. This man with the spongey nose aroused my suspicion immediately.

Feverishly and apprehensively I tried to recall what I had said, how he had listened, remained silent, or smiled, and what had been concealed behind that smile. Bathed in sweat, I repented the error of my ways, cursed myself and made a vow never to say anything ever again. Lord God almighty, why had it happened? What good had it done anyone? If I hadn't met him and spoken to him, how marvellous everything would have been now!

Your index card would be lying somewhere in the general file, or possibly in the special one, sleeping peacefully and not bothering anyone. It didn't jostle for attention, didn't pop out or burst into flames, and yet of all the cards it was this sleeping, meek, forgotten one that was fingered, taken out, and then used to locate your old, bulging personal file on the shelves or in a cupboard; your face would look out at the person who opened the grey document case, and he, giving the photograph a cursory glance, would become absorbed, leafing through the documents and reading your life: a life disfigured by grammatical errors, its reflection grimacing in this anonymous distorting mirror, the most up-to-date attraction of the greatest of all the great epochs of mankind. You would have no inkling of this, not even the slightest intimation; you would hurry to your various rendezvous, sit in restaurants eating fish in aspic, read Andersen's fairy tales and live that elementary, minimal, provisionally permitted life; and you would be contented and sometimes even happy, lulled by youth, health and hope.

Sometimes at night or even during the day in some noisy, cheerful street a sense of impending disaster would bear down on you and you would feel as if it were hanging on your chest like a dead weight and breathing into your face. What was it? A mirage? Fear? Nerves playing up? Or telepathic waves communicating an event taking place that very moment in an office somewhere — an office that was clean and of lofty proportions, like the hall of a crematorium?

Basically I had always expected it to happen, but when it did, I was quite incapable of believing that it was happening to me and not to anybody else.

A human being can get used to anything. A human being is a machine which rapidly readjusts itself as it goes, and does so quite openly, with the most unflagging determination. Yet nobody can get used to that, just as nobody can get used to the idea of death; although we know death is a reality, is unavoidable and comes to all of us, we cannot imagine ourselves lying dead in a coffin, and respond to the thought of this with equanimity and a strange insouciance, as if we were invulnerable.

I raised myself on one elbow and looked out of the window from behind the curtains. My watchman was still standing by the gates. He was watching everybody who entered or left the courtyard; some became aware of this recording gaze and looked back again once they had passed him. Others did not notice anything, but walked into the yard as if they were blind, carrying their string shopping bags and briefcases, their bits and bobs and illusions; one even stopped and asked him for a light. He scrutinized this passing freak attentively, as if photographing him from head to toe, then calmly and with unconcern took out his matches and handed him the whole box. The passer-by struck a match, lit his cigarette, returned the box and with a nod of the head continued on his way along the street, unaware of who it was he had been in contact with.

How Ovid sensed that he was there I cannot say. Whether there was telepathic communication between these people, or whether Ovid's single eye was so trained and proficient that he picked up and understood everything immediately. The fact is that Ovid began walking to and fro past the gates with a greater sense of urgency than usual, clearing the snow with a wide wooden shovel around the spot where the other was standing. Then, abandoning all subterfuge, he simply went out and also stood by the gates, level with the object of his manoeuvres, glancing repeatedly in his direction with the good eye not affected by a cataract. But evidently my watchman was from another, higher department inaccessible to janitors. He turned away and looked in a different direction or simply took a stroll to the corner and back without looking at Ovid. The most surprising thing was that Ovid put up with all this and understood all its high-level, momentous implications; in any other instance he would have asked rudely, "What yer standin' there for? Show me yer papers!" — yet on this occasion he simply disappeared, vanished into thin air. If he wasn't needed, if he was surplus to requirements, then there must be a reason.

Nor did it even occur to anyone to ask "Who are you?" Intuitively, almost on the basis of hereditary instinct, all immediately understood who this was, where he was from, and why he was there. It seemed that people were no longer just learning this at their mother's knee, but that it was already beginning to be transmitted through their genes, where some sort of mutation or deviation had taken place, some re-grouping or transfer in the age-old chain of nucleids that was perhaps no more than microscopic and yet already highly potent, seriously affecting the whole organism.

If he had come, and was standing there, watching, then there must be a reason.

By now they had simply become accustomed to somebody standing by the gates. In any case, there was always somebody they didn't know hanging around the gateway who as things stood didn't interfere in their affairs — and thank God for that. So let him stand there getting wet through in the rain and snow, and much good may it do him, if there's a reason. It was a matter of no concern to them, citizens going about their purely personal, family business, on their way to or from work, to a cinema or bar, to a wedding, or to the cemetery. And they looked the other way to avoid becoming involved or mixed up in this affair, to avoid registering that someone was standing there, waiting for someone else — waiting with good reason.

And yet, however much they might try to avoid it, he would leave a dull and washed-out imprint of himself in his sealskin cap and overboots, like a snapshot or one of those while-you-wait photographs they used to have at fairs; nevertheless they would walk past without letting on —

independently, proudly, pretending to be taken in — and then after all would be unable to resist a backward glance. They would go up the iron staircase, with an effort now, and panting, as if they had just climbed a hill, and on entering their room would at once rush to the window where, maintaining a low profile against the wall, they would stand for a while looking at the man by the gates, studying him thoroughly, and as they made their observation they would conjecture as to who could be on the receiving end; only then would they turn to their domestic affairs: frying a chop in margarine, studying for Party education classes on Stalin's History of the Communist Party of the Soviet Union, or listening to the Pyatnitsky Folk Choir on the radio, all the time feeling uncomfortable, and now and again, pressed to the wall, peering out of the window to see what was going on.

For some time I had sensed them passing by in my general vicinity, yet keeping a wary distance. Sometimes there would be a sudden penetrating glance from someone in a crowd, a glance that was directed straight at me; yet while I was disconcertedly looking this way and that, trying to find that someone, he would melt away, and I was left with the conclusion that I was possibly imagining things. On other occasions he was lying in wait for me in the entrance when I arrived to visit some friends, although it may be that he was waiting for someone else. Whenever I picked up the telephone, I could almost hear him breathing.

"Do you have any problems with mice?"

A woman was standing at the door with a tiny red mousetrap. It was so tiny, it would have been more suitable for catching beetles.

My room had always seemed to me like a trap that I had been chased into, and from which there was no way out. Yet after the meetings I would always slink back to this loathsome narrow room with its gloss-painted walls, this smoky den crawling with cockroaches and bed-bugs. It was after all the only den in the whole city, and now perhaps in the whole world, where I could be alone, face to face with myself, with my gnawing despair, my amazement at the absurdity and nonsense of what they were doing to me, and with my pain. Here I could rest up and lick my wounds.

A foreboding of what was bound to happen and could not be averted was ever present. Sometimes it seemed to gutter, to be on the point of going out, and appeared forgotten in the hurly-burly of living; but in reality it never disappeared: it merely slumbered, and there would come a time when it took hold of you again with renewed vigour, and again you would be waiting, registering every glance, looking round in the street, waiting to see who followed you when you turned a corner. Whenever you got into a taxi you would as a matter of course glance through the rear window to check whether you were being tailed; and if on entering a cafe or restaurant and sitting down at a table you suddenly noticed eyes watching you, or an ear cocked in your direction, you would try to recall whether the person in question had been there when you arrived, or had appeared after you. Yes, sometimes this foreboding would burn low and gently gutter, but never once did it disappear completely: lightly covered with ash, it smouldered somewhere in the deepest depths inside you. It was you.

All the time you felt, with a certain unease and for some reason even alarm, that you were guilty — guilty without having committed a crime; and you awaited punishment. Punishment was inescapable. It would come, sooner or later. Each new morning was only a reprieve.

And now it had happened. Now I did not need to worry any more, for everything else had paled into insignificance before that monstrous reality.

I no longer had the strength to be afraid; fear and the

ability to endure pain were beyond my powers, and I felt apathetic about everything. Let everything take its course, it was all the same to me: at least I had nothing more to fear.

He was standing right under my window, walking on stilts, peeping in at the window, and there was no way I could escape, nowhere I could hide.

I looked in the mirror, and my face appeared strange, distant, from another life. Perhaps it's always the case that when you look at your face for a long time, it seems like somebody else's. That nose, those eyebrows, those eyes, those ears — was that me? Was it really me? The one who was constantly talking to himself, shouting inwardly, thinking his innermost thoughts, each day, each morning mumbling through a replay of everything, once again taking stock of his life, drawing up new plans, considering new alternatives, and all the time maintaining a flow of sparkling repartee and protest, all internal? How numerous they were, those unmade speeches and rejoinders, those cries of indignation and pain that had never been heard, those secret thoughts that nobody had been aware of and were now forever buried and forgotten!

When alone you would reassure yourself, feel sorry for yourself and suffer torments; and all the time you would be waiting, waiting, waiting for something, patiently enduring in this hope. In fact you ended up allowing yourself to endure anything. You didn't even notice how your face had changed: you failed to register any of the changes, you became inured to them, reconciled to them; and all the time you thought that you were still the same person — that you were you.

Had that really been me chasing a hoop down the steep incline of Upper Street, running the length of Hetman Street to Vocational Comprehensive School No.5? Was I that boy sitting under a green lamp, carefully applying transfers, in the old, cheerful and melancholy house in Zlatopol Street?

That was me, that boy marching in the dusty, vociferous,

demented ranks with his smoking paraffin torch held aloft, bawling: "Down with monarchs, rabbis, priests!" — the boy who thought everything was child's play and a bit of a joke, and didn't give a toss for anything: "We'll smash the old world, and we'll build a new one!"

I had enjoyed standing for days on end in the noise and cigarette smoke of queues by the dirty brown walls of the Kiev-Pechersky Youth Employment Exchange, fervently dreaming of becoming an industrial pattern-maker.

And it was I who had come to Moscow and, riding on the running board of a ringing, jingling tram over Borodino Bridge, along the narrow, cramped corridor of the Arbat and through the flea-market on Hunters Row, had come out into Theatre Square, to the venerable white stone walls of the Bolshoi Theatre; and I had suddenly felt that I had been here before, as if I had always lived here, so familiar had everything seemed.

Later it was I who had waded through the Trubezh marshes under German flares; and I who had stood in front of the baying crowd at that fateful meeting.

All this was me. Whenever I look in the mirror, I both do and don't recognize myself, always. How many lives does a person live, one or a thousand? That meek little boy in a sailor suit and that youth in riding breeches and boots seem complete strangers. They run, shout and wave their arms like people in some old film.

Hunters Row with its corn-chandler's shops, carcasses of red meat, unplucked turkeys and geese suspended on hooks, and fumes from sizzling pancakes; displays of books laid out for sale on the pavement by the Kitaigorod wall, stretching as far as the Commissariat for Heavy Industry on Nogin Street.

Jangling bells of over-filled trams; sirens of red fire engines; the incoherent cries of women selling pies, of ice-cream vendors and purveyors of kvass; shrill voices of urchins with toffees on hawker's trays — all this made one's head spin. And all the time there was an uneasy, anxious anticipation of something new, something never experienced.

Everywhere you went in Moscow there were construction trenches. The sour smell of dug earth, of ungalvanized, rusty, cold-looking pipes — all this I breathed in eagerly.

I spent a lot of time standing by the towers sheathed in fresh yellow planking which had sprung up, strange and intrusive, right in the middle of the city, in courtyards and in squares. Here with feelings of eagerness, envy and elation I would watch the lads and lasses come up from under the earth and into the light of the street in their wide-brimmed hats, tarpaulin capes and clay-covered rubber boots; there, under the earth, they had been engaged in mysterious, momentous activity, and now, emerging into the light, they walked along the sunlit street proudly, independently, not mingling with the common crowd, different from everybody else, and feeling themselves to be knights *sans peur et sans reproche.*

I too wanted to work underground, by the dim light of wire-caged lamps; I too wanted to lie on my back and, holding a pick above my head, to hew into earth, rock and clay; I wanted to go through quick grounds and emerge into the outside world in a wide-brimmed hat, tarpaulin cape and wet, clay-covered rubber boots.

Evening in Tverskaya Street: stretching away up an incline, the narrow street was full of glittering lights, sounds, the ringing of tram bells; filled with their glowing gas, neon tubes shone brightly, unfamiliarly, magically; the doors of festively lit restaurants, hair-dressing salons and shops banged open and to; newspaper sellers were shouting: "Evening News, Evening News..." There was a large excited crowd thronging the street.

Enthralled by this noise, this bright activity, I breathed in to the full the electrically charged air of the crowded street, with orange and green letters flitting past and changing colour, and in the evening twilight there seemed to be a louder, shriller note to trams ringing their bells, cars sounding their horns and clouds sailing illuminated above the city.

Ah God! All around in festive exultation Moscow shimmered with iridescent lights — brightly, freshly — glowing with the light of thousands upon thousands of windows that touched the heart with their warm and inviting appearance. But I wanted to go to the tundra, the Kara-Kum desert, the North Pole, to experience intolerable hardship which would demand all my strength, all my unquenchable thirst for life.

The column of an evening rally was parading with torches down Tverskaya from Strastnaya Street. It was International Youth Day. Parades then were still free of the iron discipline that came later, when Red Square was in a state of siege and a curfew was enforced in the city centre; the column with its red flags moved freely, flowing like a river along the streets, and one could join it, marching in its ranks under a placard proclaiming: "Down with Chamberlain!", emerging into Red Square to gather by the Mausoleum rostrum and listen to speeches.

Youngsters were marching at the head of the parade, students of workshopschools from the 'AMO' and 'Hammer and Sickle' factories, wearing unbuttoned blouses and cloth caps: adolescent workers in the 1930s, who had rallied to the red banner in their most impressionable and idealistic years.

I walked along after them and stood by the Mausoleum in the light of flaming torches, listening to the speeches. And when the speeches were over, the torches had been extinguished, and over Red Square rose, like an archer's bow, the slender sickle of a new moon, I stayed on there, alone. By now it was night.

I left the square and walked onto Stone Bridge. All around, far and near, were millions of lighted windows, as if the starry heavens had descended onto the city. From the dark waters under the bridge came a muted gurgling, and I could hear my heart beating.

The desire to study and to work underground or go off to the ends of the earth were tearing me apart, and I didn't know which way to go.

I heard the telephone ringing as if through a padded wall.

"It's me, Arkady, " somebody shouted down the line. "Well, how are you — still alive?"

I made no reply.

"I see, " he said.

We were both silent for a while.

"Any news?"

Again I said nothing.

"I see," he repeated.

There was a further interval of silence.

"Good or bad?" he asked cautiously.

I remained silent.

"I see," he said.

The electric silence of the line bore down on us like a thousand-ton weight. I thought I could hear the breathing of a third person on the line, as if he or she were chewing a smoked sturgeon sandwich.

"Well then, ciao," he said and rang off. I heard the short bleeps. I listened and listened, and wept.

It was as if all the despair I had felt during my life had been concentrated in this despair, all the terror in this terror, and all the hopelessness of days and nights in this unbounded hopelessness that could no longer be endured.

I felt a sudden urge to pray: no, not to God (of whom I had no knowledge or memory, who had never appeared to me either in dreams or when I was awake, and who from childhood on had been the object of my mockery), but to that supreme, all-seeing, all-forgiving being, that equity of love which must after all exist on earth — it was to this that, weeping and sobbing, I was drawn to pray passionately, frantically.

What had been the point of burning with ardour, trembling with joy, believing, loving — only to end up one awful, desolate and cheerless day — this raw, cold day — being hunted down into this prison cell?

It was raining. At Sokolniki Circle cabbies sat hunched under bast mats and sacks, perched high on the boxes of their cabs.

One of them twitched the reins with a flourish and straightened up. As he did so, the bast mat fell away, and his dim outline swam into view.

"Need a cab, young comrade?"

Solitary pedestrians walked past, their heels clattering on the wooden paving boards. People were queuing at some standpipes, their buckets rattling. Yellow lamps had come on at the snack bars.

A boy, a pupil on the late school shift, ran past with some books tied with string; he looked round and stood for a long time, watching the cab go. Where is he now, that boy on the late shift?

Now that rain seems like the nebulous network of time, through which I glimpse evening, dim lamps, the illuminated windows of blocks of flats with families sitting at their evening meal, and nobody going out.

As if from a great distance I hear the rattle of wheels on cobblestone, cries of newspaper sellers, a deafening sound of car horns from the infrequently passing vehicles, and the cabman with his outsize peaked cap pulled down over his eyes, giving a long, plaintive account of collectivization in his village.

We drove into a wide main street. The windows of a commercial shop shone brightly through the rain, with yellow tailor's dummies, wearing hats at a jaunty angle, their wax faces following us as we passed. There was the clatter of cabs and a ringing and jingling of overcrowded trams; the pavements were thronged with people walking along under umbrellas; and over all this hung a vapour, a reddish evening mist; and a burgeoning hubbub of sound filled the air — church bells ringing, the blaring of new silver-gleaming loudspeakers, and brass band music: everything that finds such a joyful resonance in a young person's heart, eliciting an even more intense feeling of joy and love of life in response. But I was leaving all this to go on a journey.

My train left from the Yaroslavl Station.

Brightly lit trams passed under a bridge; the city lights became few and far between and looked somehow dim, suburban and god-forsaken; then they disappeared, and all that remained was the sky lit up in the distance. In the depths of dark fields shone the lights of villages, at one moment rushing towards the train and at the next flying away; and it seemed as though they had been lit for your benefit — it was difficult to imagine that they would continue burning just by themselves and for their own sake after you had gone, those gay and sad village lights. A train going the other way flashed past with a thundering roar, and it was as if with this sound everything that lay in the past was being swept out of your heart and you were gradually being transported to a new life.

There was a dank autumnal gloom that had a feeling of irredeemable finality about it. Dark fields, copses, the distant lights of the provinces, yellow as dandelions, all came hurtling towards the train, and it felt as if I was travelling back to my childhood.

Marshland with icy tussocks: wretched, dismal tussocks; ever the same little villages of wooden buildings, black and wet; peasant log cabins with low windows Archpriest Avvakum gazed out of in the 17th century; and the same place names: Lower Paloma, Neya, Svecha... A thousand years before, too, a cow had stood here just like this one, lowing on the same theme.

Of what concern were your fantasies to all these black huts, all these people sitting with wooden spoons at their black earthenware pots? What you saw was the familiar sight of a man staring at you goggle-eyed through the window, unable to understand what you wanted, what you had come here for. He just went on shovelling down his food with his wooden spoon, quite unconcerned...

Within you there arose an intense, fervent impulse: to bring light to these peasants' houses with their rain-blackened straw roofs, these dark settlements forgotten by the rest of the world that seemed to have fallen into the marshes out of the sky — to transform them into cities and lead these people in their homespun caftans and bast shoes to a new life...

Now my familiar spirit was not standing by the gates any more but on the kerb, looking at the new multi-storey building on the other side of the street with its large windows and balconies. Was he wondering who lived there? Or did he simply take pleasure in this new building — in its superior balconies and the sumptuous filigree of its decorative towers — well aware that generals and ministers lived there, and thinking of them with respect, with not a trace of envy, and not even dreaming of being allocated a room in such an apartment block? When he had had his fill of gazing at this latest wonder and basking vicariously in life at the top, he turned his eyes to our windows.

Did he know which was my window? Did he find it a pain in the neck, stoically marking time there by the gates, chafing against the boredom of waiting? And did he like his posting, did he value it and consider himself superior to everybody else on the grounds that he kept an eye on them, and not vice versa? Or perhaps he was already fed up with the power he wielded and yearned for nothing more than to be transferred to another, quieter line of work that didn't involve such brazen behaviour, where he wouldn't have to stand in the wind getting frozen through, in obscurity, constantly expecting a rocket from his uncouth bosses.

Suddenly he turned his head to the right and spat three times: either this was a habit of his, or he had decided something in his own mind. Strangely enough this made him seem somehow more familiar: just like an old friend.

As recently as that morning I had not known him and he had known nothing of me; now there was nobody in the whole world more important for me than he.

The whole of my life, everything that I might still do, see and endure — all my love, panic, fear, illnesses, enthusiasms, discoveries — were in his power.

When he had finished his cigarette, he flicked it into a litter bin; then he moved to the kerb and, waiting until the last of a stream of cars had passed, stepped out and calmly crossed the road. On the other side he stood on the kerb again and began looking at our building, at the windows. For a moment or so our eyes seemed to meet; he wiped his nose on his sleeve, hoisted up his trousers, turned and walked calmly to a telephone kiosk. In the kiosk he slowly dialled a number, waited for a reply, and then spoke for some time, talking calmly and seriously about something. He may have been giving his superiors an account of his observations and conclusions, or possibly he was telling an aunt about his children, what grades they had got at school; in any case he listened for a while to something the person at the other end was saying, and then replaced the receiver. After this he stood in the kiosk for some time without doing anything, then dialled another number and this time, as soon as he started speaking, immediately began to laugh and continued to do so for the duration of the conversation. Perhaps they were telling each other funny stories, or recalling some highly amusing private joke, or just chewing the fat; on the other hand he may have been talking about me and finding this so funny that he was convulsed with laughter. But then, sobering up, he left the kiosk. He took out his packet of cigarettes, lit up against the wind, crossed over to this side of the street with his glowing cigarette, and walked up to the gates again; here he looked patiently and indifferently at the passers-by, but they did not look at him.

The Ring Road reverberated and shook with the traffic, and every so often in the lively stream of vehicles a small snow-covered lorry would sweep past with black crape on red calico along its side. It would drive past at speed, carrying a glossy silver coffin and wreaths with lifeless flowers, around which the mourners sat on stools arranged as in a conference room, staring at their surroundings, chatting and laughing. And immediately behind, with no demarcation between life and death, came a tanker bearing the inscription 'Live Fish'.

All day long I had kept catching glimpses of that small lorry with black crape on its side in the general traffic, until eventually it seemed as if it was the same funeral party going round the city, round and round in circles on that dark, yellow day.

I lay on the bed, obsessed with the feeling that all this was happening not to me but to someone else. Again I had become detached from myself and was standing somewhere to one side, observing this person who was 'I'; I saw him lying on the bed in this room that shook with the roar and rumble of the traffic, waiting, waiting until they came for him; and even when they arrested him and took him away, I, the observer, would be safe and would just watch him being taken away.

All the time I had the feeling that somebody was eavesdropping at the door. I stood up, walked quietly to the door, carefully removed the catch and banged the door furiously, with all my strength. It opened and slammed to again like a gunshot; but there was nobody in the corridor. I lay down on the bed again, and once more I had the feeling that someone was listening.

I could feel time itself flowing, passing, on the move, as if an alarm clock had been set in motion and was counting out the seconds; either that, or it was my heart beating.

I caught the sound of lost time: those thousands of days, thousands upon thousands of hours and minutes that flowed and ran like sand in an hourglass, slowly but inexorably, unceasingly, and went on running until the day came when all had run out, down to the last grain.

I lay on the mattress that had been somebody else's, with springs that had come out all over the place while the original owner was still alive, and I thought about my life and how particularly badly everything had turned out in my case. Yet perhaps it is the same for everyone, only each person thinks his situation is unique? You constantly search for the mistake in your life and ask yourself when and where it was that you — you and nobody else — made that one mistake. You calculate how everything might have turned out if at this or that time you had acted differently, had gone not where you did but somewhere completely different, or if at the very beginning of your journey through life you had encountered a person who knew everything, who had taught you at the outset how to develop strength of character, to read the best books, value your time and not waste a single moment on frivolous pursuits or idleness, and to value that which is truly valuable: that mythical, non-existent person who is good and great, that teacher nobody has yet come across in real life — each individual has always worked out everything alone, making all his own mistakes and finally realizing that he has bluffed his way through life or frittered it away.

Or perhaps in fact you are not to blame at all; perhaps however you personally might have arranged things, you would have ended up all the same lying here with your head buried in the pillow, spinelessly pondering on your life, seeing your whole life as nothing but a chain of mistakes, failures, absurdities and humiliations.

The telephone rang.

"Hi there, laddie — what are your plans for this evening?"

"I don't know," I said.

"Who does know, then?" she asked.

"Not me, that's for sure."

"My dear, I can see you're not in a good mood. Take some medicine, have a rest, and I'll ring you back in two hours."

A series of rapid bleeps indicated that she had rung off.

Now I turned my thoughts to the girl friends I had known....

The winter's day dragged on as if it would never end. I kept dozing off and dreaming; I may have been moaning in my sleep, in fact I am sure I was, because every time I woke up I seemed to hear from that mysterious lost realm something like the echo of a moan uttered the instant before. Outside the window it was grey and wintry, and I lay there listening intently, trying to remember where I was...

...Through the din of the street, the rattle of window-panes, the familiar and accustomed sounds of the apartment, the humming of water pipes and the banging of doors I suddenly picked out the sound of footsteps: squeaking, stealthy footsteps coming towards my room, out in the poky little corridor. So this is how they do it, I thought: quietly, simply, without ceremony — and no chance of escape.

I did not hear them open the door. Unexpectedly and without a sound they appeared in the room through the wall.

I lay on my bed, and they were standing over me, lean and wiry, wearing for some inexplicable reason the green caps of border guards; and I was saying to them (not with my voice, not out loud, but mentally): "So this is how it happens." They said nothing but waited... One of them looked at me politely and grinned sardonically.

By now I was aware that I was dreaming. And as so often with a recurring dream that has been haunting you for a long time, you pray for it to be really just a dream and for it and everything else to end happily this time. And at this point, at this precise moment, I realized that once again it was a dream playing its tricks.

I drifted from this sphere to another.

I was drawing up in a cab at the station: that familiar old yellow-brick station — 'first class', 'second class' and the black luggage registration desk — and at the same time it was unaccountably new and modern, built of concrete and glass, with coloured stained-glass windows. Inside there was a comforting smell: samovars, oak benches, way-bills — the smell of childhood. Here too was the businesslike Party office with slogans all over the walls, and for some reason a school friend of mine was sitting there, with a child's round face yet wearing a dark grey, narrow-waisted home guard blouse and grey puttees. I had on the long overcoat of a young cavalryman that reached down to my ankles, and the two of us were walking along together, discussing the principles of optical reflection and looking for a cab.

Then I was standing at a presidium table that was covered with red calico and had a greenish jug of water standing on it, and I was being hauled over the coals. The setting was familiar: a lofty hall with wooden panelling, galleries and carved beams on the ceiling. And that humpbacked little man with red eyes like a rabbit's kept asking the same question over and over again, in a voice that sounded like a cock crowing: "Have there been any warnings?"

Then the one who was myself said, perhaps not in words but mentally: "You can destroy my spirit with fear and a feeling of uncomprehended and unacknowledged guilt arising from each word spoken (and even from those that remain unspoken), and from each action, thought or glance. You have most likely achieved your purpose: this you know and accept; and yet it is not in your power to make of me a lickspittle and a moral cripple, and this too you know and must accept."

And at that moment I saw this alter ego: pathetic, sleepy, helpless, lying on the mattress with its protruding springs, his head on the grimy, soiled pillow-case. "So this is how it happens," I thought again, at the same time saying hoarsely and indistinctly, "What's going on?" — and woke up.

As always after sleeping in the day, I lay for some time in a state of numbed weightlessness, unaware of time, not realizing or sensing where I was, who I was, what I was, or which city I was in — as if I had just been born; as if I were lying there prostrate, crucified; as if I had risen from the grave.

Only gradually through the numbness and weightlessness came a feeling of the reality and gravity of being and, like a light breeze running ahead of this, a sensation of recent disaster — just a sensation, just a hint — until finally I was hit by the full force of the earth's gravitational pull, crushing and stifling me.

The first sound I became aware of after the stupor induced by sleep and unconsciousness was that of the radio. Its familiar, burned-out, unconcerned voice was droning on as usual from behind the wall. And I had neither desire nor reason to pay any attention to those words, which were the same as they had been the day before, and the day before that, and the previous year: cotton-wool words, words that were empty shells, words that filled the air to no effect.

Gradually I began to feel that they were not even being spoken by a human being. The voice had no intonation, nothing betraying the personality of a speaker. It sounded as if it was the black disc of the loudspeaker itself that, having been set going once and for all, was now warbling on like a cuckoo irrespective of whether anyone was listening or not; it seemed that it would never stop, that it would continue like this always, for the rest of my life. It seemed that even if everyone died it would carry on broadcasting in the same even, calm, precise and imperturbable tones; and gradually I was overcome by bewilderment and a feeling of impotence.

Now I became suddenly and clearly aware of something which for a long time I had unconsciously felt, sensed, and known in my heart: I should never have ventured into this whirlpool, got trapped in this bottleneck, this idiotically jabbering mill; should never have sat through those meetings transfixed with fear, letting my nerves become racked with fear and senseless guilt. On the contrary, I should have done my own thing right from the start: reading, reading, reading; observing, observing and working — nothing else but that: reading, observing and working — and living life to the full, living life from one minute, one second to the next: that life which I had despised, looked down on and foolishly avoided, always pinning my hopes on the future, on tomorrow and the day after tomorrow, leaving everything for later, and only coming to my senses when this 'later' was already a thing of the past, and he who had bestowed the gift of this unique life had already opened his mouth to proclaim, "Sorry, time's up!"

Somebody knocked at the door — or perhaps they hadn't, perhaps I had only imagined it? No, somebody was tapping at the door, quietly and timidly.

"Who's there?" I called.

"Open up. What's the matter, can't you be bothered?" came a whining voice from the other side of the door.

A youth stood smiling, out in the poky corridor. He was extremely thin — almost flat, as if cut out of plywood — wearing striped pyjamas and black knitted cotton gloves. It was Pasha, one of the neighbours; he wore the gloves to stop bacteria getting on him, and he never took them off, even in bed.

"Excuse me, do you have any blotting-paper?" asked Pasha.

"No, I haven't."

"Well then, could you let me have four thimblefuls of bread?"

He looked at me with his melancholy eyes.

"No? Well, lend me a light-bulb until this evening."

He gave a strange smile.

I suddenly had the feeling that he knew something which nobody else had even guessed at, and I was distinctly uneasy about being left alone with him and his half-smile, half-grimace.

"Go away, Pasha; I haven't got anything."

"Well then, let me use your phone."

Without removing his black glove, he dialled a number: cautiously, intently, and grotesquely slowly, as if he had not only to remember each number but add it to the one before and the one following to produce a total, and then calculate something else from this. When somebody answered, he said

"It's me, hee-hee..."

So in this vast city of millions there was one soul who took an interest in Pasha; there was at least somebody on his wavelength who listened to his 'hee-hee'.

"How's civilization?" asked Pasha, his face taking on an attentive, alert expression.

The person at the other end said something in reply. Pasha listened, and then said, "Degeneration of the Moscow population — well, amen to that! Hee-hee..." and put down the receiver.

Through the window, which was grimy with mud from passing vehicles as well as being covered with ice, came the fading light of the winter's day, filtering slowly in as if through a sieve.

My faithful friend had not moved from the gates. He took some papers from his pocket; they might have been post-office receipts, or perhaps a haphazard selection of telephone numbers, or papers he had used to wrap his sandwiches or a toffee-nut bar purchased on the way here. He looked through these papers, tore some up, screwed up some others, and went and threw them in a litter bin. However, one paper he folded neatly, put it away in an inside pocket and fastened the pocket with a button. Finally he turned out the yellow lining of another pocket, shook it out, and then put it back as it was before; after which he stood quietly for some time, looking at our windows now and then, and even yawning a couple of times.

I continued observing him.

Now he twisted his arm round, looked at his watch, held it to his ear and then, revealing a calm, unfussy character, started slowly winding it up. Even at a distance I could count him turning the winder thirteen times. When he had finished winding it up, he listened to the watch again and for a while seemed reassured.

Suddenly and without warning he detached himself from the gates and after a backward glance strode off at a fast, energetic pace as far as the corner, and then returned to the gates at the same brisk pace; after this he marched to the corner and back once more, and again took up his position by the gates, standing there motionless, blending into the crude red-lead paintwork. This may have been his stint of keep-fit, or possibly he had had to spy out the lie of the land for some reason, or perhaps it was just because he had pins and needles in his feet or was frozen through, poor fellow, standing there outside other people's gates in that ersatz sealskin cap which must have been useless for keeping warm in.

Now he was carefully examining his overboots. First he studied the right one, then the left, and then put them together and subjected them to common inspection. Perhaps he didn't feel too snug in these new government-issue boots: perhaps they were uncomfortable or too small? After all, at the stores or shop where the boots had been issued to him they were not exactly punctilious about ensuring a proper fit. Or perhaps he had a blister or sore spot; or he had just had a sudden urge to wiggle his toes and at this very moment was performing that ritual, that pleasurable act: was engrossed in it, quietly enjoying it.

Now he took off his gloves and blew on his fingers, and then thrust his hands into his coat sleeves, warming them with his body; for a long time he stood like this without moving, completely absorbed in his own warmth.

I looked out of the door at the back stairs. It was quiet there, and cold, with a haze of cigarette smoke.

Two youths in peakless caps were standing on the middle landing, puffing away at cigarettes in silence.

"What time is it, three?" one of them asked.

"That's right, three," the other replied.

"Fuckin' hell," said the first one.

Then there was silence once more.

I lay down on the bed again and saw everything in a waking vision.

I saw them ringing the doorbell — a long, inordinately long ring — and everyone asleep, only myself awake, knowing that it was for me. Another ring: no reaction on my part, only a determination not to go to the door under any circumstances. And then a continuous ringing that just went on and on, as if a tram had stopped in front of the door and no-one would let it through, followed by banging of doors all along the corridor, the shuffling and flip-flopping of slippers, whispering, then a rattling of the door-chain and the front door being opened, and I seemed to hear the wind on the stairs and an unfamiliar voice, loud and peremptory, saying: "Go back to your rooms," and then silence; and I heard the thumping of my heart, the distinct sound of approaching footsteps, and Ovid's voice: "This is the one!" — and a loud threefold knock at the door.

Or perhaps they would simply arrest me in the street:

suddenly, on a fine sunny day, a public holiday — would drive right up close to the pavement and in an affable tone of voice call me by name from the car, inviting me to join them in the car for a chat, as if they were old friends; and would then drive off with me to a place where the iron gates opened up with a clang. Or they would arrest me at the theatre, during the interval. This too was fairly common practice. They would suddenly come up and grasp you by the elbow in a friendly manner, with a smile, and then whisk you off to the manager's office to clarify certain matters; an hour later 'Sleeping Beauty' would seem like a fairy-tale dimly remembered from childhood. Or they would get you in the train (this one they were particularly fond of, priding themselves on their own ingenuity). You might have thought they could pick you up at the station in Moscow while you were heading for the platform. But no, they let you board the train, arrange your luggage on the rack, travel a few stations, peacefully drink tea served by the train attendant and nibble rock-hard railway biscuits, lie down between the cold, starched, government-issue sheets, and doze off, lulled by the motion of the train. And then in the middle of the night there would be somebody rapping at the door with a key: "Open up, ticket inspector." And there he would be, the inspector, peeping out from behind the train attendant's back in a peaked cap with dark-blue piping, and he would stride into your compartment with the words: "ID, full name, get dressed." By this time the train would be slowing down, and at some out-of-the-way, dark, obscure station with one solitary lamp illuminating the gilded statue of Stalin in the public gardens outside you would be led away in the rain, along the sidings to some remote location.

Why did they have to do it exactly like that? But then if they did, they must have had their reasons. It wasn't just to show off.

Of course, all this was well known to you already. You

had heard it all so many times before in its various permutations. It had happened to your elders and betters first: those who had guided your first steps in life, taught you how to work, defended you when you were attacked at meetings, and later who had put you up for Party membership and spoken up for you during the purges; they had been the first, and then it had been the turn of your contemporaries: the ones you had shared a desk with at school, gone to target practice with at army summer camp and got tipsy with at parties. You had seen all this with your own eyes. Only this time it was happening to you — to you in your one, unique life: you would have no other.

Come to think of it, the feeling of fear was the main, predominant element in your whole life when all was said and done. There was more of it than all the rest put together — anger, grief, or joy; and it was this feeling of fear and despair that had shaped your life and coloured it through and through with its own greyness.

Everyone pretended that they personally were not affected, not only when they were with others, but on their own, even at night when they lay awake thinking about their own and other people's lives, and about life in general. This made it easier and less complicated for them to put their conscience on ice or stifle it completely, to brush aside the inevitable and keep it at arm's length, all the time pretending — sincerely believing — that they were not affected. What was the point of all this? In truth there was none. Then where was the logic of it? Again there was none. It never ever helped anyone. And so, deceiving themselves, they lived for the time being in this mirage, this looking-glass world.

So far you had been spared. And so there was still that yawning chasm, like the one that separates life from death.

I was tired.
Now I was prepared for anything: prepared to accept it

all without surprise, without complaint, with nothing more than pain and fear — although perhaps even without these.

Once again the funeral march was heard intermingled with the roar of the street, the braying of car horns, the clatter; it swelled and then vanished again with the speed of sound.

It felt as though nothing, absolutely nothing, would survive this moment, that everything would come to an end in this winter twilight that was so dead, so yellow and gloomy, with the walls transmitting the muffled sounds of distant, sickening shouts and squabbling from the kitchen, and the overheated air congealed, petrified.

I touched the central heating radiator and at once became aware of the unbearably stuffy heat.

I climbed up on the table and opened the ventilation pane. I was convinced that he knew which window was mine and that he would now see me opening it. So what — to hell with him. An icy wind with snowflakes blew into the room, and I breathed it in, breathed it in greedily, insatiably. And gradually I felt somehow better, calmer, as if I had drunk of strength and desperation. To hell with him, to hell with him, to hell with him...

Somehow I had grown more resolute; everything began to appear less gloomy, hopeless and final.

At that moment the telephone started to ring with a piercing, savage, screeching tone. I had never heard such a disturbing, peremptory ringing tone in all my life.

A plaintive female voice came floating from somewhere in the distance: "There's a call for you." And immediately after this someone ringing off, and a series of rapid bleeps.

Now I began to rack my brains, agonizing over who it could have been. A secretary? The operator? Who had wanted to speak to me, and why? Who needed me, who had remembered me on this weird, turbulent day and hour of my life? Or perhaps there was no tick against my name on some list where I was still included? They had needed to tick me off the list, urgently. And again I was overwhelmed with fear and uncertainty. Again the telephone rang stridently.

"Hold the line, please: there's a call for you."

After this I heard Katya's dear voice, sounding rather distant: she was calling from out of town.

"Was it you trying to get through to me a few minutes ago? It was, wasn't it?"

At once I had become in some way calmer, had become in some way tuned-in again to a world where there were people: sisters, brothers, loved ones; where there were so many voices, whispers, intonations; where there were questions and answers, dignity, tolerance, respect. Did all that still exist? Did it?

"What's up, have you been asleep?" she asked.

"No."

"But why does your voice sound so strange? Are you ill?"

"No, I'm not ill."

"I don't recognize your voice. Is it really you?"

"Of course it is."

"Come on, what's up with you? Are you in trouble?"

I was silent.

"Why don't you say anything? What's happened?"

All the time I seemed to sense the presence of a third person on the line: I thought I could detect his breathing, his attentiveness.

"Nothing's happened."

"I'm worried about the state you're in. I'm coming over straight away."

"No, don't do that."

"Yes, I'm coming."

"Please don't."

"But I have to see you," she said.

"What about?"

Now it was her turn to be silent, and mine to ask.

"What's happened?"

"I can't talk about it on the phone."

"Has something happened to you? Eh?"

The only reply was: 'beep-beep-beep-beep...'

I couldn't tell whether she had hung up or that other, third person had cut us off; and I felt even more apprehensive.

Over recent days some sort of finch — a modest, grey little bird with a tawny breast — had been in the perverse habit of flying into my room through the open ventilation pane, perching now on the coat rack at the back of the room, now on the bookshelves. Suddenly I would hear the fluttering of wings, and there would be the little finch, looking at me in dumb amazement as if he wanted to tell me something. I would be afraid to move, to startle him, in case he started flying about in a panic and injured himself on the stone wall. I would just give him a gentle, friendly whistle, at which he would immediately fly out through the ventilation pane and be lost to sight. But the following day there would again be a flutter of wings, a living palpitation, and there he would be once more looking at me with his sad, surprised expression, wanting to tell me something. He had come with such persistent regularity each day that the thought began to form in my mind that this was the soul of someone long since dead who had once loved me and who was now visiting me, trying to warn me of something. Yet today for some reason my little finch was just not to be seen: why didn't he come? This too seemed a bad omen.

First of all I would disappear from the register of tenants. Instead of delegating this task to his secretary or the aged book-keeper, the manager of the apartment block would himself silently strike me out, putting a cross through my name, and then with a knowing smirk forget me. No, I hadn't left, hadn't moved to another flat or another town, hadn't even died: I had simply never existed, had slipped into the register of tenants by mistake.

And then they would hastily, feverishly, stealthily delete me from all the lists containing my name, lists where my name had been neatly ticked off: membership dues, party work, meetings, party seminars — where I had received reprimands both informal and formal, the latter recorded in my personal file. Even my personal file would disappear.

Perhaps only my library ticket would be left to gather dust in the library for some time, and then even that would disappear, and I would be forgotten for good; information about which books I had liked reading, what aspects of life I had been interested in — neo-romanticism, neo-realism, or even socialist realism — all this would disappear. For some time afterwards letters, postcards and perhaps even money orders would continue to arrive at my address, but somebody would pick these up with their finger-tips as if afraid of being burned and take them to the house management so that they could be forwarded to the relevant authorities. As for my newspapers and magazines, they would be passed around the flat until the subscription ran out.

All this I saw clearly, and I was gradually learning to live with it. My psyche was readjusting itself as it went, avoiding any head-on confrontation.

Some people would come (strangers, not locals) and affix a large, flat wax seal to my door; and in the sealed-off room the telephone would ring laboriously for long periods and at night would suddenly weep, moan, or wheeze like someone with tonsillitis, with no reply other than the sealed-off, irreversible silence, the significance of which was quite clear, and which everyone would quickly come to understand. Possibly some lengthy trunk call would burst in all unaware and unthinking; but it too would remain unanswered. And gradually the telephone would ring less and less frequently, until it became mute and fell silent completely. The only exception might be if some brief, stray call to the wrong number slipped through, or if an old friend from schooldays or a comrade from the war, in Moscow on business and unaware of anything, were to ring.

Most likely, however, collective resolutions would be passed as soon as the seal was on my door, to the effect that my telephone be moved out to the hall or kitchen; and then the same replies would be heard day and night: "He doesn't live here any more," and, "I'm telling you in plain language, there's no-one of that name here." And the significance of this would also be clear and require no translation.

I saw all this as clearly as if it had already happened. I saw life after my departure: parts two, three, ten, which nobody had yet filmed. One day, in the morning or at midday, representatives with briefcases would arrive, accompanied by the house manager, the janitor, and neighbours co-opted as witnesses; they would break the seal in accordance with correct legal procedure, open the door into the musty room, and then spend a long time making a meticulous inventory of the contents, calling out as they did so: "One armchair, used... one mattress, used... one electric light-bulb, hundred-watt."

Outside the window there was a start and a flash, a greenish mist drifted past, as if a prolonged-action German flare had gone off, and the room became bright and dead.

The street lights had come on.

I got dressed and went to the communal kitchen. It was full now, not only with those who were always at home, always at their cooking pots and washtubs, but also the ones who had just returned from work and had straight away set about peeling potatoes, cooking fish or mincing meat.

Women were frantically pumping up primus stoves — frantically as if wrestling with demons — or were regulating the flame on paraffin stoves, with the sooty smoke billowing up to the ceiling one moment and dwindling and dying away to a tawny flame the next; while one of the male residents was deeply engrossed in tinkering with a device reminiscent of Watt's locomotive. There was silence: that tense, mean-minded kind of silence that, sparked by a single word, can explode like dynamite and turn into a brawl, a conflagration or a denunciation with far-reaching consequences.

Without looking round I started to close the door, and had a sense of everyone keeping still, pretending not to be there; the only sounds to be heard were the hissing of primus stoves and the sizzling of meat in frying pans. It seemed that everyone already knew what the score was, and the space around me seemed to have expanded, leaving me trapped in a bewitched circle: a vicious circle with no way out. I left the kitchen without looking round, banging the door as I went, and heard someone say behind my back: "How'd you like a bang on the head like that?"

The same two callow youths were standing on the middle landing, puffing their cigarettes and spitting out strands of tobacco.

"Is it five yet?" one of them asked.

"Nearly five," replied the other.

"Fuckin' hell," said the first one.

Then there was silence again.

I went down the iron back staircase through a mess of potato peel, vomit and muddy snow, and pushed open the heavy door. As I did so, I caught a sudden glimpse of a black cat and, dazzlingly close like a flash of light, its pale, puffy face, strained with anxiety, its piercing eyes, and its eyelashes wet with snow.

I fancied that in its surprise the cat was about to say: "Hello," but then thought better of it; it sprang awkwardly to one side like a wounded hare and began darting hither and thither. I felt sorry for it and wanted to say: "It's all right, it's all right." I walked past, pretending not to notice.

Outside in the yard was our resident dog, standing there on its bandy legs. Nobody knew where it lived, and it was fed and kicked alike by all and sundry. As I passed, it lifted its head and fixed me with its free gaze, "No, you don't know anything yet," I said to the dog soundlessly. It ran after me; I looked round, and there must have been something in my eyes that made it stop — as if to say "What is it?" — and not go any further.

I wondered how he had found out that, of the various entrances, this was the one leading to my place; after all, when I had entered the courtyard he had been hovering on the other side of the street. Perhaps he had already been to the house manager's office to make enquiries and then sought me out from the verbal description he had been given.

Through a semi-basement window of the vocational school, students could be seen playing table tennis by electric light: two were prancing like kittens round the table with their bats; and all this was from that other, forgotten life I had left far behind, as if from a film seen years before. In this film there drifted across the screen a watchman in a cap with ear-flaps, a huge half-collapsed snowman with pieces of coal for eyes, a woman hanging out washing in the wind who greeted me and then eyed me strangely when I failed to reply. From the entrance to a scientific research institute emerged members of some commission, carrying briefcases and looking worried. Under the archway the postwoman rummaged in her bag and handed me a letter in an official green envelope, which I put in my pocket without opening.

I walked underneath old, dirty kitchen windows that were boarded up with plywood or stuffed with pillows, trudging through dark trampled snow, and skirting a white, snow-covered little public garden with one sickly fir tree. I came not to the gates but, via a brick archway, into the inner courtyard. A monumental concrete or plaster statue stood in this courtyard:

inscrutable, grey, darkened by snow, rain and wind, so that it was no longer possible to make out even the facial features, let alone the sculptor's intentions. People said it was Ordzhonikidze, although at times it seemed like Stalin himself standing there with his hand thrust into the breast of his coat, while at other times it seemed to be just a symbolic representation. The statue had been moved here from some square because of restoration work; it clearly had no business standing here in a back courtyard next to iron litter bins.

Several healthy, strapping young fellows with nascent moustaches, wearing the black uniform caps of technical school students, were playing some childish game, squealing and laughing inanely and chasing each other, reminding me of orphans from a children's home. And I envied them, as I had before, so many years ago. Why couldn't I be an orphan, a homeless waif? Then I'd be able to take everything in my stride and not give a damn about anything.

I walked past the canteen, where clouds of steam redolent of cod and sauerkraut were billowing out as if from a bath-house. Through the windows I could see the serving counter, a barrel of beer from which the froth was being pumped off, tall pot-bellied beer mugs, and bare tables without tablecloths at which students were seated in groups of six or eight, tucking into mashed potato or semolina with their tin spoons, and washing this down with runny jelly from chipped glasses. As in a dream I circled the block, passing through the intercommunicating courtyards. The open gates appeared, and the street swam into view. I did not look behind me as I walked, yet I could sense that he was following me.

I wondered what he already knew about me. What had informers told him about me, and what was he obliged to pass on?

I joined the queue at a trolleybus stop. A trolleybus drew up, and everyone boarded it. I stayed where I was. The trolleybus moved off, and without looking back I continued on my way; as I walked I was blinded by the sight of an intrusive Party slogan in neon lights on the roof.

There was nothing out of the ordinary about any of the people. I saw their faces as they ran across the street or drove past in cars; all were in a hurry to get somewhere, and at the end of their journey they had someone waiting for them. I should never be like them, never again.

All the time I was walking I felt as though I were on a lead.

I stopped at the 'Gastronom' food store, intrigued by a curious sight. People were running into the shop in a strange agitated fashion, as in some old silent film starring Max Linder, and running out again in the same jerky, speeded-up way, as if something quite undreamt of was on sale there. I took a closer look. A painter in a cradle suspended over the door was wielding his brush, and everyone was trying to slip past unscathed. I too ran into the crowded store, into the stifling crush and noise. Somebody was making his way through the crowd with a green balloon on a string that bobbed along near the ceiling. People carrying string bags heavily laden with oranges and tins of food pushed on regardless with resolute expressions, fighting their way to the counters.

Steering clear of minor turbulences and eruptions around the cash desks, I squeezed through the crowd to the vodka and cigarettes section, where I became penned in on all sides and suffocated by the reek of alcohol on people's breath. There was a whole battery of empty bottles on the counter, which the sales assistant and a customer were vying with each other to count, confusing each other and getting mixed up in the process, so that they had to keep on starting again, while from the crowd came shouts of: "Give it a rest!" There was no sign of the sealskin cap, so I relaxed in the crowd for a while and then began gradually to extricate myself. When at last I was disgorged by the crowd and I found myself with space to breathe again, I was afraid to look in the direction of one of the marble columns; I felt that there was something not quite right there, but I looked nevertheless, at which moment something fast, agile and predatory hid behind the column. All I managed to make out was the top of a black cap.

Then I darted behind a column as well and watched him closely from this vantage point. He looked round and was suddenly unable to see me anywhere, then looked in a different direction and again could not find me; I saw him become agitated and start twisting around as if in a whirlpool, searching for me, and gradually he began to move around to my side of the column. Then I shifted my position to the other side. It was like a game of cat-and-mouse: a peculiarly mid-twentieth-century game of cat-and-mouse.

I finally emerged from my cover, and when he saw me in the open and vulnerable, he pressed himself against his column to avoid being noticed, took out a cigarette and then his matches, but decided against lighting up and put the matches away again, leaving the cigarette unlit in his mouth.

All right, come on, I screamed at him soundlessly, come here and say everything in front of all these people, and I'll say everything I have to say to you. Let them see everything and know everything — let it all go hang, let it all be done with in an instant.

All my hatred was focussed on him, on his pale face, his air of harassed solicitude. If only at that moment I could have pushed my way towards him through the crowd, seized him by the throat, shouted out, appealed to the people and, not holding back my tears, exclaimed: "What do you want? Why are you following me?" But between us there lay an abyss: the abyss of state secrecy; and I could not talk to him as one human being to another.

I joined the queue at the cash desk, and from time to time looked out of the corner of my eye to where he was standing.

I examined his pale, lifeless face, which was strained from the effort of his vigil, and I don't know why, but I fancied that his voice too must be lifeless, and high-pitched like that of a eunuch. I had never heard his voice and probably never would. We were at close quarters and could see each other, but it was as if there were a thick sheet of armoured glass between us.

He stood motionless while the crowd of people drifted and flowed around him, jostling with their elbows, exuding odours of pepper vodka, perfume and validol. A woman glanced at him and clasped her handbag more closely to her breast; someone dug an elbow into his stomach; someone brushed against his face with a string bag containing eggs that they were gingerly holding up over the crowd; but he did not take his eyes off me.

When I had managed to pay, I took my receipts and moved on. I did not look in his direction any more. It was all the same to me now. I walked on as if blind.

"Stop pushing, you lout," said a woman. I glanced at her briefly and made no response. She simply belonged to another world.

"That's right, don't bother to apologize!" she screamed at me.

I turned round to look at her. Her eyes had a crazed glint, her hair was dyed, and there was something false about her whole appearance; I had the feeling that she was in fact an agent who was on duty here.

A crowd had started to gather. A sales assistant stopped slicing sausage and stood there with his long thin knife, waiting to see what would happen.

"I'm sorry, I didn't mean to," I said.

"Go home: you can push and shove as much as you like there," she said. And she walked off with a strange hobbling gait, dragging her low-slung posterior behind her as if it had been stuck on.

During this contretemps my faithful follower was standing right opposite us, pretending to queue for pies, watching us; he seemed to be trying to read our lips to see what we were talking about. I looked at him through the haze of the shop; our eyes met, and for an instant we each saw into the other's inmost being. And we both turned away, as if startled by this.

This happened again a couple of times as I wandered through the shop to buy things in different departments and became aware of his sealskin cap. Now he was trying (just as I was myself) to hide behind an absent-minded expression and not look in my direction, but we were connected by invisible highly-charged wires that stretched through the crowd in the shop, and there was an incredible telepathy at work: "Are you there? Are you there?" And as we moved about, the two of us were suffering torments — were horribly constrained, bound vertically and horizontally in the same magnetic field, and driven by powerful, relentless, implacable electromagnetic forces beyond our control.

I went out into the street with my purchases; and at once, as if it had come specially for me, a trolleybus glided to a halt at the stop, and its doors opened; but I looked the other way and crossed the Arbat, heading for my block of flats.

What was he following me for? After all, I could have told him everything myself. I could have told him at what time I got up, or when I went to the communal kitchen where people did their washing, cooking and gossiping, telling each other in conspiratorial whispers where buckwheat porridge concentrate was on sale; I could have told him how I brewed tea, fried potatoes, and then lay on my bed for the rest of the day reading *Vanity Fair*, or *The Cherry Orchard*, or *A Farewell to Arms*; I could have told him who I was friendly with, or what cigarettes I smoked. I had no reason to conceal anything. Why did he have to follow me?

And again I thought: I should turn round here and now, go up to him, grasp him firmly by the arms and, looking straight at his pale face, into his piercing eyes, say quietly: "Why are you following me, what do you want? I'll phone Beria..." As if I had a chance in hell.

Or perhaps it would be better to take him aside and say calmly: "Look here, pal, there must be some misunderstanding. I assume you must be looking for someone else: it can't be me, do you understand?"

But I didn't do either of these things. I walked along the street, pretending to be calm, as if I didn't suspect a thing.

I was not even surprised at what had happened. Yet there was pain and dismay that it had come so swiftly, with such unexpected speed. All my life I had had it trailing behind me like a shadow, but even so its final advent had been unexpected.

Anyone who has not been accustomed to that since childhood, anyone who has not grown up with that, can never comprehend the dull ache, the sheep-like acceptance of the inevitable.

I could not see him now: he was walking along behind me, somewhere in the crowd, and I could feel this, as no doubt one feels a gun held at one's back as a tiny cold circle between the shoulder-blades.

People came towards me: faces flashed into view, caps and hats floated past; wet snowflakes began to fall, and umbrellas appeared; buildings passed by in the shape of truncated cones; long queues stretched back. They were speculative queues: nobody had any idea yet what would be on sale.

I walked and walked as if through a submarine world of silence, under the enormous pressure of water a kilometre deep. Suddenly I followed an urge to deviate from my path; there was an instant clamour of cars sounding their horns, followed by a shout: "Come back here, citizen!" and I seemed to wake up to find myself in the middle of the road with cars snarling and belching fumes all around me, while on the pavement a crowd had gathered. The familiar sealskin cap was also to be seen sticking up out of the crowd, as well as several others like it, and suddenly it appeared as if everybody was wearing the same type of cap. I didn't look more closely, but returned to the pavement, where a police sergeant was waiting for me. He raised his hand to the peak of his cap.

I slowly undid one button of my coat, took my internal passport out of the side pocket of my jacket, and handed it to the policeman. He read my surname, then slowly leafed through the passport, handed it back, and saluted again.

Disappointed, the crowd dispersed. The sealskin cap had disappeared, and I walked on with the passport in my hand. Then I stopped next to a drain-pipe and put the passport back in my pocket, my hands trembling. A piece of ice that had broken off the roof came rattling down inside the drain-pipe.

I crossed the street, and although I knew and sensed with every nerve in my body, with the sum total of my despair, that I must not go home, nevertheless I obediently dragged myself towards the familiar red-lead-painted gates, as if guided by an inner, unconscious force of non-resistance and driven by the whole of my preceding life.

I threw my bits of shopping down on the window-sill. I couldn't have eaten anything. Pulling down the blind I stood by the window. Yellow, deadening light filtered in through the crack; the street boomed and shuddered from the passing traffic, and I had the feeling that everything was careering out of control into the jaws of hell.

With each passing minute there were more and more vehicles, sending out low beams of light from their yellow headlamps and throwing up a spray of muddy slush; from time to time the traffic streaming in both directions would suddenly come to a standstill, filling the Ring Road across its whole width and spilling out onto the pavements. Then something would suddenly stir into juddering motion, and the turbulent, roaring stream of traffic was unleashed and flowed on again in both directions, following various routes, heading for various destinations.

The black stream of people on the pavements was also becoming thicker by the moment. They came gushing out of every main and service entrance, scurrying out of all the doors and gateways like scalded cockroaches, and, caught up in the current of the evening river, flowed on in a dense mass, skirting eddies that suddenly blocked their path next to little shops, stopping for a moment to ask: "What are they selling?", and then either came to rest as they joined the queue or ran on to the various stops, overtaking each other on the way, to form long meandering queues that obstructed the pavement and changed their configuration from one moment to the next; and when a trolleybus arrived they bunched together and pressed forwards, holding string bags containing bottles of milk over their heads, pushing each other aside with elbows, bags and briefcases, scrambling up onto the footboard, clinging on as they went, cramming themselves in, and through its brightly-lit windows one could see the trolleybus shaking its contents down flat as it moved along in a series of jolting stops and starts: every time it braked, people fell against each other, as if packing into each other, creating more space; and the dark trolleybus, bulging with people, manoeuvred its way sluggishly through the roaring traffic.

Where were they all going, where were they hurrying — and for what? Surely there was nothing worthwhile awaiting them at the end of their journey? It seemed that all they wanted to do was to escape from this street as quickly as possible, and that if they met with no mishap here, they would find happiness there, in the other streets.

Suddenly I heard the sound of loud laughter just beneath my window. A few youths and girls were standing by a street lamp, eating pies which they had bought from a fat woman in a white overall; they were talking to each other about something and laughing.

Why were they laughing so loudly? How could they laugh and stand there munching pies and swapping anecdotes? Were they really so unaware of everything, could they really not see this yellow, dead, dreary light, these yellow, dead clouds? Not see that everything was finished?

Yet although it seemed as if the world was coming to an end, high up over one of the roofs some gay, festive letters in neon lights lit up and began to run from right to left: 'Cheap, convenient, fast'.

And there — in the evening that had now come into its own, in the jungle of twinkling, trembling, flashing, blazing lights — life was going on as usual.

Someone was living it up at a party, perhaps the first he had ever been to in his life; someone had stayed on at the office alone and was bent over a sheet of paper, composing an anonymous denunciation; someone was watching Maeterlinck's *The Bluebird* for the first time; someone was having his arrest warrant written out; someone else was having her hair permed and waved; in the heat of bakeries, bread was being baked for the following morning; at an abattoir outside the city, a herd of mud-caked, exhausted, obtuse cattle, unfed before slaughter, was lowing; someone was speaking first words of love to someone else: ardent, devoted, heartfelt, faltering words for a lifetime and until the end of time; in little churches services were being held by the dim light of a wax candle; by the light of blazing chandeliers meetings to mark some jubilee were proceeding with a ceremonial gravitas that smothered all living truth; and someone was walking devastated out of cemetery gates; three-man tribunals were working impersonally and methodically, enclosed by the silence of fortress walls; and somewhere out in the woods on the outskirts of Moscow an old poet who would be hounded in years to come wandered along wintry paths, murmuring poetry with every last breath he could command.

The city of six million souls had begun its evening life, austere, boisterous or weary; and nobody knew (nobody wanted to or could know) that somebody was suffering and dying alone in his room, in one of Moscow's millions of poky rooms: this was of no concern to anyone. And life continued running on all cylinders, because it can never stop, because whatever might happen — be it earthquake, plague, purge, pogrom or eclipse of the sun — people still want to eat, sleep, enjoy themselves, love, hate, envy, and propagate the species.

A street lamp was shining right by my window, filling the room with its dead, bluish light. A faded brown spot on the ceiling showed up, also a spider that had expired in its web, and something else cowering in the atomic flash of the street lamp.

The street roared, snarled and hooted like some demented out-of-tune brass band; it rumbled and shuddered, transmitting the vibration through thick stone walls, roof rafters and the stone foundations of the ground floor, where chandeliers belonging to the retired, camouflaged operetta singer could be heard tinkling.

I could not believe my eyes: either I had gone mad, or the street had gone mad, or the man at the gates was not at all what I had taken him for. I could clearly see him performing a Russian tap-dance, which he did unostentatiously yet quite openly, dancing nimbly and skilfully, almost professionally; I could almost hear the tapping of his heels. What was he at? Either he suddenly felt in a very good mood, or the sound of some tune had carried along the street to where he was standing, or else he was just raising his spirits and keeping on his toes. I was agog with curiosity, unable to take my eyes off his feet darting hither and thither. I felt I wanted to laugh and cry at the same time. So even he might be human after all.

Perhaps he played the accordion in his free time, or the balalaika, using a teach-yourself manual; perhaps he even sang as a tenor, perhaps he rocked his baby in its pram, singing a lullaby. Yes — a lullaby. And then swilled vodka, munching bites of pickled cucumber between gulps.

On Sundays he would go fishing and sit watching the float — watching until he had spots in front of his eyes. Or perhaps he was tired of contemplative pursuits, not to say fed up to the back teeth with them, and spent his leisure time quite differently, in such active pastimes as going to the races or gambling at cards.

He too had once been a boy, after all: had gone to school; run errands with an oilcloth shopping bag, in the city or along some village cart-track; swotted up multiplication tables on the back of his arithmetic exercise book; written an essay on 'The Character of Pechorin'.

Now he took a vast handkerchief the size of a headscarf out of his pocket and, covering practically the whole of his face, began to blow his nose. I fancied I could even hear him sneeze. Then he pondered something, paused for a moment, and suddenly, quite unexpectedly, tied a knot in one corner of the handkerchief as a reminder of something or other. Old chap, you're a man after my own heart...

Did you get into this line of work voluntarily — did you follow your heart, so to speak? Or was it a case of having no other alternative? Did you get your call-up in one of those sudden, quite unforeseen emergency mobilizations? Or was it one of those perfunctory postings that take place when they're filling gaps with anyone to hand? Did you know, did you understand exactly what was involved?

Powdery snow began to fall, rapidly bleaching him white, so that he seemed to stand out and become conspicuous in the opening of the gateway, and people hurrying past sometimes turned round to look at him. And then he stirred himself and began to walk about.

Now he was acting out the part of someone going for a walk: a working man who had come home at the end of his shift and was taking a stroll round the block where he lived, walking beneath icicles that glistened in the light of the street lamps with his hands behind his back and his sealskin cap pushed back on his head.

I woke up suddenly, as if I had been jolted by someone from within. There was somebody in the room, standing there like a dark shadow in the light from the window.

"What is it? Who's there?" I cried.

"You've been moaning in your sleep. I thought you were ill."

"But how did you get into the room?"

"Through the door," replied the figure in a quiet voice.

"What time is it?"

"It's only eight o'clock."

In the doorway stood the retired operetta singer, large-framed and bony, looking like an old clapped-out nag; her face, ravaged from the effects of stage make-up, gazed at me with a sad expression.

"There's something I have to tell you."

She closed the door carefully behind her and then stood for a long time, listening for something.

I could hear my blood pounding.

Then she said, "It's not really my business, but I feel I must warn you."

"Why, what's happened?"

She raised a finger to her lips and again stood listening for something.

"They've been making enquiries about you here."

Something seemed to snap inside me, but I asked nonchalantly, "Who's been making enquiries?"

"That janitor fellow asked if you were at home."

"Why, what does he want to see me about?"

"There was a man with him," she said vaguely.

"What sort of man?"

"In plain clothes. I think he was from the local police station."

I said nothing.

"From the police station — a short fellow with fair hair."

"And did he ask about me as well?"

"He didn't say a word. But I reckon he'd told the janitor what questions to ask. I feel obliged to tell you that."

I assumed a nonchalant expression.

"So let him ask questions, what's that to me?"

"I just thought you ought to know," she said quietly. "He also asked what visitors you have."

"I'm not really interested," I said.

"I understand," she said. "Good night. You ought to do something about it, all the same."

Do something! What, run away? Vanish into thin air? Immure myself in the wall? Turn into the Invisible Man? This last idea I found definitely appealing. I had once seen a film of The Invisible Man: he would take some tablets and then melt away, turning into a phantom, into air, after which he could walk through walls. I could still remember his voice: mysterious, prophetic, a voice from nowhere, from the void, the demonic laughter of retribution. He was here, there and everywhere, blowing up bridges and roaring with laughter. He left dark footprints in the snow, the only thing that gave away where he was, and the people chasing him shot in the direction of these footprints. And when the bullets found their target, my goodness, did he scream!

I lay there fantasizing about being invisible: I was walking unhindered past that hapless fellow hugging the wall by the entrance in his sealskin cap, and he had no idea; now I boarded a trolleybus and stood hanging on to a strap, and nobody round me knew that I was there, on my way to that place.

And now here it was, that huge stone building in the spacious square; now I was walking unseen past the guard and then a second guard, and going up a wide marble staircase, my footsteps noiseless, ghostly, as if I were not walking, but hovering through the air; I walked down a long corridor with a row of tall oak doors, entered various rooms, opened cabinets, until at last there it was: an old grey document case with a black rubber stamp — 'To be filed in perpetuity' — and my photograph on the cover. Goodness knows where they had got hold of the photograph: it was completely unfamiliar to me. Such a calm, unsuspecting face; and yet at that very moment they had been photographing me. And now I was leafing through the grey file, turning the pink and blue pages that had been sewn into it, finding out things about myself that even I was unaware of. I read denunciations and was quite taken aback to see who had written them. What unexpected hands revealed themselves here!

I drew the curtain back a fraction and took a look at the street. He was not there. I scrutinized every entrance of the generals' apartment block on the other side of the street, every lamp-post, every shadow that he might be hiding in, merging into. No, he was nowhere to be seen. I studied the queue at the trolleybus stop: perhaps he had insinuated himself into the queue, assuming the role of a passenger waiting for a trolleybus, only to stay behind at the last moment when the trolleybus left and then hide in the queue again? No, he wasn't there either. A trolleybus drew up, and its doors opened and devoured the whole queue; at the now empty stop a snow-storm began to swirl. Neither was he among the people walking their dogs: their pugs and fox terriers.

There had been years when I had asked myself: "What

are they after? What have I done?" Now I no longer had such thoughts, but not because I had fathomed those twin mysteries, I had not; nor did I fathom them for a long time afterwards, and even today I have probably not got to the bottom of them. No, I had become shrouded in a mist of apathy: the impossibility, inconceivability of struggle; a spineless, pathologically extreme submission to the flow of events; the sense of being trapped in a dead end, with the early dusk of a winter's day crowding in, to be followed by the long, unending night with its silence, submissiveness, striking of clocks, random cries, random whistles, and swishing of random cars.

Evening Lights

The sky above the courtyard was almost black; the dusty light bulb by the entrance shone dimly, as if somehow sunk in oblivion, speaking of the futility of living, of going on and on like this, suffering in solitude: it just wasn't worth it.

Walking across the yard at an angle, I approached the gates stealthily, with a feeling of apprehension. There was nobody there. I glanced at the other side of the street: it too was empty. I put my head inside the entrance, and there was such a gross, dank stench of dogs and urine that I could have howled out loud.

I started walking slowly along the building, keeping close to the wall. I had just come out for a breath of air — why, surely I was still entitled to a breath of air? This was my daily exercise. I stopped by a poster, looking right and left out of the corner of my eye. Nobody. Then I walked as far as the corner and took a peep into Glazovsky Lane. Empty. After this I went back again, and then on to the Arbat, where I looked across to the corner opposite, next to the 'Gastronom' food store. There was a man standing there; he glanced across the street in my direction and then turned away.

I walked along, aimlessly examining the shop windows. In the pharmacy on the corner of Vesnin Street there were, just to cheer everyone up, a few dismal rubber bulbs, with the cold nickel of some surgical instrument as a garnish. Next came 'Clocks and Watches': a million dials, all showing the same time. Now I was already at the health-food store with its eye-catching display of imitation joints of meat, after which came winking neon lights.

And suddenly I saw, coming towards me, myself. Bathed in a garish green light, I was standing in my grey raglan coat and fur hat with ear-flaps in front of the long, brightly lit street mirror of a hairdresser's salon; protruding from a slender support in the shop window was a head with an affected, arch expression and permed hair henna-dyed to a fiery red, above which a small poster advertised: 'Six-month perm with two months' guarantee'. Without any conscious act of will I entered the world of the barber's shop: warm and redolent of eau de Cologne and pleasant childhood memories. There was no queue. The gloomy long-haired barber languidly worked up a lather, just as languidly lathered my cheeks, examined me in the mirror first from one side and then the other and, sticking out the tip of his tongue, proceeded to shave me rapidly, finishing with a few languid flourishes of the towel. His girl apprentice, who was staring gloomily out of the window at the street, said, "Goodness, what a lot of unshaven men there are walking around."

At 'Embroidered Goods' I crossed the street towards the second-hand shop. A lady's shoe lay on some black velvet, pining, while next to it was a man's white felt boot, as if a couple had eloped and inadvertently left their worn footwear behind in the window as material evidence. Then came the orange, glowing aquarium of the pet shop with goldfish drowsily entangled in red aquatic plants.

A man wearing an old black hat and a pince-nez who was walking in front of me stopped suddenly by the kerb and lurched forwards: his hat fell into the slushy snow, and it was impossible to judge whether he was drunk or ill.

Just then a police sergeant came running from the cross-roads.

"What's going on here, citizen? Why are you violating traffic regulations?"

"I'm not," said the man quietly.

"Come along with me, citizen." And he took hold of his sleeve.

Two men in overboots gently pushed him, urging him to move on.

"Let me go!" he shrieked, pressing himself against the wall. "I'm a member of the Russian intelligentsia."

"We'll see about that at the station," said the sergeant, now taking the man's arm in a ju-jitsu grip.

"I'm tired. I'm ti-i-ired!" protested the member of the intelligentsia in a cat-like wail.

A traffic controller who was sitting in his blue cylindrical booth on the corner next to the tinned goods store listened intently for some time, then leaned out of his window and blew a summons on his whistle, aimed in the general direction of Smolensk Street; an answering signal came back, and there were more whistles from a different direction.

"Ah, how tiresome I find these peasants with their whistles," said the gentleman wearily, and then fell silent.

The sergeant listened to this lofty protest with a stony expression, then started to drag the man into a gateway, while the two in overboots searched him as they went, roughly groping at his chest, back and legs.

A crowd gathered.

"What are you pulling him like that for? He might be ill," said a woman with a shopping bag.

I had the impression that they were about to drag me away as well, so I slipped into the 'Science and Knowledge' cinema.

I peered through the window of the ticket office; the woman selling tickets seemed to be sitting a long way away, as if seen through the wrong end of a pair of binoculars.

"One, please," I heard my own feeble voice saying: it seemed to be coming from somewhere far off.

A prodigiously fat usherette in Soviet nylon stockings stood in the doorway, barring the door with her stomach; she tore my ticket with her pudgy red fingers, breathing a hot, furnace-like blast over me; I squeezed past, brushing against her soft belly, and entered a dimly lit, cold, dirty foyer that stretched out like a tunnel and smelled of beer and stale sandwiches, where youths with cigarettes between their teeth languished and fretted. All of a sudden a bell rang, a red light came on over the entrance, and everyone started jostling and pushing past each other, pouring into the narrow auditorium, where it was dark and cold and the air was thick with the vapours of people's breath; everyone had just managed to find a seat when the lights dimmed and the screen lit up.

I looked around. Nobody was looking at me. I quietly stood up and made my way through the phosphorescent, sunflower-seed-chewing, toffee-sucking, sneezing, coughing auditorium, past the luminous screen and towards the red light over the exit, then down a long, grimy, broken set of stairs gloomily lit by a lamp caged in iron mesh, and through some winding alleyways with dustbins, to emerge into an unfamiliar, quiet back street that was blanketed with snow, leaving an Indian dream in colour behind me in that vast building, in that narrow, cold auditorium.

Basement windows, laid bare in the garish light, revealed the impoverished, desolate life within: tables covered with oil-cloth, open wardrobes and children sitting over their schoolbooks, chests with old women sleeping on them, unspeaking, sequestered shadows, old men in nooks and crannies smoking cautiously and guiltily, and cats — for some reason there were cats everywhere.

I came to a trolleybus stop. A trolleybus drew up, the doors opened, and with a backward glance I jumped in. The doors gently closed, and the trolleybus moved off. I peered through the rear window: a car was persistently following the trolleybus — following sedulously, without dropping back or overtaking.

Suddenly I noticed that the conductor was looking at me: he was standing in his place in the corner with his bag, staring at me with a strange canine grin over the heads of the passengers, over their caps and hats — staring fixedly just at me and no-one else, as if he had mistaken me for a friend of his. I stood up and headed for the door, but the conductor continued to look steadily at me, as if he still took me for a friend and was surprised that I didn't recognize him. By now I had forgotten where I was and where the trolleybus was going. Incomprehensible signs flashed past, occasional pedestrians ran past, and everything was strange and sinister. I stopped by the door, saying nothing.

"Perhaps you can tell me, citizen, who's going to buy you a ticket: Pushkin?" said the conductor unexpectedly from the back of the trolleybus.

The talking suddenly stopped, and all the passengers pricked up their ears.

"Yes, you in the rabbit-skin hat: you're the one I'm talking to," said the conductor.

Passengers with newspapers stopped reading them and looked at me.

"Wearing a fur hat, too," said a man in a dark-blue cloth cap sitting in a seat reserved for mothers with babies.

The other passengers looked at me in silence.

"I'm sorry," I cried, handing the conductor a crumpled rouble note.

At that moment the trolleybus braked sharply, and the passengers all went tumbling into one another; the doors opened, and a man entered the trolleybus and gave me a searching look. Before the door closed again, I jumped out onto the pavement; the conductor gestured at me, holding up my rouble note and ticket, and then the trolleybus glided off, taking the man with it. Through the glass I could see him move to the front without looking round and then sit down. My heart was palpitating, as though a pigeon had flown inside my shirt.

The car that had been following the trolleybus was not there any more: it had just vanished.

I turned into Borisoglebsky Lane, which was dark and empty. There was a service in progress in the Church of Saints Boris and Gleb. A persistent fog hung in the air, unmoving, tinged by the light of a yellow street lamp, and there was a blue cast to snow on the roofs of buildings, glimpsed through the bare branches of trees. The pink columns of an aristocratic mansion had the appearance of an old faded oleograph.

A little old woman from pre-revolutionary times emerged from a small, peeling outbuilding; she had a mauve dog with her, a pomeranian, which barked at me hoarsely, in a quite modern manner.

In the dull light of the street lamps everything had become hushed, had nestled up to the gates, taking on diffuse, mysterious outlines.

Ah, what a secluded spot, tucked away here in the snow! And with what explosive force you could feel the oppressive spirit of the age, could feel the life that would carry on here when you had gone: the same little street of stone buildings, the service going on in the church, the swirling snow, the ashen windows of the houses — only you would be missing from all this.

A snow-storm was getting up, and the narrow street began to howl like a braying trumpet. Staggering along completely encased in snow, a man was struggling through the white spectral shroud that swathed the street, roaring a popular song as he went: "Whoever steps out along life's path with a song on his lips..."

He repeatedly fell to his knees, scooped up snow by the handful and champed away at it, then pulled himself to his feet again and, spinning round on the spot, walking in zigzags, sometimes even going backwards, kept on shouting: "Whoever steps out with a song on his lips shall never come to grief..."

When I drew level with him, he looked me straight in the face and, breathing out hot fumes of raw alcohol, said with conviction, "Shall never come to grief," trying to hold on to me as he did so.

The door of a telephone kiosk slammed shut in the wind, and the telephone suddenly started ringing — strangely, feverishly, eerily; it rang and rang, sobbing, choking, as if calling for help, calling upon anyone nearby to lift the receiver and listen to somebody's cry or warning, or perhaps their whispering.

It was strange and fanciful to think that in this same life there were green, tranquil streets and gardens with roses and jasmine.

I was walking through a meadow, through the tall grass, brushing white umbelliferous clover blossoms with my hand; nearby, like the sea, was a field of millet, waving in the breeze — a breeze redolent of pine trees and wild strawberries; and grasshoppers were chirring, so many of them that they did not even acknowledge each other: every blade of grass had its own grasshopper, each one intent on forging its own happiness.

I found it quite impossible to imagine that I, who had walked through that meadow, was the same person who now, on this damp, grey night, was making his way along the lonely winter street, past greenish lamps, closed gates, dark windows.

I marched on and on: down frozen back streets, skirting any dead angles, letting the fresh air blow into the recesses of my despair and fear; past blind windows which, so it seemed, had never contained any life; past black icy doorways that stood wide open; from time to time dazzled by a brightly lit shop window or deafened by the squeaking door of a pub from whence poured, together with a hubbub of drunken talk and laughter, clouds of steam smelling of beer and mushy peas.

And I had the impression that I was alone, alone in the whole city: that nobody was concerned (or could be, indeed) with what I felt, and that I was fighting my battle on my own. I also had the feeling that every dingy corner, every shadow, might come to life, turn into the man in the sealskin cap and come after me in hot pursuit.

The electric clocks in the streets were showing different times, and this too I found alarming: it seemed strange, deliberate and sinister.

The blizzard pushed me along from behind, trying to hustle me into a cul-de-sac, as if manhandling me into a prison cell.

Somewhere the snarling of a stray car could be heard; somewhere violet flashes flared up from a tram; with a sigh, snow crept down a roof and fell, and then there was silence. And suddenly there would be the sound of someone moaning and giggling in some randomly chosen entrance, living life for all it was worth.

Ahead of me an old man was struggling along in a heavy fur coat, an equally heavy boyar-style hat, and galoshes. He walked slowly, as if stumbling. I overtook him and looked at his face, which was grizzled, grey and marked by illness. As he walked he gasped for breath: he not only had difficulty in moving, but in breathing, just living in this world — even getting through this minute was torture; and I thought: am I too going to end up like that one day? Shall I too have to tread this via dolorosa on a winter's night, in the teeth of a blizzard, struggling for breath against life's burdens, holding an empty string bag? For the moment I had forgotten everything that had happened to me that day; it had all receded into the distance and seemed unimportant and paltry compared with this.

An unexpectedly strong gust of wind slammed the door of a telephone kiosk with a report like a gunshot, making me jump. Then the wind blew the door back and banged it again, and again, like a madman; fragments of glass rained down, and I felt as if this was being done to me.

That strange, enduring emotional aberration: when you are in low spirits, when you are unhappy or ill, you think that the whole world is feeling jaundiced, despondent and tired of life.

By now I had come out onto the broad Ring Road, and it was as if I had been swept out onto a big sparkling wheel, round which flew thousands of fleeting lights, catching up with each other, merging and separating: yellow, blue and white. It was like a fireworks display.

And again, as so many times before, both reason and instinct told me that life has no knowledge, or desire for knowledge, of what you feel and endure, but is a law unto itself, and always will be. Everything will continue, everything will be repeated, even your own life will be repeated in thousands upon thousands of variants; and yet nobody will ever learn a thing from any of this.

A young couple were strolling along ahead of me. They stopped at the window of a furniture store, arguing as they chose furniture; after this they stood for a while near a high-rise building, saying how nice it would be to have a flat there; then they stopped at a post office to read the timetable of the motor vessel 'Rossiya', and said how nice it would be to take a trip from Odessa to Batumi in June; and in front of a dark entrance, after talking for some time, they parted.

The giant swings and the big wheel in the park stood frozen into immobility, looking like iron dinosaurs. My heart was filled with aching, as if I was the only one left from those far-off days when the wheel had turned, the swings had flown up to the sky, fireworks had gone off, and it had been carnival time;

when in the early hours I had come to our student hostel in the forest outside the city, and in a clearing there had been the glistening of yellow buttercups and the sharp scent of fresh yellow dandelions, and life had been never-ending, the sun had risen over the forest, a cuckoo had called from the twilight, and I had counted the years. On that morning the war had begun.

The wind forced me into an open telephone kiosk; I partially closed the door and stood in the freezing kiosk, wondering whom to ring.

A multitude of voices came to life: "Hello! Yes? Who's there?" God, it was hard to imagine that it was warm and cosy at the other end of the line; hard to imagine a shaded lamp, books, tea in delicate cups, normal human life. And I had the overpowering feeling of being like a stray dog.

Finally I dialled his number, and the familiar neurotic voice replied: "Hello." Then the voice was silent. I could hear breathing, as if steam were coming out of the phone. I said nothing and replaced the receiver. So he was all right.

I walked over a railway bridge. A strong, gusting wind blew unrestrained. I was alone on the bridge, which moaned and vibrated.

As I reached the outskirts of the city, the moon was hanging in the sky, surrounded by a yellow aureole, and the snow glittered and crunched underfoot. In an open field behind a dark cluster of long, low barrack huts shone the lights of some new residential blocks.

The two-storey villa was lit up with the warm, inviting lights of contemporary lamps, modernistic in their design.

I entered the spacious, spick-and-span porch that still smelled of paint and a certain long-forgotten cleanliness. My helpless agitation and nervousness were deadened by the silence and warmth.

The door, which was lit by a concealed bulb and lined with olive-green artificial leather, had gleaming on it a brightly polished brass plate engraved with a facsimile of the occupant's signature, like those old plates that used to hang on the doors of provincial gynaecologists or barristers. But this one was very new, showy, one might even say insolent. My heart sank. Faced with the olive-green opulence of that door I was keenly aware of my own insignificance and lack of success.

Before ringing the doorbell I breathed in and out deeply several times, and only then pressed the button; my ringing was answered by the barking of dogs.

The door was opened by a maid, and immediately two setters appeared on the threshold, for all the world like two brothers. The house smelled of repose, established warmth, varnished parquet, good pipe tobacco and coffee.

The master of the house, in a quilted pyjama suit of silky wool and wearing spectacles with a thin gold frame, was sitting at a desk in a deep leather armchair, a restored antique, reading a brand-new weighty tome with a dark-blue cover which I recognized as the latest — thirteenth — volume of Stalin's works.

He did not look up at me immediately; only when I had said, "Hello" did he put the book aside and say, "Greetings, old man. Do have a seat."

His face had noticeably changed: it was now pale, puffy, care-worn, inhabiting a higher world closed to me.

He left his desk and sat opposite me, and for a moment the old close camaraderie and trust reasserted themselves, as if we had just come out of the Law Institute student refectory after a meal of beetroot salad, pearl barley soup and stewed dried fruit.

"Well, then, how are those precious liberals of yours?" He removed his spectacles.

"What do you mean, liberals? They're just honest, decent people."

I took out a packet of 'Belomor' cigarettes.

"They're a pack of idiots. But to you they're romantics!" He laughed, flicked a flame from his cigarette lighter, gave me a light and then lit his own cigarette.

I had forgotten my reason for coming.

We sat in silence for a long time; he puffed at his pipe and did not hurry me.

Then I launched into an account of what had happened to me, during which he calmly observed me from his vantage point, from those inaccessible dizzy heights where the air is rarefied.

Gathering up the last shreds of humane, youthful feeling still remaining in his heart, he reached out for a brief moment to touch me with his hand: a hand that was warm and trembling, somehow soft and irresolute, somehow frightening in its trepidation, and yet comradely.

"Just give up seeing Lyusin," he said suddenly.

"Why, what's he done wrong?"

"I don't know, and I don't even want to think about it. I'd advise you not to think about it either — just stop seeing him!"

His voice had broken into a falsetto screech. When he had composed himself again, he said mournfully, "We've all got our heads on the block."

The setters circled round him, beating their tails, licking his hands whenever they came near him.

Just then the telephone rang with an irritable, shrill tone, and downstairs a second telephone on the same line could be heard trilling away as well. He picked up the receiver: "Yes?" — and at once his face took on a tense, uneasy, dismayed expression. His wife was standing in the doorway, looking at him. He listened, saying nothing but: "Yes, yes," over and over again; then he covered the mouthpiece with his hand and said quietly, in a trembling voice, "They're asking me to make a speech about the Jewish doctors' plot." He had gone as limp as a wet rag.

I shook my head, but his wife whispered, "Say yes, for goodness' sake!"

He removed his hand from the mouthpiece and said, calmly and firmly now, "Yes, send me the documentary material."

His face had taken on the appearance of an earthenware mask.

He sat down in his armchair again and was thoughtful for a while. Then suddenly his features twisted into a scowl.

"I told you not to hob-nob with Lyusin. How many times did I tell you!"

His face was distorted with hatred towards me. Everyone knew that he was friendly with me, and he knew that everyone knew.

"I told you it would all come to no good — didn't I tell you that?"

"I suppose so."

"What do you mean: I suppose so? Idiot! If you're so stupid, you can see that you get out of the shit yourself, damn you — there's no reason to pull others in with you."

"I'm not pulling anyone in."

"Then why did you come here?"

There was a whining note to his voice, a certain pathetic whimpering, as if everything that was painful and humiliating, all his suppressed fear, had now suddenly broken through to the surface. With an effort of will he subdued this and said wearily, peaceably, as if worn out: "Go away somewhere, disappear for the time being. Hell, what other advice can I give you."

"I understand," I said.

"Keep out of sight, wait for all this to blow over," he said without looking at me.

"Do you think it will blow over, then?"

"This madness certainly can't go on for ever."

"Is it madness?"

"What do you think?" He gave me a searching look.

"But you're participating in it."

He held out his hand in a despairing gesture, as if to say: "What can I do?"

His attentive, anxious face had become sharp and grey.

"You must do as you see fit — I haven't said anything to you."

He rose, and I followed suit.

He held out his hand, which was cold and rigid, with unbending fingers.

I began to walk down the carpeted staircase.

"You haven't been here," he said from the top of the stairs.

The two setters stood at the bottom, watching me attentively and expectantly.

...And sitting in his silky wool pyjamas and his thin gold spectacles, as soon as night had fallen and the noise had abated from the continuous traffic rushing down the main road, down towards the Moscow River, he, sitting motionless in his armchair, holding the new weighty tome with its dark-blue cover, no longer taking in what he was reading, listened intently to the cars driving down the road. Ever since he had been told how his friend had been arrested at dawn, how they had come for him in an official car, he had been unable to sleep and would sit like this for nights on end, waiting, listening to that far-off sound like a bee humming that would arise somewhere up there in the distance, and then become more and more intense, filling the night, coming closer and closer, right up to his window, into his very heart; for a moment his heart would stop, then the car would speed past down the hill with a squealing and whimpering and recede into the distance, to fade away somewhere beyond the cemetery, in the jungle of the night. But already a new bee would be hatching up there, and again he would listen, eagerly awaiting its approach, as with a howling sound that became more and more intense the car came closer and closer, right up to his window, into his very soul. And he would be counting the cars all night until dawn, counting the cars and waiting for his. Only when the trolleybuses started their sighing, when the first voices — spirited, resonant and clamorous — were heard in the street, and dark figures began to walk past with their string bags as yet empty — only then did he realize that he had been spared this time; and taking a sleeping tablet, he would fall into a ghastly leaden sleep filled with dreams of exploding cars.

The city had come to a standstill, had frozen.

I recalled how as a boy I had once travelled to the city from my small town. It was there, from a sixth-floor window in Tarasov Street in Kiev, that I had heard the sound of a great city for the first time: that sound permeating the air — ubiquitous, all-pervading and heartening — that is woven from the strands of car sirens, tram bells, the shrill clanking of carriages negotiating a turning circle, various enigmatic rumblings, car horns, the heavy rolling of trains on railway track — everything that charges, as if with gunpowder, a young heart open to everything and ready for anything. Then life had seemed never-ending.

That was long ago, so long ago.

Low clouds, dirty yellow in colour, from which dry, gritty snow fluttered down at intervals; yellow street lamps; the dull yellow windows of blocks of flats and frozen yellow windows of passing trams; the snow-storm whistling along close to the ground — all this cast such a blight of oppressive, unrelieved, manic despondency, that I threw what reserves of strength I had into footslogging on and on, not looking where I was going, concerned only to keep on without stopping, without thinking how it would end.

It seemed that the city itself, this ancient, centuries-old city, had knuckled under. It had grown sombre: the streets were dead by ten o'clock in the evening; dingy shop windows displayed orange-lit imitation goods; dimly lit cinemas showed the same film, *The Siskin*, all over town; display cases held grey, identical-looking newspapers; the same stony portrait was repeated thousands upon thousands of times, insensate and fading, like the pulse of someone mortally ill — all this drove one to despair. The night was heavy and oppressive, as were the stone buildings, and ahead of you someone was hiding behind stone piers, waiting; the whole city seemed to be nothing but one grey mass from which there was no escape, and wherever you went, whichever way you turned, there would be the same yellow, fading sky closing in, the same grey, hopeless walls and yellow street lamps; and always there was somebody lurking round the corner, watching and waiting for you.

All this would hit you suddenly, like a tornado. Emptiness, deafening emptiness. As though all the air had been pumped out of the city, and without warning the street had silently receded into the distance, and the buildings were left standing like stage scenery after the end of a play, of no interest or use to anyone.

Somewhere a light would come on in a window high above the street, and it too would be lifeless and deliberate, and one would have no sense of the life and fate of a particular individual being played out behind it at that very moment.

Traffic lights went on and off; cars sped past soundlessly in the streets; somebody in a state of some agitation was running over the road at an unauthorized crossing place; a couple stood on the kerb amidst the crowds thronging the street and gave each other a hasty kiss as they said goodbye; a gold-braided commissionaire was refusing someone entry to a restaurant.

What was it all for, what was the purpose of it all?

Everything seemed to be part of the same superfluous, hackneyed, tedious mime show. From time to time I would snap out of it for a brief moment, and everything would come to life and give tongue, as in my childhood and youth, with a shrilling of police whistles, hissing of car tyres and pealing of good old tram bells.

As I reached the city centre, however, I was overcome by a strange feeling of illusoriness and improbability, and at the same time of having seen everything somewhere before but without having fully understood it or engaged with it emotionally: the uncanny feeling that I had missed out on all this, had not lived it out to the full, and yet that now it was something of no further concern to me, but — in the cadaverous light of these fluorescent lamps — something diffuse and dim, like the image on a radar screen, making headway somewhere through fog and gales, through spray and lively winds, independently of me and not for my benefit.

It is extremely frightening the first time this happens to you, the first time you are dazed by this feeling of emptiness and apathy: it feels like the end of everything, as if you are staring into the void. However, with time it passes, it quite simply passes, and you can't even believe it has happened to you; but then it comes back and hits you again — dazes you — and you wait and wait, saying, "It'll pass, it'll pass." And it does.

On this occasion I had already had some experience, so I knew that I had only to be patient for a while and not panic, and it would pass, would be removed, like a cataract from the eye, leaving no trace.

Yet all the time life is passing, oozing away as if through a sieve.

In the past I had always had a feeling of elation and fascination in the city centre at night — as soon as I came out of the metro into Revolution Square it would all be there: the city lit up by night; a haphazard crowd, animated and excited, of unknown suitors, cuckolds, lovers and onlookers; and that feeling of expectancy in the air, the expectation of adventure. I would immediately take in and comprehend everything, readily noticing a smile, a fleeting sidelong glance, the funereal figure cut by someone waiting hopelessly; I would size up the situation and be able to see what was going to happen: who was simply hoping for manna from heaven, who was in with a chance and having luck at that particular moment, and who had the skids under them. Whatever category they filled, they were all in a state of intoxication, galvanized by the bright lights, by the nervous tic of the street by night, drawing me too into this shining wheel.

I would take deep breaths, revelling in that sparkling, stimulating air, the lustre of street lamps, the lustre of nylon stockings, buccaneering smiles, the hot fumy smell of diesel oil at bus stops, the silky rustling of women's raincoats, the businesslike leather scent of briefcases carried by men on official assignments, the bright, vulnerable colour of the first daffodils. "Daffo-deels, daffo-deels, vio-lets from Crimea!"

And a voice from the crowd, countering ironically: "Come on then, let's all take a stroll along the pier!" And I would join the rest in strolling up and down the pier: slowly, independently, taking a good look at faces and legs, sauntering to the end and back again, getting worked up and all on edge, as if I were waiting for someone, as if I knew exactly who it was, as if this person I was waiting for also knew and was already hurrying here in a packed metro carriage, a long-distance express bus, or a trolleybus. And: the incandescence of neon; a pair of carmine lips; the incredible swaying motion of a woman's walk, luring you on, as if into a hidden trap.

I never experienced loneliness, united as I was with hundreds and thousands of others just as lonely as I was: people I knew and people who were strangers, and even those I could not see in other streets and squares, whom I could nevertheless sense to be on the move in heated throngs, following the current with clattering, shuffling feet, swept along by the hope of striking lucky, of making a pick-up (that undying hope which sprang eternal in my breast too), all fused into one mass by the neon luminescence lighting up the night, by the sheen of evening street lamps, the sheen of leaves, and by that elusive, unspoken, undeclared, unvoiced, propitious something that is always there, alive, swirling constantly, permeating the air of the great city.

The lobby of the Moskva Hotel was clean, warm, very grand-looking, and empty, like a polling station the night before elections.

In a recess at the end of this long hotel lobby a small spotlight picked out the marble figure of the Generalissimo, standing tall and erect in his greatcoat, and glimmering. To the left of this, behind the hotel pharmacy, he was there again, this time wearing a tunic, sitting next to Lenin on a wide garden bench, the two of them apparently in an amicable attitude, with their arms round each other's shoulders, chatting intimately, inseparably; and it was not he, but Lenin who was listening attentively, leaning towards him with an air of marmoreal complicity, hanging on his words of wisdom. And there he was again looking out from a vast painted panel on one wall, standing behind the blinds of his half-open study window, a pipe in his mouth, gazing pensively and sagely over the Kremlin walls tinged red by the rising sun, out towards the city basking in the radiance of his life on this summer morning. Everywhere there were potted plants: pale winter hydrangeas; and a solemn, funereal silence prevailed.

A few night travellers with painted plywood suitcases, making their way through gloomy shadows in between the marble columns, headed for the brightly lit reception window, where they made an enquiry; having received an answer, they moved away from the window and stood looking disconcerted. They seemed so absurdly out of place and vulnerable, standing there in their long black and navy-blue coats and with their wooden suitcases, in the soaring, cathedral-like lobby, in the warmth of its radiators, surrounded by palms in green tubs, and with the marble generalissimo looking down on them from the full five metres of his height. After putting their heads together in a brief, subdued, provincial conclave, they marched off in single file, past the silver-braided commissionaire standing by the entrance, and — clutching those unmistakably Russian wooden suitcases — walked out one by one into the swirling powdery snow.

Things were quiet at the receptionist's window: one might have thought that rooms were being allocated by a celestial bureaucracy, and that from time to time the phone would suddenly ring with a message from some seventh heaven ordering a block reservation. Even if (as did sometimes happen) some wild unshaven provincial, in the capital on assignment, should accidentally blunder into the hotel, wearing galoshes over his boots and carrying a bulging briefcase, or perhaps with a pince-nez like Chekhov's holding a travelling bag, and should ask: "Do you have any rooms?", he would be told: "We don't take bookings."

How strange, how coldly alien they now seemed, these grandiose marble columns, these galleries and high stucco ceilings, as if this were the palace of some shah, of a Harun al-Rashid; and yet during the war, after I returned from partisan warfare, I stayed in this hotel for some considerable time, returning to it each day as if it were my home. For a moment I had the sudden feeling that I was staying here now as well, and that at any moment I would enter the warm, cosy lift to go up to my floor, to my room; and then it all became impossibly distant, as if it had happened in some other country or some other century.

I sat down in a soft leather armchair and felt calm and contented.

...It was New Year's Eve, and party guests were arriving at the Moskva restaurant. In front of the main entrance, which was brightly festooned with seasonal illuminations, police sergeants were checking people's invitations.

Meanwhile in the hushed, deserted hotel three young men in steel-grey covert-cloth suits, new socks and new patent-leather shoes were ascending the marble staircase. They had taken off their coats downstairs, and when the commissionaire had asked: "Which room number?" they had said nothing, only looked him straight in the eye; and he had nodded, obediently taken their identical coats, all made at the same outfitter's, and their identical velour hats, handed them their tokens with a bow, and then with a serious, gloomily solemn expression watched them go.

They entered the heated festive crush of the restaurant via a service entrance and, striding with assurance between long banqueting tables that shone white and immaculate and groaned with the usual superabundance, made for a distant corner where a small separate table awaited them.

There they sat, looking like triplets with their grey eyes and blond hair curled in identical styles, clinking their glasses together formally, officially and a trifle sadly, drinking sweet port and off-handedly nibbling soya chocolate sticks, at the same time smirking enigmatically and languidly — perhaps because they found it amusing to be drinking, or perhaps for some other reason known only to themselves.

Why had they been brought here and provided with port and soya sticks, all paid for by official order? Who was celebrating and drinking away the last hours of freedom in these first hours of the New Year? Had they perhaps come for those three in pressed suits who were sitting on their own, apart from the rest, on tall bar stools with round leather seats, vigorously clinking their glasses together and muttering to each other gloomily, scarcely audibly?

Those on bar stools were my friends and I. We had no invitation cards — those long glossy cards with their gothic script and colourful pictures of New Year trees. We had also come in through that inside entrance as if we were hotel residents, newly arrived by train from Eastern Siberia; and when the Kremlin chimes had sounded and the band had let rip, we had run through a veritable fireworks display of confetti and flying champagne corks to slip behind a thick curtain; and that moment of full-throated jubilation, when all one's past years, all one's misfortunes, losses, pain and despair are suddenly and instantaneously forgotten, and there is only the future: already upon us, seen from on high, to the blare of music, in the nimbus of the chandeliers' hot light, and, as always and forever, holding out the promise of hope and happiness — that moment we spent behind the thick curtain, with only a chilly restaurant window for company, gazing out at Manege Square, which was silent and swept by eddying snow, and where a lone trolleybus, empty and frozen, was gliding past the dead street lamps like a toy.

But as soon as the first gust of excitement had passed, and the dancers rose from their tables, we left our hiding-place and set off down the stairs towards the bar, the three of us, smoking our cigarettes with a free-and-easy manner and assuming the air of invited guests who had tired of the jollifications.

Sitting on tall round bar stools with cherry-red leather seats, we clinked glasses and toasted the New Year with champagne. We drank to those who were not with us, and (articulating our toasts in whispers, or rather with lips and eyes alone) we drank to those who were being arrested that night — being dragged away from New Year trees and festive tables, having their medals and decorations torn off, the epaulettes crudely ripped from their shoulders; then we drank to those who had only had their arrest warrants written out that day, then to those who would have them written out tomorrow, and then to those who had only just been denounced anonymously. So we sat there, drinking...

"Who are you waiting for, citizen?"
The receptionist was standing in front of me; she was

dressed in a severe dark costume and gave off a strong, cloying scent of perfume.

"Who are you waiting for?" she repeated.

"Myself," I replied abruptly.

"That's against our house rules."

"What is?"

"Do you want me to spell it out for you, citizen — move on, or if you prefer we can discuss it elsewhere."

"Where's that then?"

"I think you know," she said.

I stood up and left quietly. The receptionist kept her eyes on me until I reached the doors, as did the commissionaire in his silver-braided peaked cap, standing by the entrance with his hands behind his back; and I left feeling as if I had stolen something or at least planned to do so.

Snow-laden lime trees glittered like tinfoil in the park on Theatre Square, and through the snowflakes falling slowly on the darkened city the Bolshoi Theatre with its columns dimly floodlit from below appeared as if in a picture from the last century.

I walked through the park, where the snow lay in deep drifts; along one of the railings stretched a column of long dark limousines with cream curtains.

This was clearly a far cry from the usual cheerful, chaotic scene, the regular evening convergence of ballet-lovers on the Bolshoi. It was a precise, almost military formation of identical limousines placed at fixed intervals, each with its paintwork gleaming like a mirror and without a scratch, each palatial in its dimensions. Even from a distance one could feel the highly charged electric field that separated them from the rest of the world. These were cars that had come down from roads at dizzy heights, from those rarefied expanses where no police direct the traffic, while our earthbound highways stood in reverence at the sight of their yellow headlights and coded number-plates framed by a border. They were not cars, but instruments: if one got near them one could smell, not burnt engine oil, but clean metal, the heavy cloth of greatcoats, asceticism, omnipotence.

These limousines would glide up to a special private entrance, and He would emerge, alone, like a god, followed by his aides-de-camp walking in file like apostles; and all around there would be deserted streets and a wary, magnetized silence.

Whenever these limousines gently drove off and then sped uphill with yellow headlights blazing and klaxons dinning like the croaking of so many frogs, they would be followed at the same speed by a line of Pobeda cars with Mercedes engines; and the cavalcade would sweep through the sleeping city noiselessly, like greased lightning, through traffic lights switched to green.

The chauffeurs in their leather coats and ministerial deerskin hats were standing bunched together in their little group, as if they were all members of the order, welded together (more firmly than any modern welding process could achieve) by their sworn complicity and by the perks and privileges of their special confidential status. They were not the main players, nor their assistants, nor even the assistants of those assistants; they were mere ancillaries, yet even so they were in the state service, and even when not working they inhabited that other, special, ozonized top-level world; and now as they talked among themselves they did so as if silently, as if without opening their mouths. And the silence was so immense, so deep: everything had been turned to stone and struck dumb. In the sky above the columns the horses had frozen in mid-flight beneath the dark, tattered winter clouds, and it seemed that at any moment they would be unable to endure this oppressive silence any longer and would fly off with the clouds, off into the great untrammelled universe of the sky.

Over by the steps of the Bolshoi Theatre several police

sergeants were pacing up and down, wearing coats of a superior quality not normally available to sergeants; while some silent dark shapes loitered, as if there by chance, in shadows next to the columns and under the snow-covered lime trees.

I stopped for a moment, bewitched by the Corinthian columns and low-lit horses of Apollo, bowled over by the eternal and majestic simplicity of their magical proportions; and already one of the shapes in a long coat was coming towards me. I came down to earth again and began to move away. It seemed as if the trees themselves were watching me sullenly and disapprovingly, also that the path that wound its way through the snowy park was leading me somewhere I had no earthly reason or necessity to go, and I tried heading off at an angle into the virgin snow; however, this felt utterly absurd and ridiculous, as well as looking very suspicious, so I continued plodding along the lonely, well-trodden path. A mysterious force was tugging at me, pulling me between the white trees and towards the columns; trying nevertheless not to look at the columns, or the cars, or the sergeants in their thin coats strolling up and down the deserted avenue in front of the columns — in fact not looking at anything, but just keeping my head down — I crossed the empty space in front of the Bolshoi Theatre, walking as if through a minefield.

The man in the long coat followed me with his eyes, and the chauffeurs in their ministerial hats looked round at me — almost all of them simultaneously — subjecting me to a searching gaze. I walked on as if beamed up to a high-voltage cable and crossed the road towards the Central Department Store, where in large windows that appeared greenish in the artificial light dummies were standing to attention, their faces like glazed earthenware, their lips carmine, as if made up with lipstick, the jackets on them stretched to bursting point by their broad manly chests; they also seemed like agents in disguise who had been assigned to stand in shop windows. I walked on in the blaze of neon lights and began to see double and even triple, until I reached the shadows on the corner of Kuznetsky Bridge Road. Only then did I feel how the tension had diminished and how tired I was.

I turned onto Kuznetsky.

The street was dead now; it was overhung by heavy buildings with caryatids that weighed down oppressively on me, and only the light, elegant dolls in the tall, mirror-like windows of the Fashion House injected an element of frivolity into this dismal street that was as dead and deserted as a graveyard; they spoke of the vanity of life, of the reduction of everything in this world in the final analysis to a charade acted out by puppets.

The main "Gastronom" food store was already closed. It was that final moment when the sales assistants were removing hams and cheeses from the refrigerated display cabinets and women working at cash tills were counting the takings; at the entrance a doorman in a sheepskin coat was appealing to latecomers in a considerate tone of voice: "No more now, please, citizens." Just then a low grey vehicle marked 'Liaison Service' drew up in front of the shop, and a money-collector got out, wearing a leather jacket with a flared waist and carrying a canvas sack; he rapped on the door with a key, and the doorman opened up from inside.

Everything was shut and in darkness: shops, cafes, snack bars selling pelmeni or pies; only the ice-cream kiosks were brightly lit, and there was also a man looking pinched with cold who was selling the new academic edition of Dante from an open stand. I stopped and leafed through some pages of the Inferno.

There was a light on in a tobacconist's kiosk on the corner, and through the iced-up window a little old man wearing glasses could be seen among the many-coloured packets, looking rather flummoxed as he clicked away at the beads of an abacus. I tapped gently at the window, but the old man didn't even lift his head. Then I knocked harder and shouted: "Belomor!"

The old man jumped as if someone had shouted: "Fire!" and looked up at me with startled, sad eyes, in which one could see his unhappiness at finding the till short of cash. Miming my urgent need of a smoke, I repeated: "Belomor!"

As if under hypnosis the old man slid back the little hatch and without a word chucked out a packet with the familiar blue lines representing canals.

"Thank you, thank you very much," I said.

Through the glass I saw the old man apprehensively shake the abacus and start all over again.

I lit up eagerly, drawing the smoke deep into my lungs several times, and at once I seemed to feel better, as if I had spoken to an old friend and he had managed to calm me down a bit.

I walked through stonily vacant streets, deserted as during an air-raid warning, that seemed as if they had had their heart and tongue removed. Long, antiquated shopping arcades built in neo-classical style; all those little drapers', haberdashers', drysalters' and hardware shops; millionaires' residences — all without exception were now occupied by various minor official organizations (some of them exceedingly minor).

Stretching in a never-ending sequence were the dark, dead windows of countless ministries and government departments (which had proliferated, gemmated from each other, been divided, re-united and then split up again, and become swollen and dropsied), also of various so-called voluntary societies which were nothing more than empty facades — just a signboard, staffing list and letter head; these had deluged and filled to overflowing former inns, arcades, boyars' residences, cabmen's taverns, military academies, brothels, palaces, peep-shows, restaurants, hotels and dancing schools, seeping into ancient walls, into the towers large and small of the Kitaigorod Wall, the cellars and underground vaults of Maroseyka, Varvarka and Solyanka Streets.

Each entrance displayed a vast number of signboards and plates jostling for space one above the other — haughty gold ones, small ones, some grey and insignificant, some that were puny excuses for signs — all proclaiming in intricate Tartar-style lettering the presence of various trusts, agencies, offices, bureaux, branches. And through the windows could be seen ink-stained office desks, glass-fronted cabinets stuffed with files, iron safes. Desks stood in the entrance hall and under staircases, almost spilling out into the street. Everywhere there were checkpoints — booths with little sliding glass hatches — as in a prison camp. Iron gates would open with a clang, and couriers would drive out in cars or on motorcycles.

I came into Nogin Square. Here was the vast building of the former People's Commissariat of Industry, where Sergo Ordzhonikidze had once presided as People's Commissar, and which I had come to from Siberia as a teenager, together with some furnace-workers and steel founders. Now it housed the Ministry of Coal, the Ministry of Oil, the Ferrous Metal Industry, the Non-Ferrous Metal Industry, and assorted directorates; and the whole lot was lit up — was ablaze with light — and seemed to be humming like a beehive.

Stalin was not asleep; nor were his ministers, nor their deputies, assistants, advisers, secretaries and stenographers; nor were the chief accountants, chief geologists, chief steel founders, chief rolling mill operatives, chief technologists, messengers, canteen assistants, army bicyclists, medical orderlies, high-frequency telephonists, guards; nor, the length and breadth of our great country, were the secretaries of regional committees, the commanders of military districts, the managers of factories, of mines — the whole country had reorganized itself, adapting its day and its whole life to a routine dictated by the metabolism of our insomniac Generalissimo.

As long as he was not asleep but up and on the go somewhere, standing by a globe and smoking his pipe, nobody could remain calm or feel anything but trepidation in their heart; nobody slept — they all waited, sometimes just sitting at their desks, watching the telephone.

I walked up Solyanka Street, then Pokrovka. The streets were dead and the windows of shops too brightly lit: their light was lifeless, senseless and somehow feigned.

I walked past a stationery shop, and in the neon light all its beautiful and remarkable wares were so clearly visible: open cases of drawing instruments with compasses and dividers on green or black velvet, magic lanterns, penknives. And I took it all in with the excited enthusiasm of boyhood, savouring it, possessing it, holding it in my hand — and suffering pangs of longing.

To tell the truth, I had never had any of this. How was it that I'd missed out? Now I walked along the street, pondering on the number of magnificent and marvellous things that had passed me by. I had never had a kaleidoscope, never had a gun or a reflex camera, never raced through the streets on a bicycle, wearing a cycling cap and glimpsing mirages in the heat haze. In later years I had never once sat behind a steering wheel, had never felt the gentle, obedient quivering of an eighty-horse-power engine and then driven past nocturnal buildings, nocturnal shadows, along the asphalt highway, whether to some specific destination or not.

And there's something else: Madrid, Rio de Janeiro, the Canary Islands, the Balearics, Tierra del Fuego — they do actually exist, don't they? Or was all this just on that blue map of the world, there, in my childhood, in the stationer's shop?

Somewhere in the side streets off Pokrovka a police whistle

shrilled, followed by what sounded like the crack of a gunshot; and the empty city's nocturnal fear, its stony terror, seized me, propelling me forwards towards the light, towards the broad Ring Road as wide as a river.

The snow-storm swirled as if in open countryside, and the street lamps receded in the mist, glowing yellow and distant.

A lone trolleybus with snow on its roof was gliding along, frozen, making a crunching sound. It looked as if it had blundered into this wide road by mistake and now, feeling bitterly cold in the whistling, exposed wind, was in a hurry to get down to Orlikov Lane as soon as possible; and one could imagine a warm refuge waiting for it there at the end of its journey. After all, it couldn't just carry on going round and round in the snow-storm like that forever.

The street was spacious and empty, with an air of free-and-easy living; fronting the pavement were the marble entrance porticos of some new residential blocks for the party elite, and the wide orange and blue windows of individual apartments in these buildings shone with a warm, cosy light through the swirling snow, speaking of tranquillity and enjoyment of life; while next to them in sharp contrast were the dull, narrow, unwashed windows of poky little rooms in communal apartments, above the flimsy curtains of which one caught glimpses of shadows on the walls, with old furniture all around. And I recognized my own life, irredeemably hopeless and dingy.

Entering a solitary, forgotten telephone kiosk, I dialled a number. From the dead, icy receiver I heard: "Hello, who's there?"... I listened, greedily absorbing that peaceful, homely voice, and then quietly hung up. I didn't have the strength to speak: everything had gone numb inside me. I walked on past darkened shop windows. Suddenly a wailing, jangling din started up right next to me, making me jump. The massive black iron box of a police telephone on the corner was whooping frantically, shuddering and vibrating.

A traffic policeman in huge felt boots and a sheepskin coat had left his post and, covered from head to toe in hoar-frost, was walking slowly towards the sound of the alarm. He opened the iron box and took out the receiver, giving me a sideways glance, and I quickly walked on without looking round, so that no-one should think I was eavesdropping.

I don't know why, but any time that I feel out of sorts and depressed I make for the hustle and bustle of a railway station, drawn, as if to the source of my own life, to that electrically charged atmosphere of expectation and hope; and I am excited and reassured by the mirage of renewal, by the illusory feeling that if only one were to get on a train and leave, there would be a fresh start to everything — that it's all just waiting to happen somewhere out there, in the far blue yonder.

This is evidently a habit shared by that whole generation which started out in life with farewells at railway stations, which in its youngest and most impressionable years broke with everything that had gone before — with its childhood and adolescence, its home, its first teachers — for good, for keeps, for ever and ever.

To this day I cannot help being stirred by the distant whistle of a locomotive in the stillness of the night, although by now I know well enough what the invariable outcome will be. On its highest and most poignant note the whistle sweeps you off and on into open fields, into the distance, beyond the forests, beyond the horizon, and you have no strength — you simply have no desire to resist: each time you imagine once more that it's all just beginning, that it's all ahead of you, that it's all just waiting to happen.

Kalanchevskaya Square with its three railway stations was brightly lit, living its unsleeping nocturnal life. Passers-by were darting hither and thither, and all the time there were cars arriving at the station or leaving.

I headed for the Kazan Station. A fat woman checking

tickets at the entrance barked: "Tickets!" I said I had one and went through without stopping. I was hit by the smell of soot from the engines, disinfectant, nappies, and air that was so thick inside the station that you could hardly breathe it in — it was almost like steam.

As with people, so with stations: no two are alike. For example, the Leningrad (or as it used to be known, October, and before that, Nicholas) Station is a swanky, aristocratic one which has about it the feel of important business, of official assignments; it is empty and echoing: the passengers — film stars, academicians, generals, foreigners — arrive by taxi just before the departure of the 'Red Arrow', carrying briefcases or small artistic suitcases, and go straight to the platform, never dropping into the restaurant on the way; rarely will you encounter a passenger carrying a bundle or sack. The Kazan Station, by contrast, is a folksy, plebeian, multi-ethnic station — a station for passengers setting out on long journey to distant republics who carry enormous wickerwork baskets or wooden suitcases with padlocks, and who arrive well in advance, perhaps even a whole day before their train is due to leave, and use the station to live and sleep in.

By the main wall stood the Leader in marble: unassailable, five metres tall, wearing a calf-length greatcoat and semi-military peaked cap, his hand tucked into the breast of the coat; and around his pedestal swarmed and seethed the travelling populace, clamouring and buzzing, picking at hard-boiled eggs and peeling oranges, snoring, brooding, falling asleep, waking up, and feeling miserable; but he gazed into the distance, only into the distance, his hand tucked into the breast of his coat and his disdainfully stony face directed above their heads, seeing what nobody saw, or could see.

Here there were aged men like pilgrims, Siberian peasants in sheepskin coats and deerskin boots, Uzbeks in their colourful quilted robes and embroidered skull-caps, sailors of the Pacific fleet, women from Ryazan, Kalmyks, tribesmen from the Altai, workmen from the Urals, Astrakhan fishermen, river folk from the Volga — the whole of Russia was here, thirsting for a change of scene, driven by the urge to move on; they all had their various dreams, hopes and illusions shining before them like the lights of a locomotive.

Passengers were sitting or lying on the bony seats of long brown oak benches that displayed the crest of the People's Commissariat of Transport on their tall backs; some were sleeping, others had set out provisions on their suitcases and were having supper, while others simply did nothing, but just waited in a state of torpor.

Above sleeping children many-coloured balloons swayed from side to side on strings: masses of them, red, blue and green, all over the station concourse. It seemed as though they were the children's dreams. For some reason there were lots and lots of ring-shaped bread rolls — nearly every other person had a garland of these rolls; and there were also string bags containing ripe oranges and sacks which from their appearance held long white French loaves.

The station was filled with the continuous restrained buzz of nocturnal conversations, and the windows were rattling and vibrating.

"Shush now, or I'll hand you over to the policeman," said a woman to her child, who had just woken up, and the child became silent, gazing in enchantment at a blue dream with crimson edging.

A slip of a girl, chilled to the bone in her little fur jacket and thin shoes, was warming herself by a metro ventilation grill; skinny, with the cheeky snub-nosed little face of a corrupted doll and green eyes, she looked frozen through, vivacious, artful. With a kind of brazen unconcern she fired glances at pot-bellied types on official business as they walked past with bulging briefcases, or at various flashily dressed spivs, and sniggered; and then all at once she would exultantly produce an affectionate smile, a sweet childish smile, for somebody young and attractive.

She looked at me and raised her eyebrows in a surprised sort of way, as if passing on a secret sign.

I slowed down, glanced at my watch and stopped to peer earnestly and anxiously through one of the wide windows, looking out at the street as if expecting somebody, as if somebody were due to arrive any moment now.

She was one of those vagrant girls, one of that unhappy legion of orphans who came to Moscow to become film stars, some travelling with seat reservations and some without any ticket at all, and from whose ranks hard-up artists still chasing fame were in the habit of picking up live-in models.

They had no fixed address, no residence permit, and sometimes not even any identity documents, just their birth certificate. They would doss down at the places of other girls or old women they had casually befriended, sleeping in the cubby-holes of lift attendants and Tartar janitors, or on some occasions just with a man they had met in the street, or sometimes even in the stairwell of a building, right at the top in an unfrequented passageway leading to the attic.

They would usually gang up with other girls who were the same size as they were, and then swap outfits. If you looked carefully, you would see the same skimpy jacket, tatty plaid skirt with a fringe or little bronze horse on a chain, worn by different girls in turn.

They would usually congregate in the mornings, coming together from the various parts of the city where they had spent the night in fitful sleep, all except those who had been summoned by postcard to attend at the film studios on that particular morning, or were going there in response to an advertisement or at the personal invitation of a film director they had happened to meet (or cameraman, studio head, assistant, lighting technician — or even just some con-man they had bumped into); or those who happened to be enthroned somewhere in Sretensky Lane or Maslovka Street or in Izmaylovo that morning: in the nude and shivering with cold, posing for some artist, or sculptor covered in clay or plaster of Paris, who because of his youth and the fevered excitement of his working didn't feel the cold; or who that morning were crowding around the entrance to the personnel department of the Central Department Store or the Fashion House on Kuznetsky, or were jostling with all the others in the noisy, unrestrained hurly-burly of the actors' employment bureau on Neglinnaya Street, trying to get taken on as Soviet 'gerls' in unofficial music-hall shows, with illicit jazz bands, or as snowmaiden assistants to Grandfather Frost. Anyway, the rest would gather in a bunch early in the morning at some pre-arranged rendezvous where it was nice and warm: at the Central Telegraph Office or the Central Post Office, or at some snack-bar selling pies or pelmeni on Petrovka; and when everybody had arrived they ransacked all their pockets, digging out the small change — silver, and in some cases even notes — and put it into a kitty to pay for tea and hot pies all round; while consuming these they discussed, debated and planned where and how to spend the day, and then used the toilet to swap blouses, shoes or sweaters.

After this they would pop into the shop, even though they had no more than a packet of cheap cigarettes and a box of matches in their handbag. The evenings would find them in a cocktail bar, perched on high revolving stools with their legs crossed and cigarettes in their mouths, talking about this and that and sipping some greenish cocktail through a straw.

"I've smartened up his image."

"And I'll just have to grin and bear it tomorrow," replied another girl, gloomily.

They were never to be seen in a single group together at night. They would scatter all over the city, but mainly within the confines of the Ring Road, where in tiny rooms in communal apartments there lived all those artists, film and stage directors, operetta singers, actors, lawyers, librettists, dancers, sketch writers, sculptors, legal advisers, simultaneous interpreters: members of the free professions, bachelors old and young.

I continued to look out of the window. Snowflakes were falling, and the pavement outside looked empty and inhospitable. I took a cautious sideways glance at the young girl, and as if she were already prepared for this and had rehearsed it all in her mind beforehand, she smiled openly and vivaciously, as if to say: "You're not really waiting for anybody — why don't you come here instead, and we'll have a talk? You see, I'm just as lonely and fed up as you are."

I understood, and signalled back in the same Morse code: "I'm coming," and moved towards her like a moth towards the light.

"Hello, good evening," I said.

"Hi there," the girl replied.

The mascara had run from her eyelashes, which were wet from melted snow, and she consulted her make-up mirror to carry out a minor repair.

"Shall we have something to warm us up?"

"Why not."

She took a couple of sweets from her pocket, popped one in her mouth and gave the other to me.

"It's a long-playing one," she said.

The sweet, a glacier mint, was cold and took a long time to dissolve in the mouth.

"What's your name?" I asked.

"What's yours?"

I told her.

"Well, my name's in that opera, Eugene Onegin. Have a guess."

"Tatyana?"

"Brilliant!" she said, impressed.

"So where do you live, Tatyana?" I asked.

"My boy friend's just got married, the sod," she said without malice and burst out laughing.

"So where are you going to sleep?"

"Why, d'you live on your own?" she asked.

A rather swanky, conceited-looking sort of fellow suddenly appeared in the deserted entrance hall of the metro; he was covered with a dusting of snow and wore an astrakhan cap with an indented crown. I took an immediate and instantaneous dislike to him. (Why that style of cap? It was well known that they all wore the kind with ear-flaps — or perhaps he was one of the top brass?)

Wet from the snow, he walked across to a telephone booth, taking long energetic strides, then closed the door of the booth behind him and began dialling a number. He was on the phone for a terribly long time, yet didn't speak at all. I could see quite plainly that he didn't even once open his mouth, but kept putting the coin in and dialling the number; and whether because it was engaged or there was just nobody answering, he kept replacing the receiver and then immediately starting all over again. And all the time for some reason I had the impression that he was looking in our direction over the top of the dial.

"What does he want of us?" I said.

"I couldn't give a monkey's," said Tatyana.

She bent down and, as she was straightening her stocking, clumsily and as if by accident lifted her skimpy skirt a fraction higher; and etched in blue above the stocking was a tattoo: 'So few years lived, so many errors made'.

"Perhaps it's you he's after?" I said.

She shrugged her delicate shoulders and, laughing, said: "So what — I'm not scared."

Ah, if only I too could have said: "I'm not scared," and in the same defiant, glib and detached way!

But I was scared — very scared; and everything kindled by this chance encounter — the flushed excitement that had taken me back momentarily to that old, familiar and pleasantly cheerful world of carefree living — had all suddenly cooled and melted away; and all that was left was that round face (which I had come to hate by now) behind the glass of the telephone booth, like a wound-up mechanical doll, endlessly turning the dial.

"Anyway, I'm off now," I said.

"Where are you going?" asked Tatyana in surprise. "And what for?"

"I've got to go."

I ran down into the metro and looked back once again at the end of the corridor to check whether the swanky fellow in the astrakhan cap was tailing me.

Had he really had to make such an urgent phone call at this time of night and then been unable to get through, and was this why he'd been so on edge in the phone booth? Or had all that been play-acting, and had he in fact been waiting for me? Or perhaps for her — waiting until she was free, until I'd agreed to her terms or not as the case may be, or until she'd got fed up with me and seen that I was a dead loss, when she would turn her attention to him? This would explain why he'd kept turning in the booth, showing off his astrakhan cap from the front and in profile. I wondered what had happened after I'd left: had she given him the same smile and gazed at him with the same intimate eyes as she had at me, having in that instant forgotten completely and for all time that I even existed?

The metro carried me off into the distance, with only lights in the tunnel to be seen through the windows: flaring, fading, swallowed by darkness; and when the train stopped, people got on and people got off, and brightly lit platforms, white and red marble, glided past.

A sparrow had inexplicably managed to fly into the metro and get as far as the platform. It was a common grey little urban sparrow, its feathers ruffled with fear, clearly unhappy; and a supervisor in a red peaked cap was shouting at it and shooing it away with his signalling disc, as if it were threatening to cause a derailment. The sparrow, however, darted nimbly back and forth, flying between the marble columns and sculptured symbols of modern society abutting on them. Frightened and dishevelled, it landed first of all on a miner's lamp, then flew to a steel founder's round hat, then alighted on a border guard's sub-machine-gun, then sought refuge behind a partisan's dog. Passengers stopped to observe this elaborate chase. Finally the little sparrow flew up high and for a long time beat its wings against the stone vaults, trying unsuccessfully to find a way out into blue sky.

I looked round, to be struck immediately by the sight of a face gazing at me attentively. Whether this was really so or I had just imagined it, I began to panic again: I hid behind a column and waited to see whether he would appear, whether he was waiting for me. Then I got into a train that wasn't going in my direction.

Wandering through labyrinthine passageways, I ended up somewhere strange. There wasn't a soul there — only marble columns, and behind them an endless marble corridor with bluish buzzing light. A cold dead wind began to blow, I couldn't tell where from: it felt as though it were coming from a marble sarcophagus. And I was suddenly overcome by a feeling of the end, a feeling of doom. I raised my eyes and read: 'No entry', 'No exit'.

I tore back again, heading for the escalators. They had already stopped operating. I started running up one of them, towards the blue light at the top. I was running to get out, as if scrambling out of a well.

A policeman in a thick navy-blue coat was standing at the top. He glanced at me and went to open the heavy entrance door.

I walked out into an unfamiliar, dimly lit square and saw tattered, dark, rapacious clouds scudding across the sky; and I heaved a deep sigh. How dreary they were, those blocks of flats, so distant and of no concern to me, and the cross roads, and all this life that knew nothing of me and of which I knew nothing.

I got on a trolleybus. It glided through unfamiliar streets and stopped in a dark, forgotten, lonely back street. This seemed a good place to get off. Rushing for the door, I suddenly thought I saw somebody waiting for me in a recess next to one of the buildings: standing with his back pressed to the wall in the shadows of the recess, waiting for me. And I recoiled so abruptly that the door banged shut within an inch of my face; the driver looked round angrily, and the passengers grinned as if to say: "That'll teach you to nod off." My heart was pounding like a drum. How on earth could he have known that I would decide to get off at that precise stop? Or were they waiting at every stop? And did they know everything in advance, everything in the world, including things about yourself that even you didn't know yet?

For a long time after this I sat quietly in a corner of the trolleybus, not daring to get off. Mysterious nocturnal streets floated past; many times the trolleybus stopped, turned off to the right or left, glided past some long factory buildings. People got on and off, and I examined them carefully. Illuminated shop windows flashed by, and dark, grey, sleeping rows of buildings.

By now it seemed as if the trolleybus had lost its way and was going round aimlessly in circles, with the street rushing past, merging into one blurred building, like a grey stone scroll unfolding: endless, hopeless; parsimonious dim light; mute silence; and soothing, patient sleep, broken into by the driver sounding his horn, the clicking of the gear lever, and a discreet, gentle hissing as the doors opened and closed.

When I came to, the dark ribbon of the Moskva River was in full flow, with tufts of mist above its black waters. By the stone parapet, welded into ice fringing the river bank, stood the Seagull' restaurant; a triple light shone out through the iced-up panes of its little narrow windows. For a moment I was deafened by the frenetic music of the restaurant's jazz band. Spread out on the far side of the river were the free, snow-covered woods of the Sparrow Hills, and as always I felt a hankering to move out there and thought how stifling, how terrible, how wrong-headed it was to live in the stone canyons of the city.

At one of the stops the trolleybus emptied, and I was left on my own. At this point I had the impression that the conductor, with his bag slung from one shoulder, pretending to be asleep, was actually keeping a watchful eye on me from behind deceitfully half-closed lids. I stood up and walked to the door, trying to keep my eyes from meeting those of the deceitful conductor. And then I suddenly noticed that the driver, looking in the rear mirror above his head as he turned the steering wheel, was also watching me most attentively as I moved towards the door. Phantom buildings flashed past; the conductor and driver were in league, taking me by a predetermined route to the required destination.

The trolleybus went round and round, turning this way and that like a cat on hot bricks, driving into lonely nocturnal streets that were deserted and cheerless, as if the houses in them were really mausoleums and gravestones; and then suddenly a square: a burst of incandescence, a blaze of neon light, a bright and colourful urban merry-go-round — but also deserted, gloomy, meaningless.

I stood by the door, waiting to get off.

But the trolleybus sped down a long unending street without

stopping, carrying me away, with only the hissing of its tyres to be heard.

All at once the lights went out in the trolleybus, and the street broke loose, as though it had been snipped off, or hurled away by the force of an explosion; a dark open field sprinkled with stars floated gently towards us, and the trolleybus, skirting a little park, came to a sudden halt.

"La-a-ast stop," the conductor announced in a nasal voice, before finally falling asleep on his leather seat, with his ticket bag on his chest.

In all this vast country, throughout the whole land-mass from Batumi to Chukotka, there was, it seemed, nowhere for me to hide or find refuge. I could have gone to my sisters: as a matter of fact I had four, all in different towns; but their addresses were all recorded on numerous forms in the personnel department, and I would have been tracked down immediately.

Or what about other relatives? I didn't have any; that is, I probably did — uncles and aunts, cousins and second cousins who no doubt were grown up by now and probably had grown-up children of their own — but most of them I had never known, while any that I might have known I had either long since forgotten or not seen for years; I had taken no interest in family relationships, considering that sort of thing outdated and worthy only of my derision. To judge from my own example, it seemed to me that there were no family ties left at all in our country, that they had long since been severed, fragmented and completely shattered: first by the Civil War, when brother had fought against brother; then by the class struggle, when sons had not been answerable for their fathers, and when sons had denounced their fathers to the authorities; and then by the numerous mobilizations and evacuations, by the undermining of all the foundations laid down by our ancestors, and by fear. Fear drove a wedge between brothers and sisters within the family; everything dissolved and vanished in its sulphuric acid: love, affection, gratitude, mutual assistance, and succour, and conscience. And anyway, who needed me in my present state at such a period of heightened class tension?

I felt deeply uneasy, surrounded by this night, by these frozen back streets with their dim, gloomy lamps. Only now could one see what an old, weary city this was: a city that had endured everything, had put up with everything, and was now doggedly and patiently enduring this cold, empty, hopeless night as well. Yet what was the point? Wouldn't it be exactly the same tomorrow, and the day after tomorrow, and in a year's time? Even ten years from now there would be the same empty, icy, blizzard-swept night.

Suddenly I emerged into a wide snowbound square with a frozen pond. I swept the snow off a bench and sat down under some trees. The wind moaned above my head. I thought I could see stars falling.

Ranged on all sides were houses of deathly appearance, standing in strange and startling juxtaposition: palatial residences of the old aristocracy, stone-built and of pleasing proportions, cheek by jowl with dreary red-brick tenement blocks blackened from the soot of portable stoves; then a grey, bare, rational le Corbusier box that had gone up in the Thirties; and a massive new concrete block with decorative columns and turrets, containing flats reserved for generals. Windows on the various floors now lit up, now suddenly went dark: the mysterious life of the night, unknown to me and alien, flared up and died away, flared up and died away; and this was like Morse code, like dots and dashes, dashes and dots: as if the lights of the city were communicating with one other, flashing some arcane message unique to them and destined to pass into non-existence. Some of the windows, however, blazed steadily throughout the night. Whoever was there was having a party or swotting for exams; perhaps somebody was dying, or saying goodbye before going away for ever; or perhaps a search was being carried out.

How long the night is when you are not asleep! Longer than a whole lifetime.

I sat on the snow-covered bench somewhere in a public park, unsure of my exact whereabouts. The city did not exist, the night did not exist — nothing existed. There was just some kind of vacuum in time and space. Something within had been stretched to breaking point, had snapped. All my resources had been drained: I no longer wanted to think, to endure, to try to escape.

I did not have the strength to get up and walk; falling snow was beginning to blanket me, and once again all around me everything had been struck blind and deaf.

A cat ran past, then turned back and stopped in front of me. A black cat in the snow, with green eyes. Its green eyes flashed in the darkness, communicating a silent message to me, and I suddenly fancied that it had taken me for a cat that was just pretending to be a human being. I stood up, shook off the snow and walked on. The green eyes followed me for a long time.

The Milky Way, a pall of dust over the city, inched slowly towards dawn; a solitary neon light glimmered and pulsated aimlessly, tinting adjacent roofs with a scarlet twilight.

I was so tired that I felt nothing any more, but moved along the pavement like a disembodied shadow, not caring where I was going. From somewhere came an unexpected spring breeze, bringing with it a smell of the thaw: of meltwater, willow branches, freedom and all those dear things which I had once known and had now learned to do without.

And I had a sudden vision of quiet snowbound streets, yellow lights, crooked tinplate signs and an air of remote seclusion that was so resonant and fresh, so splendid, that my heart felt a stab of pain. Had all this really been part of my life? And had it all gone forever?

Slowly the street began to emerge, pale blue and unfamiliar, from a watery realm beneath the waves; while the houses stood with a glum expression as if expecting something from me. As if swept along on a current, I drifted through lightly falling snow with a hint of blue, to find myself in the familiar surroundings of Arbat Square, which, as in a fairy tale, lay spellbound in the white hush of dawn.

The outlines of the city blurred, looming through the light morning mist of bluish snow; and everything appeared unreal: not only this morning at the end of the night, but the previous day and the whole of my life as well.

This was me: me, walking along the dawning, deserted street; reflected in the early-morning shop windows along with clouds and extinguished street lamps; breathing in the fresh morning breeze. I seemed to see myself from the outside.

Blanketed with virgin snow, the Arbat stretched into the distance, and only the odd forgotten street lamp was still living its sad, nocturnal, wasted life.

No trolleybuses were running yet; so far only the first black, hesitant figures carrying string bags, in a hurry to join queues, were emerging from dark entrances and gateways. Then the first bus came along the street: it stopped at a crossroad, and several policemen in sheepskin coats jumped out, laughing and joking, while one wearing a longer sheepskin coat who had been standing at his post boarded the bus, to be met with ribald jests and expletives from those inside; then the bus drove on, and I saw it stop at the next crossroad, where once more several policemen came tumbling out before it drove on again.

Some road sweepers were bearing down on me, looking like angels in their white overalls and wielding their brooms with a flapping motion as if they were wings.

And then there were those strange, pathetic, solitary figures in beaver hats and overboots, hanging around, shifting from one foot to the other in gateways and chain smoking; their faces wore a dejected, cheesed-off expression, and at this dawn hour they looked like unfaithful husbands who had been locked out. They all looked at me as I passed, but this didn't bother me any more. No longer afraid of anything now, I examined them with brazen curiosity, and some turned away and looked in another direction.

Now I was back at the pet shop, with its goldfish in orange glowing water, surrounded by green and violet water plants. It didn't matter to them whether it was night or day, whether we were in the nineteenth or the twentieth century, whether mankind was thriving or in a parlous state: they carried on with their silent, monotonous existe ce, living their anonymous, onerous, miniature lives.

I stood looking at them for a while, and suddenly felt sorry for them. What were they darting about for, where were they in such a hurry to go, what was the point of all their hustle and bustle, and where would it all finally end?

I passed the window containing clocks and watches. Lots and lots of clocks and watches, all showing the same time in expectation of some important and inexorable event. Then came the old Arbat pharmacy: a restless, disconcerting half-light in the duty pharmacist's room, and in the window the assertive red rubber bulbs of enema-syringes.

Now I could see the grey building of our house, looking calm, as though nothing had happened. It had been like that throughout the night, as it had in the distant days of the Revolution and the New Economic Policy, 1937 and the war, living apart from and independent of the people who lived in it. Now in the dawn it was particularly apparent that, built of stone, indestructible and impassive, it had no wish or inclination to know anything about those people.

This frozen, dead house was quite alien to me. If there had been anywhere else to go, I would never have come back here.

Instead of approaching the house directly, I crossed to the pavement opposite and looked up at my window, which seemed to be filled with dark water. I felt that there was someone lurking there, lying in wait for me. Reaching the corner, I turned back and again looked at my window; and again I had the feeling that there was somebody in there.

Snow began to fall: no angry, stinging blizzard this time, but quiet, fluffy, gentle snowflakes, as in childhood or a fairy tale. And suddenly I felt happy and at peace. I stopped to gaze at this magic snow, at the brightening, swirling sky. I took off my hat and stood like this in the falling snow, resting after all the alarms, the fear, the ups and downs of this troubled night; and I vowed most solemnly that if everything turned out all right this time I would live, live each minute, each second, each moment of time — fast-flowing, exquisite, sublime, eternal time.

Slowly I climbed the back stairs, which resounded with that ponderous clanging that iron gives off at night.

This was the only time when even a communal apartment was quiet: when the radio and all the gramophones were silent and all the mincers asleep. And yet this silence had a deceptive feel to it: it was as if everything were filled with detonating gas and one had only to light a match, or shout, for it all to wake up, ignite, explode and be blown to smithereens.

I tiptoed quietly past the silent doors and could hear snoring, people moaning in their sleep, and the scrabbling of mice.

Old Mrs Soroka hadn't died yet, but was in the kitchen, simmering her soup; and the sickening, glutinous fumes of boiled-down fish bones enveloped my face as if with gum, making it difficult to breathe.

The old woman glanced at me with her light-blue, weathered eyes and said nothing; it wasn't even clear whether she had noticed me, or had just turned round at the noise. Her hands were worn from years of work, swollen and crimson, like a lobster's claws, and her overall complexion was reminiscent of a ham. I pushed the heavy kitchen door, unlocked the door into the dark, poky corridor with a large key, then another door with a small Yale key, and entered my room. It had been waiting for me; it was always waiting for me; it was frighteningly empty and bare. I had the feeling that something had been going on in the room during the eternity that I had been away: no doubt some shadows of my past life here, echoes of conversations, reflections of myself in the mirror had been alive in the room during all that time, acting on their own initiative while I was away; and now that I had appeared, this had all died away, subsided and become silent.

Sickening vapours from the fish bones being boiled down had seeped into the room through the cracks and keyhole and collected in a suffocating cloud.

It was quiet, and the street lamp by the window shone with a cadaverous light. I heard a clock striking nearby, followed by another in the distance. The unseeing, unseen, suffocating cloud hung there without leaving the room, choking me. And there was nothing in the world apart from this cloud.

It was good that it was getting light now, that soon the sun would be rising over the rooftops and I should not feel so afraid; and perhaps there was still life to look forward to, if not today, then in any case tomorrow: we had to hope, for hope was the only thing nobody could take away from us. Hope was no illusion: an illusion was something quite different, something imagined, uncertain, chimerical; while hope was an adamantine reality. So I sat there, trying to convince myself.

Now in the utter stillness of the dying night I suddenly heard the entrance door downstairs open with a squeaking of hinges and then slam shut on its tight rubber spring. Then silence and, clearly, the sound of footsteps on the iron staircase. No, I hadn't heard any footsteps, I'd just imagined it; and I started counting: one, two, three, four, five... Just as I reached fifteen, somebody came in — he was already upstairs and would ring the bell at any moment. I listened intently, but the bell didn't ring — perhaps it was broken, in which case he would be knocking at the door any moment now. Again I listened, but there was silence. Perhaps they were standing at the door; perhaps they had a skeleton key and at any minute would unlock the door themselves...

'To Be Filed in Perpetuity'

For almost all of his conscious life, for as far back as he could remember, he had been pursued by an enigma: some unknown, undiscovered transgression that was buried somewhere in his grey personal file — that file which he had never seen in his life and probably never would.

It might have taken the form of a denunciation written by a friend on a sheet of paper torn from a school exercise book, or a report submitted on an official form, or a telegram with the red rubber stamp of an administrative department. Or perhaps it was just his imagination that there was one single transgression; perhaps it was constantly being renewed — perhaps it was immediately replaced with a new one whenever it had withered and become obsolete and ludicrous.

This undiscovered, hidden transgression followed him from town to town by invisible paths and with the speed of a despatch rider; and every time his name cropped up — whether in connection with a new job or military rank, an award, special privilege or permit, or a passport for foreign travel — then at once the Morse signals would start to tap out, sounding the alarm.

And this transgression, undiscovered and unreal, like his own shadow, followed him constantly, passing from youth to maturity and middle age without ever growing old, and would probably go with him into old age; one day in winter, decked out in full-dress uniform, it would probably join the crowd following his coffin, mingling with the dark overcoats and beaver-lamb hats; and, stopping at the side of his grave, it would not be content until it had heard the thud of frozen clods of earth on the lid of his coffin; only then would it depart with a sigh, to sleep in the hideously grey cardboard file specially reserved for it, which bore the stamp: 'To be filed in perpetuity' and a photograph of its owner: young, carefree, full of youthful faith and dreams.

Boris YAMPOLSKY (1912-1972) was a prolific novelist and journalist in the late 1950s and 1960s, but his major novel, *The Old Arbat* (*Moskovskaya Ulitsa*), written in the 1960s, was banned by the censor. It was kept safe by writer friends, and published only with the coming of perestroika.

The Old Arbat examines the inner state of a hunted man, his fears and his loneliness. In this respect it recalls Raskolnikov's tortured wandering around St Petersburg in Dostoevsky's *Crime and Punishment*. Unlike Raskolnikov, however, who really was guilty of murder, Yampolsky's hero is innocent and only wishes he knew what his supposed guilt is all about. At the same time he is not at all surprised to find himself being followed and hence, no doubt, doomed to eventual arrest. He has seen it happen to other, equally innocent people, each of whom was sure his own case was a mistake, that he would be released shortly, and that all the others in his position really were "enemies of the people". Yampolsky's hero has no such illusions. He knows what awaits him once the KGB get him in their clutches.

When he reads in the newspapers about the Jewish "Doctors' Plot" he knows that his days too are numbered.

First there are strange telephone calls whose purpose is obviously to soften him up. He is openly followed wherever he goes. Next his friends abandon him, and he is left completely alone with his thoughts and fears. Like Yampolsky himself the hero saw action in the Second World War and was fearless, but now, in the Stalinist atmosphere of witch-hunting and political intolerance, he is paralyzed by uncontrollable terror. It is impossible simply to disappear, there is nowhere to flee to, and no one to turn to for help.

Yet at some point his hopelessness produces an inner freedom which gives the hunted man strength to resist. Yampolsky's anatomy of fear evolves into a description of how to overcome fear.

For reasons of space the novel has been considerably abridged for this edition leaving out flashbacks into the hero's past: the revolutionary enthusiasm of the 1930s and the difficult but heroic war years. Also deleted for this edition are most of the scenes in the communal apartment and the portraits of its residents that reflect, like a drop in the ocean, the whole society in the grips of totalitarianism. The whole novel is 300 pages long.

SUPPLEMENT

Facts Supporting Fiction

Lev Anninsky

Confessions of the Sixties Generation

From an interview with Glas

At some point practically every generation finds itself bitterly criticized for everything that has gone wrong in its time. We too blamed our fathers for all the intractable problems they bequeathed us.

The early Bolsheviks, like the early Christians, heroically sought to create a just society on earth at the cost of human sacrifice. The front-line generation fought for their socialist motherland during the Second World War. And then came the "shestidesyatniks", the post-war "sixties generation", who clung to the illusion that, given the right social reforms and wise leadership, life in Russia would improve, and that what had been built in Russia under Stalin had nothing in common with real communism.

We honestly believed in "socialism with a human face". We could not decide whether we had failed to realize mankind's age-old dream of a just society because human nature was not up to it, or because our leaders were useless. But we knew no other system and tried doggedly to improve the only one we did know and within which we had grown up.

Whatever people may say today, tsarist Russia was not exactly a paradise either, with its anti-Jewish pogroms, its poverty, corruption, backwardness, bureaucracy, famines, and general inefficiency. No wonder all decent people wanted an end to it.

We lived in a climate of all-pervading fear. Our generation was raised on fear. I learnt to live within that fear while maintaining my inner freedom. I knew perfectly well what I could and what I couldn't say in public. For example, I couldn't mention that my mother was Jewish. It was instinctive. I knew how to behave in the company of others my own age in order to avoid getting beaten up. I knew how to live in the Soviet Union while nevertheless retaining my sanity and my secret freedom. I didn't know how many people were languishing in the Gulag, but I did know you were well advised to keep your mouth shut. From early childhood I knew you were always in danger of running into trouble with the authorities. The risk of imprisonment was very real for all of us.

I knew that the system was cruel and merciless, that it would kill you if you got in its way, and so I survived as best I could. It seemed you had either to persecute others or be persecuted yourself. Tens of millions of Russians were content to be jailers and informers, although many of those were themselves eventually jailed. Only thanks to my instinct for survival did I manage to avoid being either a jailer or a jailbird.

There were a number of careers I could have embarked on, but I knew the price. Like many other people I was approached by the KGB with an offer to collaborate with them, but my rejection was so emphatic that the offer was never repeated. There was nothing they could deprive me of. I had nothing that could be taken away.

I had difficulty publishing my essays, and they were often severely edited, so I learnt to write in Aesopian language, putting my message across by implication. Yes, I lied in my articles and public speeches, but I always hinted at the truth, and my readers and listeners got the message. I adapted brilliantly to the need to get round the censorship, nobody did it better than me. I adapted honestly to the falsehood that ruled our lives. I had always to play a role which was imposed on me, but I played it so as to indicate clearly that it was only a role.

I joined no dissident movements. Their aggressiveness was equally alien to me. I wouldn't have dreamt of openly protesting on Red Square against government policies. I had come to recognize that the system had been created to suit our particular nation perfectly, a nation which did not want to know the truth and preferred lies. The only alternative possible was downright terror and pogroms. I grew up within that system knowing just what it was worth, but knowing at the same time how to be safe within it.

Russia being what she is, I still believed we were heading towards a bright future, but my instinct for survival warned me not to try swimming against the tide. It was pointless. The system would simply crush you and move on.

Despite the harsh reality of Russian socialism we tried to find grains of truth in socialist theories, truths a decent person could identify with. We focussed on the humanitarian aspects of socialism, even when information about the Gulag started seeping out. The more we learnt about the horrors of totalitarianism the more confused we became. We retreated from Stalin to Lenin and then, as more and more appalling details came to light, we retreated back further into socialist history, to Plekhanov.

When everything started crumbling about us we crumbled too, together with our country and its ideology. But to this day we believe that socialism does have a human face. You have only to reread the classics of socialist literature. Socialism was our religion. For all its anti-Christian nature it shares many fundamental ideas with Christianity. The people who joined socialist movements were good people. Later they realized the futility of their struggle, but many gave their lives for humanity's eternal dream of social justice.

The system has been destroyed, but those who destroyed it did not recognize that it provided a refuge of sorts, and now we have no refuge and the rain pours straight down on our heads.

We happened to live in a period of historical U-turns. Any generation would be at a disadvantage under such circumstances. Our fathers believed that they had, in the main, succeeded in building socialism. So what if it collapsed later? They also defended Russia and its socialist achievements from the Nazi invasion. But today's young people say, "Why did you bother? We'd be better off now under the Germans."

It's easy enough to be brave today. Who is to say what it means to be brave today? They shout on all corners about the crimes of Lenin. I don't execrate Lenin. I didn't in the past, and I'm not going to start now. I prefer to remain true to the ideals of my youth.

I doubt that the present generation would do any better than we did. I think things would have turned out exactly the same. It's not that our generation failed to find the right way, the whole country was groping in the dark and could not see light anywhere. Russia still hasn't found the right way. She is still searching.

I agree that we were naive, ignorant and weak, but those who were not naive were outright scoundrels. They knew what was going on but kept mum. Most people knew nothing. We believed we were building a bright future. Only after the war were we less certain, but we still couldn't understand what had gone wrong. Was it the war, or were Russians only capable of heroism and incapable of day to day hard work? Was it really possible to build socialism in one country? Perhaps it could only be built in one family?

You couldn't overthrow Stalin before the country was ready for it. The statues of Stalin were toppled by the same gorillas who erected them. You can't change the character of the Russian people overnight any more than you can rewrite Russian history. It is as it is, and we had better just accept the fact. In the past falsehood reigned supreme, but like a distorting mirror it reflected the truth about the country.

Yes, Russia has had a terrible history, but I do not reject a single year of that history. It is mine and I want no other. I've always known that you can't change life on the grand scale, but every second of my life I have tried to change things for the better on my own tiny scale.

Things could only be changed on a molecular level. I'm still working on that level. There are other falsehoods we have to live with today, other temptations and illusions.

During the siege of the White House in 1993 all I thought about was that those were my children fighting on both sides of the barricades, all of them the children of my country, Russia. The only children I have, and the only country I have. That is why I didn't take sides, not then and not now.

Valery Agranovsky

excerpt from

Reminiscences of a Journalist Dynasty

My father spent eight months in solitary confinement in a basement cell of the Krasnoyarsk NKVD prison awaiting his verdict. Under the rules for solitary confinement he was not supposed to see live people. Meals were pushed in through a hatch by a warder when he had ascertained through the spy-hole that the prisoner was asleep. My father could only glimpse a hand pushing the plate. He would try to stay awake so that he should at least see this human hand, but his jailers knew that trick and were far more patient than their prisoners. God knows why they took such pains to observe that senseless order.

Very soon father lost all sense of time or of any other points of reference. He could no longer rely on the alternation of his waking and sleeping hours. His meals were invariably the same: a plateful of thin porridge, a piece of coarse black bread, and a mug of hot water. I always wondered how the people who devised this fiendish system would get on if they had to change places with their victims, something which was entirely probable in those days.

At some point my father noticed that he was forgetting how to talk. He had been talking to himself to the point that words lost their meaning. He was saved by three little grey mice that made their home in his cell. My father gave them names and talked to them as if they were human. The little creatures would run around the cell completely unafraid, and even climb up on to his bunk to rest and listen to my father's discourses with their little pink ears pricked up. When one of the mice disappeared my father took the loss very badly, seeing it as a bad omen.

One day he was summoned to the NKVD offices to meet the local investigator, who offered him tea, sandwiches and cigarettes. My father proudly refused these delicacies, suspecting some subterfuge. It must be mentioned that during his preliminary investigation in Moscow, despite terrible pressure and threats, he had not signed a single document with false accusations or denounced a single person. He was not going to give in now.

The investigator, whose name was Stepanov, announced that his case was closed and he was completely rehabilitated. Stepanov stood up, opened the door wide, and told my father he was free to leave.

It was 4 July 1942. It was not infrequent in those days for such an offer to be simply a way of tricking a victim, who was then shot as having attempted to escape. My father flatly refused to leave. What was his reasoning? God knows, but one thing is certain: he was lucky to be in the hands of a decent and understanding person. Believe it or not, Stepanov, whom I met much later after he had retired, was an honest man. He let my father stay in his office, brought him blankets and food from home, and obtained permission from his superiors for this crazy ex-prisoner to be left alone.

The next night my father only ventured to leave the room to go to the toilet. On the third night he took a few steps along the empty corridor. Several days later Stepanov brought him some army clothing, and he was now psychologically ready to leave prison. There is a photograph of him taken on the day of his release: a grey-bearded man with mad eyes who looks like the inmate of a lunatic asylum.

Stepanov also supplied him with provisions and money, and out he went into the big wide world. He was forty-five, but looked an old man. There was a cinema opposite the NKVD offices. My father crossed the square and went in. A famous pre-war comedy was showing. People were giggling, but one man in the auditorium wept bitterly: my father. He was a courageous and unsentimental person, but after all his ordeals and humiliations his wounded heart let him down. When the film was over he resolutely went to the editorial offices of the local newspaper where his name was well known. It was there they had him photographed, after which he shaved off his beard, changed his clothes, and began a new life. His terrible ordeal remained deep in his memory and was to shorten his life by many years.

* * *

...I joined my father in Krasnoyarsk that winter and we settled in a little room so small there was nowhere to put two beds, so that we had to sleep in the same one. I was thirteen at the time. It was the winter of the grim war-time year of 1942.

Now I'm going to tell you something I've always been too ashamed to confess, but which I feel I must get off my chest. One night I woke up to find that my father was not beside me in the bed. At the table, by the dim light of an oil lamp, I saw him whispering with a stranger. I could not make out any words and soon fell asleep again. In the morning I asked my father about the nocturnal visitor. "My dear boy, you've been dreaming." "No I haven't! You were sitting on this stool and the other man was sitting on that one, and the lamp was turned down. I'm in my right mind. I saw him!" "No, son. We had no visitors last night. You were dreaming."

I'm really ashamed to tell the rest. Good God! How could I think so ill of my father! I decided it most certainly was not a dream and that, since my father denied having had a visitor, he must be a spy!

The whole thing horrifies me today, but at that time it seemed quite proper, and indeed my patriotic duty, to denounce a spy when I had seen one, no matter who that person might be. I continued speaking quite normally to my father, but for the next three days could think of nothing else but how I was going to turn him in to the NKVD.

I was on my way there when I met a fellow student, Abba Schwarzman, who was famous at school for his tremendous erudition and known as The Philosopher. I told him where I was going and why, and he offered to accompany me. "Spies should be turned in to the authorities, Valery," he said with an air of gravity. "They are a great danger to our country." I imagine he too would readily have denounced his own father had the occasion arisen.

In the NKVD reception area we were stopped by a guard who listened to what we had to say, then called someone on the phone. I was taken upstairs where I told my story to an NKVD officer. As I spoke I experienced a heady delight at fulfilling my duty as a citizen. This officer called another, a tall fair-haired man, and left us alone. The fair-haired man called me by my first name, which very much took me aback, and said, "Valery, thank you for your vigilance, but we know your father very well. He is an honest citizen. Go home now, and my advice is never to mention to your dad that you've been here. It will only be one more blow to him, and God knows he's had enough of those in the past few years. Glad to meet you. My name is Stepanov."

That was how I first met Stepanov, the interrogator in whose office my father had spent several days after his rehabilitation. He could easily have made me sign an undertaking to spy on my father and my neighbours, but he just sent me packing, saving my immature soul from sliding down the slippery road of treachery.

I don't believe that an evil person can suddenly turn into a good one, or that a former communist can suddenly stop being one, or a Christian suddenly convert to Islam. The scales may fall from a person's eyes, but this is always as the end result of a tortured process of squeezing your former self, your beliefs or scepticism, your vices and virtues out of your entire system, not only out of your mind. Our whole life is spent in consciously perfecting ourselves, either in good or in evil.

Vladimir Moroz

art collector and dissident

by Anna Godik

In the 1960s and 1970s Vladimir Moroz was famous for his prodigious collection of paintings, from icons to the Russian avant garde of the 1920s. The artist Robert Falk called him "the sharpest eye in Moscow". His other closest friend was Oleg Prokofiev, son of the composer. The three of them spent much time together in museums, half-empty concert halls during rehearsals, and in artists' studios. In those years collecting such artists as Larionov, Tatlin, Kandinsky, and Malevich was to risk being accused of anti-Sovietism, another way of being branded an "enemy of the people". Soviet art galleries in those days were a graveyard as far as new and non-conformist art were concerned.

The Soviet authorities gradually woke up to the financial value of icons and the Russian avant garde, discovering that such art could be traded for hard currency. Collecting suddenly became a dangerous occupation which could get you into trouble with the KGB. A campaign was unleashed against private collections, the real aim of which was to seize those valuable works of art which in the past had been rejected by the art censors, banned, and not infrequently destroyed.

It was not long before the authorities began to take a close interest in Vladimir Moroz's priceless collection. In June 1974 he was arrested in Lvov where he had gone to meet another collector, a priest. Moroz's apartment in Moscow and his summer house in Peredelkino were searched. He was taken, handcuffed and escorted by four policemen, to Lefortovo Prison in Moscow.

This was a period when persecution of dissidents was at its height: Solzhenitsyn had shortly before been exiled, the writers Daniel and Sinyavsky had been tried some years previously, Yakir, Ginzburg and Lubarsky had been arrested.

Vladimir Moroz was not directly involved in any dissident activities, but shared the same views and was fully aware of the falsehood of the official ideology. In the stifling atmosphere of the Soviet regime, art was his only outlet. He was one of the first to appreciate and acquire the work of Ilya Kabakov, Oskar Rabin, and D. Krasnopevtsev, later to become world-famous.

"Although I grew up under the Soviet system and knew no other, I always had a premonition that it would eventually collapse. I knew that would happen of its own accord: there was no need to try to hasten it or do anything to bring it about. Little did I imagine, however, that I should see its demise in my own lifetime. I was to jump for joy."

In 1974 Moroz was accused of "anti-Soviet propaganda" for disseminating works which allegedly slandered the state and socialist system. These included his own paintings, and books by Solzhenitsyn which he kept openly in his private library and lent to his numerous friends. He was a free-thinker in a world of slaves.

During the trial every effort was made to fabricate a case for confiscating his property. His lifestyle was categorized as bourgeois, and this was amply corroborated by evidence collected by the KGB.

While Moroz refused to admit his guilt, two hundred witnesses, their names taken from his diary, were interrogated. His own interrogations lasted for many hours. It soon became quite clear to him that what his jailers were after was his art collection. He decided to let them have the lot. From then on he named as "accomplices" only people who were dead or had emigrated, so that in either case they were beyond the reach of the KGB. None of his friends suffered on his account, but there were people he hardly knew who, under duress, bore false witness against him.

Overnight his brightly coloured, vibrant world turned a dirty lifeless grey. The walls, the faces, the clothes around him all lost their colours. Visual deprivation was particularly hard to bear for an artist. Surviving a Soviet corrective labour camp was virtually impossible. People soon turned into zombies.

Moroz was determined to survive as an intact individual. In his life before the camps he had drawn sustenance from art. Now, deprived of art, he found sustenance in thought, more precisely, religious thought. His diaries, begun some years earlier and continued in the Lefortovo prison and throughout his term of imprisonment, bear witness to the intensity of his spiritual life. You will find in them no descriptions of the horrors of prison life such as abound in other writings about the camps. He concentrates on assimilating the religious teaching of Tolstoy whose books he found in the rich prison library of confiscated books.

Moroz's diaries, titled "Tolstoy in my Prison Life", are an attempt to gain an overview of Christianity, to reinterpret and cleanse it of falsehoods superimposed on it by theologians, just as during restoration old icons are freed from later accretions which distort the original image.

One day in the Gulag he made a vow that if he managed to stay alive and, God willing, go home in one piece, he would preach Tolstoy's religious teaching to other people. He has kept his promise and launched a series of Tolstoy's religious writings.

On his initiative and on the basis of his collection a museum of naive art has also been created. Vladimir Moroz and his enthusiastic followers have been collecting naive art around Russia. They organise exhibitions of naive art and are campaigning for the establishment of a public gallery in Moscow.

The latest titles from Glas

Alan Cherchesov, *Requiem for the Living*, a novel

Strange Soviet Practices, a collection

Nikolai Klimontovich, *The Road to Rome*, a novel

Nina Gabrielyan, *Master of the Grass*, short stories

Nina Lugovskaya, *The Diary of a Soviet Schoolgirl: 1932-37*

NINE of Russia's Foremost Women Writers

Alexander Selin, *The New Romantic,* modern parables

Valery Ronshin, *Living a Life*, Totally Absurd Tales

Andrei Sergeev, *Stamp Album*,

A Collection of People, Things, Relationships and Words

Lev Rubinstein, *Here I Am*, performance poems

Andrei Volos, *Hurramabad*, a novel

A.J.Perry, *Twelve Stories of Russia: a Novel I guess*

The premier showcase for contemporary Russian writing in
English translation, GLAS has been discovering new writers
for over a decade. With some 100 names represented,
GLAS is the most comprehensive English-language source
on Russian letters today — a must for libraries, students
of world literature, and all those who love good writing.
For more information and excerpts see our site:
www.russianpress.com/glas